About Artemis in the Desert

A second chance at love?
Deep inspiration for new art?

Or a soggy motorcycle journey from Tumalo to Denio to Winne-mucca to Zion, while the White-Bone Demon seeks to destroy hope?

Eliot Arden, a Seattle artisan, and Sean Frederick Wentworth, the steampunk manga artist and video producer, find themselves on the same motorcycle journey they traveled a decade before. All the forces that once persuaded them to part return again—aided now by Sean's demonically vengeful ex-partner and Sean's own penchant for living inside his own myths.

But this time, dreams and desires might heat up like slickrock in the sun. Or is that fire sparked by a 900cc bike sliding sideways down a backcountry highway?

By Annie Pearson

Rain City Incidents:
Artemis in the Desert
Nine Volt Heart
The Grrrl of Limberlost
The Pirate King

The Accidental Heretics Adventure Series:
(as E.A. Stewart)
The Blue Door
Bone-mend and Salt
Trebuchets in the Garden
Crux Lunata
Song of Valerós
The Mad Woman of La Catalane

www.anniepearson.com

Artemis in the Desert

ANNIE PEARSON

JŪGUM PRESS

First print edition: May 2014
ISBN-10: 1939423228
ISBN-13: 978-1-939423-22-1

Motorcycle icon © GoGraph.com / iconspro

Published by Jugum Press
Find ebook editions at
www.jugumpress.net

For Chip, Steve, and Bruce:
Ride on. Be safe.

Contents

1.
Lost Point Road

The cure for anything is salt water: sweat, tears or the sea.
— Isak Dinesen

ELIOT

ON PUGET SOUND, ALONG THE road that runs down the heart of Limberlost Island, the mist rose and the sun glinted across the water, strobing among the row of Douglas firs that line Lost Point Road. A great blue heron fished on tiptoes at the low tide line.

To start the day, Eliot Arden paused to visit three acres of land she yearned for, like a woman who takes the long shortcut home to cruise a one-time lover's neighborhood, remembering a too-brief night spent there. Turning off the highway, down to the end of the dirt access road, Eliot stopped her motorcycle and sat astride it to gaze across the field, spying on a little house under red cedars. She longed to wake up there each day, where the trees breathe easier because of winter fog and summer mist.

At the beginning of this affair, Eliot sought only to help her aging friend avoid foreclosure. No heroics—just a friendly attempt to keep Cora Waddington and her grand-niece Destiny safe in their home (that dilapidated double-wide just off the highway). Cora, aging faster than she'd admit, once hired Eliot to build a ramp with a rail for easier entry into her home. Then Eliot spent time fixing the drain spouts, sealing the insulated skirts around Cora's mobile home, and making a dozen other repairs in exchange for macaroni dinners and grandmotherly conversation.

When Destiny came to Limberlost, everything changed.

Now, Eliot examined that double-wide and the outbuildings like an appraiser would, guessing what a bank would require before approving a residential loan, though everyone on the island assumed that any purchaser would scrape the lot and start anew.

It didn't seem too much to ask of the universe: that twisted madrona tree hanging over the water and a ditch full of salmonberries and Nootka rose. Her friends safe in their home.

Not too much to ask; yet longing for a new kind of daily life whipped up a bubble of desire in her belly, like being in love—not the sex part, but the hoped-for shared comfort. The last time desire and friendship seized Eliot's heart in this way, she gave it up as lost to whims of Fate. She'd taught herself that you avoid disappointment if you keep your desires under strict control. This time, however, she'd never give up. She'd do anything moral to secure her friends' safety.

After ten minutes daydreaming, Eliot headed back to Lost Point Road and made the right turn onto the main highway to Limberlost Village. Cruising in the thin morning fog, she glimpsed morning light through the hemlocks. Riding a motorcycle fresh at dawn, even early in September, it's so cold that neck and knees turn numb from the onslaught of morning air.

A six-point buck dashed onto the road a few yards in front of her, the bike's headlamp flashing in its eyes. The beast skittered along the verge, close enough to reach out and touch; the plume of his breath drifted away with wisps of fog.

Hooves clattered. Fear on blacktop.

She eased off the throttle and braked gently, ready if the buck nervously changed directions again. When they passed each other, Eliot checked her mirror, but the buck had disappeared as though she'd only dreamed it.

2.
Belltown

SEAN
Friday Night

"DIDN'T I WARN YOU? Milo Speiser's a pedigreed land shark. Maybe even a sociopath."

Pete Byron yawned, then shook all over like a dog after a nap. Press events suck the life out of you. He reached over and yanked off my press-event ID tag.

Sean Wentworth, Creative Director, Laconia Media.

Former professional identity: the author and artist of Impious Aeneas and his steampunk manga friends; a version of myself now existing only in Pete's jacket pocket.

Pete draped his other arm over Jason Taylor's shoulder, who'd just shown up. My true *compadres*: Pete, blond attention-deficit ex-skate-boy and international man of docudrama; Jason, six-foot tight-and-tidy rock 'n' roll.

"Smile for the camera."

Tadeusz Nowak, my animation partner for the last ten years in London, coaxed us to the curb in Belltown so he could capture the moment. He's moved here with me to partner on this new collaboration. Bruce Lee buff (though he can't fight his way out of the London subway), Tadeusz studied his snapshot in the camera's display.

"Pete and Jason look normal," he said. "Sean looks like a punk bodhisattva, trying to be nice while the White-Bone Demon kicks his dog."

"Except the evil White-Bone Demon is a woman," Pete said. "Sean is never troubled by women. Which is why the devil cloaked himself as a man, incarnating as Milo Speiser."

"Who's Milo Speiser?" Jason asked, having arrived too late for the press event.

"The super-blond guy in there, the one doing all the talking. That dude, with fake Yakuza tats up to here." Pete sliced at his neck. He'd know: when he's not filming or showing at a festival, he's fighting a grand jury request for the identity of his docudrama subjects, who have real Yakuza or gulag tattoos.

"Milo is taking the heroes I invented on a trip to hell." I grieve for all my peace-loving steampunk heroes: Impious Aeneas with his partners Monkey King and the angel Mithra, who ride motorcycles and free the oppressed. Our team's decade-long manga and animation effort has been sold into perdition by Milo Speiser. Who discarded all my imaginary heroes except Monkey King, and then peddled movie rights, claiming my ideas were his own. I protested: "Would I ever draw wolf-spirits disemboweling women? Shapeshifters devouring children? Is Milo out of his mind?"

Pete yawned again. "In a word, yes."

Through the open doors of the event, we watched Milo in an interview, his fake European accent carrying to the street. His ambition drove his voice up a half tone as he explained the partnership with FAIL Studios[1] that would eviscerate my peaceful vision of Monkey King and flail my life's work.

My Impious Aeneas manga story has been re-envisioned by a studio committee of forty-year-olds who believe they know the yearnings of the twelve-year-old hive mind. Imagine Monkey King's live-action future, beheading his enemies left and right. A moral and artistic nightmare ripped from the loins of mild-mannered Sean Wentworth and his genius production team.

Out where we stood on the sidewalk, Pete fumed.

"Why didn't you listen to me? I told you that Milo-fucking-Speiser is a disaster on wheels."

"Because Laconia Media needed an investment partner. I had slim choices." I lie awake nights wondering if there'd ever been another solution.

---

[1] That studio isn't really named FAIL, but given what they planned to do to my work, let's just call them FAIL.

"So you invited Milo to do what Milo does, buying or swindling a reputation for himself as an artist." Pete roomed with Milo, freshman year at university, so yeah, I should have listened.

"I can relate to that kind of swindle," Jason said. "I married it."

A ponytailed guy in a business suit stopped before us on the sidewalk, doing a double-take on Jason. You often see ponytails on Seattle streets, but seldom in business suits. In fact, any business suits at all in Seattle? Not so much.

"Aren't you Jason Taylor?"

"Yeah, man. How's it going?" Jason, with two Grammy nominations, has to deal with this all the time. Me, in the U.S.? Only when I'm mistaken for a geeky Pacific Northwest indie musician.

Ponytail man said, "I've seen you play like two dozen times, man. Can I get your autograph?" He offered a fine-point Sharpie from his inside pocket.

"For sure," Jason said. "Do you have paper?"

"No, sign my arm. I want to turn it into a tat."

"Far out." When Jason says this, it means anything from "cool" to "you truly grossed me out," but you can never tell where on the spectrum. He signed on a well-toned forearm, where a Lionel train framed one side of his autograph, with a hookah-smoking caterpillar along the other.

Ponytail man tugged his shirt sleeve down and redid his cuff links. He shook Jason's hand, then cocked his head, examining me. "Are you Sean Frederick Wentworth?"

"Yes." I never get requests for tat-to-be autographs anywhere outside of Japan (where I have more fans than Jason), but I'd never say no.

Ponytail reached once more into the inner pocket that held his Sharpie. But instead withdrew an envelope and handed it to me.

"You've been served, sir."

"Far out," Pete said. But with Pete, that always means the other F word.

As ponytail-process-server guy disappeared in the crowd of commuters and homeless in Belltown, Pete watched me fold the summons and stick it into my own jacket pocket.

"You going to open it, *compadre*?"

"I don't need bad news." I retrieved the envelope and handed it to Pete.

Who studied its contents for half a second and then thumbed a number on his cell phone.

"Karl, this is Pete." He listened. Karl is the copyright and contracts attorney who manages affairs for our new collaboration. "Yeah, I knew you'd have those papers ready. You're good. Listen, Sean has an estoppel from Milo that forbids him to say anything about Laconia Media before their partnership is dissolved."

Pete held out his cell. "Karl says of course Milo can tell you to shut up."

"Not a problem," I said. "I haven't spoken to anyone but you guys. And our new work is a total secret."

Still on his phone, Pete said, "I'm sending you a picture of the rest. Milo says Sean has no artistic rights to any Impious Aeneas material. Sean receives royalties, but no new use of any characters, including Mithra and Monkey King."

"Oh man," Jason moaned. "My old label did that with the first album I released. Bad moon rising, dude."

I sucked in air like a winded runner while Pete snapped and sent cellphone pictures of the estoppel to Karl. Tadeusz cast one miserable glance my way, further sealing our bond.

Kicked in the gut: *no artistic rights to my own work.*

"Forget Milo. Forget Laconia." Pete pumped my arm to wake me from bad dreams as he pocketed his phone. "And forget Monkey and all your other imaginary heroes. We have *Riders on the Storm.*"

"*The Desert Crucible.* We took Zane Grey's title, but not his story," I said. "An on-the-road tale, adventure in the Old West. Two hundred years from now."

Our private collaboration. Just the four of us. In August, I'd optioned a new live-action/animation concept to HOPE Productions.[2] HOPE scheduled a green-lighting session for the fourteenth of September. The same day my partnership with Milo and Laconia

---

[2] Yeah, HOPE isn't that studio's real name either; it's what they represent in my mind.

ends. Tadeusz and I need *The Desert Crucible* to carry us to the next part of our lives. The part without Milo.

"Yeah, a travelogue devoid of True Love," Jason said. "Just like my real life."

"Give me a break," Pete said. "You don't believe in True Love any more than I do."

"I do," Jason said. "At least, I want to believe."

True Love—that's what his music's about, or was, before Jason's marriage to Dominique hit the rocks.

"Well, I bet—" Pete said.

"Here it comes." Yikes. If there's an edge, Pete will at least make us lean over it. Then push.

"—that our new collaboration is better than being married. Minus the sex."

"Oh, it is," Jason said. "Trust me. Invasive dental work is better than marriage without True Love."

"And yet you still believe?" Pete taunted.

"Yes, it's out there somewhere, looking for me," Jason beat a rhythm, thumb on the back of his other hand. "Wish I was riding with you tomorrow. On the road with Sean Wentworth, Tadeusz Nowak, and Peter Gawain Byron."

"Recreating Impious Aeneas's original manga journey through the American high desert," Tadeusz said.

"A great American bromance," Pete said. "Except you don't know how to ride, Jason. No motorcycles for you."

"A guy can dream," Jason said. "I'm dreaming that people like the music I contribute. Since my label doesn't want to touch it."

"And I dream that I'm done shooting video of criminal brutes doing their day jobs," Pete said. "I yearn to be on the road with Sean and the Trickster of Infinite Creativity."

"Noble goal," Jason said, jabbing Pete with his elbow. Pete shoved him back. Sheesh, guys like us, the ones from the media room in high school, the art teacher's pet, we come off as stupid when making jock moves. "You, Sean, what's your goal?'

"Yeah, boss, what?" Tadeusz prodded me. "Besides releasing our team from the iron bands of 'commercial potential' that Milo forged. What else do you want?"

"To catalog the shape of foam on water," I said, telling the truth with metaphor. "To dance with the Wu Li masters under desert stars."

Pete mimed sticking two fingers down his throat and gagging.

"Far out," Jason said.

"OK," I said, still hearing *no artistic rights* clang like a broken bell in my head. "To create and sell new work so I can hire Tadeusz and my old team away from Laconia Media. And move onto the next new project as fast as possible."

Jason fist-bumped me in approval, then picked up his buzzing cellphone. After a few seconds, he clicked off the call. "I have to go. My uncle Beau needs me. I'll catch you tomorrow."

He disappeared up First Avenue, waving farewell.

• • •

Milo exited the press event clutching a triple grande latte. He's famous for drinking a half dozen every day. Pete, hands in the pockets of his jacket, feigned surprise at seeing him.

"Milo? Milo Speiser? Good to see you, man! How's the intellectual property theft business going these days?"

That's Pete: why settle for passive-aggressive when aggressive better suits your personality?

Milo's latte splattered at Pete's feet like sea-foam after a storm.

"Watch it, *Arschloch*!" Milo Speiser, standing too close, poked Pete's chest with an index finger to emphasize his words.

"Leave him be!" Louisa said. She's Milo's personal assistant, Harajuka to the max: hair streaked purple, packed up in buns over her ears, razor-sharp bangs. Lemon-yellow eye shadow; fuchsia lips; each nail a different vibrant color. Contact lenses that remade her eyes an inhuman violet.

And white.

Really white. Cheekbones sharp enough to cut you. Like a ghost in a Japanese horror movie. Or the White-Bone Demon who chases Monkey King in novels and manga. So different from Artemis, the goddess of the wildland who visits my dreams.

Over her fuchsia Harajuka outfit, Louisa wore a long, fur-lined Laplander coat, too hot for Seattle weather, the fur offensive to Seattle tastes. "Forget him. He's meaningless in the real world."

"Thanks, Louisa." Pete pulled his shirt cuffs down, straightening them. "I appreciate you sticking up for me."

Louisa flushed crimson under her delicate ivory-toned makeup. If she possessed White-Bone Demon's power, she'd have blasted Pete with the hate of a thousand burning fires.

Milo walked away, leaving Louisa to struggle with luggage too big and too heavy for her to handle. He called an abrupt instruction over his shoulder, just as I relieved Louisa of the heaviest portion of her burden.

"Thanks," she rasped.

Milo whipped back around, scowling. He wrenched the case from my hands, but misjudged its weight so that it fell to the sidewalk with a thundering crash.

On Tadeusz's left foot.

My friend mouthed a silent scream, shaking in pain. I put an arm around Tadeusz, easing him over to a nearby concrete bench, the kind often used by the unwashed urban masses for overnight napping. Louisa and Milo quarreled through the process of loading their luggage into a waiting limo, without a word to Tadeusz.

Tadeusz's red-flushed face faded quickly to white.

"I think my foot's broken."

"Let's get you to a doctor," I said, forcing calm into my voice while adrenalin flowed. At the curb's edge, I flagged a passing Yellow Cab to take us to a hospital on First Hill. Pete and I piled in the cab. Tadeusz winced as he tucked himself in the front seat.

"What now, boss?" Tadeusz said, his face still ghastly white. He kneaded his hands, forcing that grimace of pain into a smile.

"We'll figure it out. We always do."

. . .

Since it was too early in the evening for the emergency room to be super busy, the ER crew let Pete and me sit with Tadeusz through all the waiting and hands-on torture. Pete and I told stories to distract Tadeusz, it being the kind of situation that requires *bonhomie*, whether you feel it or not.

"Guess I miss the first step for transmuting lead to gold, huh, boss?" Tadeusz tried to make us laugh (just like him) while the ER doctor studied the x-rays. "Unless we rent a sidecar. We can invent a new meaning for sidekick. You lead a long metaphysical journey in the wilds with only—"

"No long journey for you, Mr. Nowak. Only this," the doctor said, interrupting the metaphor. He held a medical boot and explained its use. "It's called a walking boot, except Mr. Nowak won't be walking in it for a few weeks. That is, if you want to avoid a cast."

Tadeusz winced again, and not from pain under the doctor's gentle touch. Tadeusz's name means "courageous heart," which he claimed when I first met him a decade ago. He's been with me through everything, a genius at both still photography and multimedia production. I'm loyal to Tadeusz, like the brother I never had.

After the long hours in the emergency room, we grabbed takeout sushi and decamped to Pete's house. Then we ventured to discuss how we'd execute the plan for *The Desert Crucible*, as if all we'd miss on the journey was Tadeusz's skill as still-camera artist.

I offered the obvious solution: I take on the camera work.

"No, Sean, you are not a cameraman. Not in any work with which my name is associated." Pete folded his arms, adamant.

Taking Pete's side, Tadeusz spoke more slowly. "You have a steady hand, Sean. With a brush. A mouse. A digitizer. But you and cameras don't understand each other."

Tadeusz sat on a barstool in Pete's kitchen, a big Velcro boot on his foot and a painkiller smile on his face, too keyed up to sleep, too doped up to be left alone. He waved away all offers to help him get comfortable, happy with the sashimi and rolls from the takeout bag.

"We hire another photographer." Pete thumbed a number on his cellphone.

"How can we bring someone on board this late and get them on the right wave length?" I ticked off the list of requirements on my fingers. "Can ride a motorcycle. Has sublime camera aesthetics. Performs well on a team."

Pete listened to the voice on the phone, one finger in the air to silence me. *Performs well on a team* isn't Pete's strong point.

Tadeusz swished raw fish in wasabi, every movement an exaggerated slow-motion capture of my hyperactive friend's usual ways.

We're like-minded, but opposites: I'm tall and slight, he's half an imperial foot shorter and broad shouldered; I'm cautious, he's curious and adventuresome; my art is influenced by J.M.W. Turner and Edo era woodblock artists, his by Jacob Lawrence. Yet Tadeusz knows me better than my own mother ever did. Here we were, in the middle of moving to Seattle as we'd discussed all year, but with our plans already upended. I made another gesture to be helpful. Tadeusz batted my hand away.

"This is me taking care of karma. Yours and mine," Pete was saying on his cell. He listened, then said, "Seven days. Photos from a bike. Easy work that pays in the range of what you require."

"I can research stock photos," Tadeusz said.

Still on the phone, Pete waved a negative, jutting with a middle finger for extra emphasis. "I owe you, and this is payback," he said to the unknown photographer. "See you tomorrow. We're on the road by ten o'clock."

"How can we possibly—"

"Stop worrying, boss," Pete said as he clicked off his phone. "C'mon, Sean. If you keep rocking like that, you'll give yourself a concussion. I have all the rigging set for video and still images. We know our journey, from start to end. There can be no failure. There's just us, on the road."

"And holed up here," Tadeusz said. In his medicated state, he apparently didn't feel the wasabi on his chin. "I can cyber-follow you all the way. And work with Jason to get the music synced."

Pete said, "We're incapable of giving up before we start."

"Our only barrier is Sean's perfectionism," Tadeusz said. He laid a sticky hand on mine, as if I were the one who needed tending.

"That green-light meeting with HOPE Productions, it weighs on me," I said. "How will we make a living if—"

Tadeusz said, "Worry about it when you get to L.A., boss. Meanwhile, we just do the work. And do good art."

"And hope it sells." That's me, scaring myself. I also worried about the pharmacokinetics of the drugs that the doctor had loaded onto Tadeusz, though the chopsticks managed to find his mouth each time he tried.

After cleaning up the sushi remains and wiping down the sticky kitchen counter, I helped Tadeusz upstairs to the guest room and left a bottle of water and his next pain dose on the night table.

Then I laid down on Pete's living room sofa and worried until dawn. For Tadeusz. For our collaboration. For everyone at Laconia Media that I wanted to save from Milo. Who would steal Monkey King's soul and leave Impious Aeneas in the dust-heap of manga history.

I lay in the dark doing what I do every night while creating new work. The story, my characters, the images: I run over them again, looking for holes in story logic, looking for new action for my characters, imagining new landscapes to draw in the morning.

Tadeusz and I spent the last year doing our best work ever to create original characters, rather than reviving any previous incarnation of an archetype, whether Asian, European, or New World. We would not re-use any previous century's superheroes, whether high literature or comics. We built a new universe, nothing like the world of Impious Aeneas. Our mixed media assemblage melds animation, video, and sound to shape a neo-psychedelic world that's the Old West two hundred years in the future. We're going for an evolve, post-punk anarchy. Not dystopian—that's been done to death, don't you think?

I invented the arch-mage figure and named him Magic Bob. He's an homage to my father in personality, but drawn large, like the all-powerful father a five-year-old sees.

Tadeusz invented Juan Vaquero as the quixotic quester. He insisted on the "Cowboy John" name, and distorted a photo of me to create the visual characteristics. It is hoped that no one notices the resemblance, because I don't want our new story deconstructed as autobiography. My life isn't interesting enough to serve as a foundation for epic stories.

We have the usual collection of *compadres* in our invented world: gamblers, reformed womanizers, troubadours. The hard part for both of us was inventing the female protagonist. Tadeusz is inclined to reinvent Valkyries and Swan Maidens. I tend to lean toward the goddess of mercy, whatever the culture. But we're good guys, I hope. We wanted a real woman. Not just breasts and legs held together with a magic power belt. We spent more than half the year creating animation where the woman stood with her back to the viewer, because we couldn't agree on a vision, or even key attributes of the character.

You'd think neither of us even knew a real woman, though half the Laconia crew is female. We settled on a composite: half Calamity Jane, half Diane the Huntress, one hundred percent self-actualized. She keeps her clothes on far more often than Juan Vaquero, who seems to be missing his pants in half the animation cells.

Here we go: our heroes roll out in the morning, on a New Journey to the West, seeking to transform the base metal of everyday life into gold, to find the philosopher's stone in the red-rock country of the neo-Old West.

Yeah, the story won't make a hell of a lot of sense to anyone until it all plays out, but we got hell-a-lot of atmosphere. And cliff hangers.

Every five minutes I closed my eyes, seeing the desert's bright light, smelling sage-scented air, hearing doves moan in the tamarisks. Hoping.

3.
Limberlost

*It is always one's virtues and not one's vices
that precipitate one into disaster.*
—Rebecca West

ELIOT
Saturday a.m.

As ELIOT CRAWLED THROUGH LIMBERLOST Village at twenty miles per hour, she spotted Roslyn Owens's pickup at Casa D and so backed into a parking space in front of the café.

Inside Casa D, seated across from Roslyn, Destiny ate pancakes and talked with her usual animation while Roslyn drank tea and nibbled from a plate of soft-scrambled eggs. Seeing Eliot, Destiny sprang with a cry from the Naugahyde booth, lifting Eliot in a high-school-girl hello hug, as if they hadn't seen each other for ages.

Though it was only last night, when Eliot stopped at Cora Waddington's house to describe her sudden temp job.

At six-foot, Destiny had a couple of inches over Eliot, with all the lank grace of an adolescent greyhound, and long dusky eyelashes that called attention to her dark eyes. Destiny stared at people when they talked to her, giving each person a sense of being the most interesting creature in the world.

"You two are here early. The market doesn't open till ten." Eliot slid into the booth beside Destiny. "Thanks again, Roz." Eliot tapped her friend's hand. Large, strong hands like hers. Eliot, who made metal-and-wood wall clocks and artsy confections, gave her metal cast-offs to Roz, who embedded pieces in the cast-stone garden steps she crafted. The Limberlost street market was a summer hobby for Roz, but a key part of Eliot's put-together micro-economy.

"This weekend is my biggest income until Christmas. You're making it possible for me to do two jobs at once."

"I can manage your booth myself," Destiny said for the tenth time since Eliot had announced the change of plans.

"Yes, except—"

"Yeah, I know." Destiny slumped in the booth. She'd laced her hair into an elaborate French braid and wore a bright-white linen poet's shirt. Her fifteen-going-on-thirty look. "The City doesn't allow underage vendors."

Eliot managed to not laugh. Drama should be Destiny's middle name. "I'm not a control freak, but humor me. Let's go over the list, so Roz knows what you plan."

Destiny sat up straight. Yanking her sketchpad from her bag, she tapped the list with a kelly-green nail as she read and then explained each item. "First, put the clocks on the back wall, so people have to go through the whole booth to get to them." She glanced at Roslyn. "That's my innovation. It's how we met, me teaching Eliot about merchandising. She used to display the clocks up front."

The year before, Destiny wandered through the Limberlost street market just after Cora had rescued her from foster care. The artsy metalwork got Destiny excited, which led to her apprenticeship in Eliot's workshop.

"Because that's what everyone buys," Eliot said.

"But a smart marketing person," Destiny tapped her nose, as the star of her own French movie, "sets the most popular items in the back. Then people have to check out everything else to get to Eliot's steampunk clocks."

Though Eliot hadn't known what to call those clocks until Destiny declared the appropriate marketing category on Etsy.com.

"Separate my projects on their own stand." Destiny glanced up from reading the list. "We track each piece with an item number. It's not like you'll cheat me, Eliot."

"Always place your name on your work. And you have a stronger statement when they're grouped together."

"OK. Also, I'm putting your newest large-scale metal sculpture out front."

"No one ever buys my big pieces," Eliot said. "It's not worth the effort to drag one out of the shop."

"Guys stop to check out the big pieces," Destiny said. "My innate marketing genius says it gets their wives inside. Someday one of those guys will buy a big sculpture."

Roz listened, mostly watching Destiny. She finally put in a word. "We'll miss you, Eliot, but we'll do fine. I'm letting Destiny run the show as you would. She's been at every market this summer, so she knows the drill."

"I'm going to start setting up," Destiny said. She scooted Eliot out of the booth, hugging her again, and then kissed both cheeks goodbye (another European movie gesture). "Call me every night. I want to tell you how much we're making."

• • •

When Destiny split, Roslyn lingered behind.

"I can't get over how she's changed," Roz said. In her paid job as social worker, she'd helped Cora Waddington get custody, and then retained responsibility for monitoring Destiny's progress.

"One more reason why we have to keep Cora in her own house. Stability is good for Destiny."

"Eliot, you're what's good for her. She's even given up faux punk fashion in favor of dressing like you. All those hours in your workshop—who'd guess how talented she is?"

"Yeah. I've known true artists before. Watching how fast Destiny's skills grow takes my breath away." Eliot spoke more softly. "Roz, please tell me what more we can do. You're the only friend I have with any ability to help."

"I'm doing what I can, Eliot." Roz nudged aside her tea cup and held Eliot's hand for just five seconds, then released it. "Thank goodness you noticed and began thinking of a solution. Her placement with Cora is tenuous. If they weren't blood relatives, the State would never have placed Destiny with someone so infirm and—"

"Broke. Poor. Nearly destitute. Supporting the two of them on a social security pittance and foster-care money for Destiny."

"We have two major problems to solve: money and her ongoing supervision."

Yuri, Casa D's gnomic owner, appeared with a pot of coffee, and Eliot refused for the third time. When he departed, Eliot said, "If I can purchase Cora's land, then at least their housing is stable. But in the long run, a seventy-nine-year-old woman can't care for a fifteen-year-old. A single thirty-five-year-old woman—me—I can handle both Cora's and Destiny's needs."

"We can prove your value in her life. It's just—"

"Yeah, my unpredictable income. Yet if the State studies all the paperwork I provided, it's obvious that I make a living wage every year." Eliot drummed the table top. "Too bad I can't show them my under-the-table handyman income."

"There's also the issue of what kind of shelter you can provide," Roz said. "Your tiny kitchenette and the miniscule bunk room at the back of your shop won't cut it with family court."

"If the land deal doesn't go through, I'll remodel my shop so they can live there. Just—Roz, I'm begging for help."

"We'll get it figured out. You're doing monstrous fine work for Destiny and her aunt now. Angels should sing your praises."

"Thanks, but I don't need praise. I need to see a secure future for Destiny and Cora."

Roslyn swished her tea, not reading the leaves but more obviously preparing to say what was on her mind. "Eliot, you're always busy doing what other people need. Don't forget to take care of yourself."

"Yeah. Pete says I habitually rescue strays. But with Destiny, it's different. I need to do whatever it takes. It's like," Eliot grabbed her shirt over her heart without meaning to, "the one time I was in love. It burns like that."

Roz didn't answer. Eliot knew Roz used silence to prompt people to say more.

"I don't mean anything skeezy. Destiny's brilliance, the fun we have working together, Cora's friendship—it's a human comfort I haven't known since—" Eliot paused, surprised at her own self-revelation. "The past doesn't matter, except someone once made a place for me when I needed it most. I owe that back to the universe."

"Pete's father?"

Eliot nodded. Stories from Dante's ranch weren't part of her social conversation on Limberlost.

"Your brother Pete came through this time," Roz said. "Offering the chunk of cash you need right now."

"Like an angel from heaven," Eliot said, "which is not Pete. It's bound to be some whacked-out job."

"Pete's doing better by people these days."

Eliot signaled to Yuri for the bill. "That's what he says. I need to hit the road. You'll watch out for Destiny while I'm gone?"

"Of course." Roslyn grasped Eliot's hand, harder than any goodbye touch. "Eliot, don't make promises to Destiny when you can't guarantee the outcome."

"I never would."

Since it was time to start tracking the expenses Pete promised to pay, she gave Yuri her credit card and then signed her name on the slip. *Eliot Arden.* A boy's name, signifying the first thing she'd done straight out of the womb to disappoint her father. Though why ponder that, this far into real life?

Cora Waddington came into Casa D just then, looking around but not seeing Eliot until Yuri pointed that direction.

"Eliot! So glad I found you before it's too late."

Nearing eighty, never more than five foot tall, Cora scuttled over to the booth, sliding in beside Roz with great effort. After greeting Roz, and after both of them remarked on the weather, Cora seemed to lose the thread of why she came in search of Eliot.

"Thanks be to all the Divine Masters!" Cora said. "Sarah Johns dropped by my house on her way to town this morning. It's celestial guidance, I tell you. How else under heaven could she know I needed a ride into town?"

Roz, Cora's next-door neighbor, claimed that she'd have stopped for Cora when she picked up Destiny.

Cora blinked. "But I didn't need a ride then."

Eliot had been watching Cora—always thinking her health wasn't what it should be—and didn't like the extra blinking and subtle hints of confusion.

"Are you OK, Cora? You seem distracted."

"Oh heavens, yes. I can't keep a thought in my head, worried that I wouldn't find you." She clasped Eliot's hand in the way she usually did when saying thank you.

"Here I am," Eliot said. "What can I do for you?"

"Let me see." Cora rummaged in her handbag, spilling a wad of crumpled tissues and a fat plastic wallet, which sprang open and rained pennies across the painted tabletop. Eliot scooped coins while Cora hunted. "Here it is. Can you tell me what it means?"

She handed over a letter with a U.S.P.O. Certified mail tag pasted on the back of the envelop. Having expected such a letter for weeks, Eliot still opened it with trepidation.

"It's not good news, Cora."

In her rational mind, Eliot understood how this came to be: just before the crunch in the last decade, an unscrupulous lender (no longer in business) talked Cora into a bad mortgage. Her husband dead, nothing to live on but slim social security, Cora Waddington had hocked her only asset. And couldn't make the payments. That's why Cora's property was on the market now. In her heart, Eliot complained bitterly that Cora had been taken advantage of—while worried that she wouldn't have sufficient money to buy the property before the current mortgage holder put Cora on the street.

While Roz held Cora's hand, Eliot explained what the letter said about the process and the deadlines, and then described the solution to Cora, who needed comfort more than details. Reassuring her friend helped Eliot quiet her own panic.

"We have ten days," Eliot said. "When I'm back, I'll have enough money to buy your house. That will halt any action on this notice."

"It's not tomorrow? Or this week?" Cora said. "What if the sheriff comes while you're gone and throws us out?"

"No, not tomorrow. Not ever. I'll be back before the deadline." Eliot added her hand to Roz's clasp. "I do not want you to worry about this while I'm gone, Cora."

"If anyone can fix our problems, it's you." Cora looked up when Yuri—who knew every Limberlost customer's preferences—set a stainless steel pot of tea before her. She slipped out of Roz's grasp to pour, her hand shaking so the tea came out in drips and splashes. "You've been so good. For Destiny. For me."

The praise made her uncomfortable, since Eliot lacked true conviction that she could deliver on her reassurances. She glanced at Roz. Time to get to this week's job, raise the cash, and then launch the purchase.

"I'm sorry, what did you say?" Cora glanced up, startled. "Oh my, I have the hiccups."

"Just that I have to be going, Cora. You have my phone number. Call me every single day."

A slip of her arm around her friend for a hug, a kiss on the top of Cora's head, and then Eliot waved to both friends. She had to hit the road. The next deadline was ten o'clock in Seattle. Not confronting Cora's evictors. One thing at a time.

At the Stop&Go just above the ferry terminal, Eliot gassed up her bike and went inside to pay. A young rider on a loud Kawasaki pulled up, dressed in battle fatigues and paratrooper boots, his bike covered in road grime, and his gear wrapped in a green Hefty trash bag lashed to the sissy bar with bungee cords. When the Kawasaki warrior came in to pay for his gas, leering at Eliot in her leathers, she didn't acknowledge him.

"You should smile more," he said, offering common advice.

As a young teenager, Eliot learned that because of her breasts and long legs, discretion served her better than charm. As an adult, she habitually rejected come-ons as not worth the hassle. Hence, all smiles were saved for personal friends.

Ready to go, she switched on her bike and buckled her helmet. The BMW—a 1977 R100RS she'd restored with serious love—hummed so quietly against the background of the Kawasaki's noise that only its gentle vibration reported when it came alive.

"Nice bike. You going over to ride on Highway 101?" the road warrior asked. "We could ride together."

"You might check that oil leak," she said, pointing to the splatter across his boot and fatigues. More dripped disgracefully from the bike where he'd parked it by the pump island.

Eliot eased the clutch out slowly, then twisted on the throttle and kicked up the gear, leaving the Kawasaki behind as she headed for the Limberlost-Seattle ferry.

...

In the Leschi neighborhood where her brother Pete had rented a house, Priuses, BMW 325s, and diesel Audis cozied against each other's bumpers along the narrow, twisting side streets. Western red cedars and big-leaf maples branched over the road and brushed the sides of houses, the maples' leaf edges yellowing, although it was only Labor Day weekend, too early to admit that fall had arrived.

Eliot coasted down the side street to the sloping driveway where Pete stood, as if expecting her arrival at that very moment.

Then all bad things happened at once, like they warn in safety classes. A dog dashed at her bike as she dodged a frost-heave pothole. The barking water-spaniel dogged her front tire as she braked sharply and then skidded in a patch of oil left by some car-jockey. As the bike slid sideways toward a parked Mercedes, Eliot put her foot down to stop the bike, which tipped onto her instead of onto the pavement. The handlebar banged her hand hard. Her leg hurt like hell, but one sound was mercifully absent: the crunch of metal against concrete.

Someone—Pete?—pulled the bike off her and hit the kill switch as she struggled to rise, unable to see past her helmet.

"Get, you hellhound!" she yelled at the spaniel, which still yapped at her bike. She jerked off her helmet and grabbed her bike to be sure it was unscathed.

Sean Wentworth held her bike. That same intimate smile.

"Eliot!" he said in that resonant, alluring voice, deeper than you'd think possible for a skinny guy. The voice that plagued her dreams. "You haven't changed a bit!"

4.
Seattle

THAT FIRST UNEXPECTED GLIMPSE OF her face came like a kick in the gut. I had no forewarning: it all cascaded back at the flash of morning light in her eyes.

The textures and shapes she created out of emptiness.

The planes and valleys of her body.

Her voice, naming the stars in the heavens.

Her embrace, the only comfort I'd ever known.

And in that flash: she found no joy at the sight of me.

Eliot jumped up from her fall, berating Pete for living amid dogs and potholes, turning an awkward moment into a joke.

"Crap way to start the day, Pete," she raved, "forcing me to dump the bike."

I pitied the dumped bike, but pitied myself more at seeing such a tragic expression on the face of a woman I once cared for.

Pete had made a colossal error.

After Eliot inspected her bike, Pete coaxed her to the patio for show-and-tell with his camera hardware. After a few staggeringly silent moments, she began to ask for details, while I missed the presentation, watching her.

Pete said, "I preprogrammed the capture processes. We carry three wireless stations, since we'll be out in the back of beyond and need to post media."

I went to the kitchen for more coffee where, unfortunately, I heard their patio conversation.

"Wasn't I right, Eliot? This is the perfect gig for you."

Silence.

"Are you OK? Did you get hurt when you fell?"

"No, I'm not OK." She sounded annoyed rather than injured. "I'm humiliated. I'm bruised. And I keep seeing pavement come for my face. My body's still scared, whatever my brain thinks."

"You'll be OK."

"My brain also thinks you're a total asshole, Pete. Why didn't you tell me what this gig really was?"

"I did." Pete played dumb, while I shared the same sense of betrayal. He said, "You just ride and snap stills. I created new wearable cameras that give full control. Just what you like."

"Where are we going, Pete?"

"And we pay all expenses. What's better than a paid ride, where you get a bundle of cash at the end of the trail?"

"Where, Pete? Answer, please."

"Dante's ranch."

Silence again.

"It's what the client put on the storyboard," Pete said.

"Sean is your client?"

"We're partners, actually, producing this project together. Plus I have personal business with Dante. Come on, Eliot. It's been a dozen years."

"Ten."

"Think of your past as a flash flood flowing under the Bridge to Nowhere."

"More like dust in the wind," she said. "Or some other dumb song from the Seventies."

"Whatever. You're free now. Dante isn't part of your long-term karma."

"Dante isn't the problem," she said. Me, Sean Wentworth. She meant that I'm the problem. "So I get a wad of cash for still shots of the high desert? In what market?"

Pete said, "We're braiding images, video, and music with animation for a web series. The animation and story are done. We compose extra art as we ride."

"I'm not an artist," Eliot said. "I'm an artisan. And I only do realism. Not comic book crap."

"Oh shut up. You get a flat-fee for your artisanry."

"There's no such word, little brother. I will get you for this one day soon. Big favor you did."

"As another favor, I just made you forget how scared you were when you fell," Pete said. "And now, forget the humiliation. Everyone drops a bike now and then."

"I don't," she said.

Done eavesdropping, I brought out three cups of coffee. Pete was explaining the details of his wearable cameras.

"Single shot. Takes a photo every two, five, ten, thirty, or sixty seconds. Press here to switch to three-photo bursts."

Eliot opened the tank bag from her bike, brandishing what must be her preferred camera. "I want control of shutter speed, aperture, exposure, range, zoom—"

Pete said, "It's the same methods as when we rode over Mount Baker last year. Except I improved the wearables after you carped about them. This'll be the easiest gig you ever had."

"If it doesn't rain," she said, accepting coffee without a glance in my direction, looking past me at Pete.

"It won't rain," Pete said. "This time next week you'll be bitching that it's too hot. Begging me to make it rain. Here, check my video gear. We'll overlay and transition from drawing to live images and back again, to illuminate Sean's underlying conceit—"

"Which is what?" she asked. Pete. She asked Pete, not me.

"That ancient spirits still live and walk the earth," I said. "If we could but hear their voices."

"Like, our cameras capture metaphoric ectoplasm," Pete said.

"Whatever." Expressionless, Eliot nested her camera back into its bag. "The itinerary?"

"We camp close to Bend tonight," Pete said. "Then race across the rest of Oregon so we can gamble in Winnemucca tomorrow."

This was ambitious riding, but Pete had discounted my opinion when we'd studied the map.

"With nothing much to do in Nevada," Pete said, "we speed through and then focus on Zion and some Anasazi ruins. That's where we capture new video to charm our audience."

"I'm eager to visit the ruins at Betatakin again," I said, hoping to revive the excitement Pete and I kicked up earlier. "You know,

Navajo National Monument. I had a great experience there once. Just sitting at the edge of the canyon is a spirit quest in itself."

No reaction. She'd transformed into a silent ghost of herself. Pete blew this one, big time.

"Come see what Sean's riding," Pete said.

In the garage, next to Pete's practical BMW K1200RS stood a 900cc Kawasaki—two actually; one had been leased for Tadeusz, but only one of the leased bikes was loaded with traveling gear.

"Nice bike," Eliot murmured, like one says automatically to a stranger at a gas station. "But it's frigging red. It'll attract every cop between here and Interstate 40."

When Pete first expressed excitement about this bike, I believed he intended to ride it. But when we packed that morning, he assigned me the Kawasaki, which is way out of my riding experience. I'd been humping little rice burners in London. People don't ride death machines that size there.

Pete said, "I can't lend him the BMW because it has the camera mounts I need. Sean's strong enough to handle this beast. As underweight as he is."

Eliot finally glanced my way, with no readable expression, no light in her eyes. I wished for a pool of kindness and comfort, like she'd let me sink into years ago. But no.

His back to both of us, Pete slapped a Monkey King sticker on the Kawasaki. He tugged at his bike's load, making sure it was secure. "Let's hit the road. We can get as far as Yakima for lunch."

I said, "I'm ready."

"Let me make a couple of phone calls," Eliot said. "Don't ride off without me."

When I went to check on Tadeusz, I glimpsed Pete through the window and, unfortunately, again heard conversation snatches.

"—and you might have warned me, Pete."

"What do you mean?" Pete asked, faking confusion. "This ride is going to be fun."

"He doesn't remind you of the stupidest things you ever did."

"Actually, most truly stupid things I did were with Sean," Pete said. "The time I rode my Triumph into the lake to win a bet, and the time that I—"

...

Their voices were lost in the garage, but by then I'd forgotten any pity I had for her earlier. She crushed my heart once.

Tadeusz hobbled in from the dining room, where we'd set up his workstations. Now he could work, eat, and sleep without tackling stairs. I'd made an online order of groceries, among other fretting about how to take care of him.

"Jason left music on the server store last night," Tadeusz said. "But he hasn't called yet. What should I do?"

"He'll call," I said. Jason is pious about showing up on time to every gig. "Meanwhile, take a guess."

"I'll do my best."

"Which is always great, Tadeusz. Trust your instincts."

"I just uploaded a test of the first voice-over," he said. Pete and I finished taping just before Eliot arrived: our first paean to riding, explicating the spiritual experience we expected on this Journey. Tadeusz nodded when I offered him coffee, which I carried into the dining room for him as he hobbled back to work.

"Close that door when you leave," he said. "I can't edit sound tracks with people talking and banging around."

Outside the closed door, I watched Eliot wander around the living room, talking on her cell phone. Pete also watched her, with that expression he uses professionally, as if he weren't recording the drama around him.

"Is Dante the dragon you're slaying on this trip?" I asked Pete. "I couldn't help overhearing earlier."

Pete banged a fist into his other palm. "Dante is selling the ranch so they can move to the south of France. His new wife Claudia wants him to donate all his art and bibelots to a wild-mustang foundation."

"I didn't know mustangs created foundations."

"Very funny, *compadre*. We'll end this trip by filming the ranch as Dante folds up twenty years of history."

"Do we need to change the storyboards?" It wasn't fair to give Tadeusz any more uncertainty, though he claimed that the pain meds didn't interfere with his concentration.

"No, not an issue." Pete rinsed his coffee cup and put it in the dishwasher. "Dante is giving everything away."

"Ouch."

"Yeah, as if he has no heirs. Dante has a massive archive, like all the video I ever shot at the ranch, including all his seminars. Plus sculptures that you and I know are ninety-five percent Eliot's sweat and blood. Selfish effing bastard that he is."

I said, "No. He always cared, always encouraged us."

"Dante claims he's your primary influence, Sean. Did you read the *Vanity Fair* interview? Dante claims he introduced blue into your palette. He acts as if you were his son. And I'm not."

"It's never been like that."

"If you say so. For me, this ride is family business. I'm seeking what Dante owes me."

"Yikes."

"Now you know my karmic risk for this journey."

"So I'm claiming a new life and you want an old one," I said. "What's Eliot need?"

"Money for some saint-like act she intends to commit. I'd help, but what do I know about saints?" Pete stretched. "Do we hit the road soon?"

Eliot joined us, tucking her cell phone inside her jacket. "Did I hear right? Dante is letting you shoot video at the ranch? Since when? He's always chased away film media with a shotgun."

"Sure," Pete said. He stuffed his camera gear into a bag.

"Prove it." She folded her arms, a familiar gesture from years before, when she bullied her brother into doing the right thing.

"Screw that, Eliot. I don't have to prove—"

"Call Dante right now," she said. "Tell him I'm coming, too. Which I can guarantee you didn't do."

• • •

"Fine."

His defiant-kid face in place, Pete dialed, flicking his cell to speakerphone so we all heard.

"*Pronto? Chi parla?*" Dante, being himself.

"This is Pete. Wanted to let you know our plans changed. We'll be there in a week."

"Peter? Your guys called—" Dante's voice scratched, broke, then disappeared.

Pete checked his phone, shook his head, dialed again. "Dante, you hung up with your ear again. What guys called you?"

"Laconia. They want to document all that happened here. You said Sean only wanted to talk about the old painting seminars."

"Our guys didn't call you, Dante." Pete's voice cracked with tension. "We don't work with Laconia."

"They're pretty eager. Milo Speiser is directing and he'll be here Sunday. That's quite a coup you arranged. Thank you."

"What coup?" Pete blanched, his face pure white except for lines of Kabuki crimson where his nostrils flared.

"A biopic." Dante sound like he was speaking from the bottom of a well. "Because Sean's Impious Aeneas artwork was born on my ranch. I'm flattered that—"

"We're doing new work." Pete strangled on the words. "Not a retrospective."

The disembodied cellular Dante blew right past that. "I promised the pre-production crew I'd give them your old footage from when—"

"That's my freaking work!" Pete slipped into full distress mode, not often seen in this decade. "You cannot give Milo Speiser my work."

"Cool down, Peter." Dante sounded hoarse, distracted—and condescending. "The forces of the universe always conspire for good. Your friend said FAIL Studios already bought the documentary, before they even shot five minutes of the ranch. He said—"

"Not my friend. Milo's lying to you, Dante. Don't talk to Milo or anyone else until Sean and I get there."

Dante chuckled, that old Coyote Trickster snicker of his. "We'll see. Art loves the camera, and you know—"

Radio silence again.

Pete slammed his phone in his palm, then sent a text to Dante:

"STOP do NOT do shit with milo"

"Sorry I doubted you, Pete," Eliot said. "He's definitely expecting you. Not me, though. Dante sounds tired, or ill, or even—"

Pete didn't hear her. "What am I, hairy-assed Esau? The new heir of Laconia is stealing my work and I didn't even get the mess of potage. Milo-fuck-me-over-Speiser."

"Who's Milo Speiser?" Eliot asked.

Pete sucked air through his teeth. "His art—"

"He's now Laconia's principal partner and creative director," I said. "My father retired and wanted to sell his part of our business. We needed a new principal to keep Laconia afloat."

"Milo imagines he's an artist. He gleans the field after a real artist already harvested the original and best ideas," Pete said. "And now he has the funding I rejected."

That caught me short. "I thought your sister Sam funded all your documentary work."

"Two former Eastern European clients—" Pete paused. "They bankrolled Milo so he could buy into Laconia Media."

"Your same gangster friends who attacked Sam?" Eliot asked.[3]

"That wasn't my fault. It was more like an accident."

Eliot remained silent while Pete raged about Milo and I pestered him about Milo's gangster underwriters. Then, without peeking up from the camera she was fiddling with, Eliot asked, "Didn't Milo Speiser take a First at Palm d'Or? The last time. When you took a Second for that Chisinau gangster video?"

"He cheats." Pete's shoulders rose minutely.

"Oh c'mon, little brother. You always say it doesn't matter if you win."

"Unless it's Milo. He's been stealing concepts and material from me since freshman year when—"

"Wait," Eliot said. "Is Milo that guy who was your roommate? The one who stole your underwear?"

"The issues and stolen material have been significantly larger since then," Pete said, as indignant as he can get.

"It's ten o'clock," Eliot said. "Are we going?"

---

[3] For details, see *The Grrrl of Limberlost*.

Pete twitched for a second. "I signed on to collaborate with you, Sean. Not a three-way with Milo and Dante. Screw 'em. Let's just do it now."

"I'm ready." I picked up my jacket.

"No, I mean we publish as we go. Instead of after the trip. If we start today, you win the Internet before the week's out. You're the master of memes and tropes."

"The details aren't nailed yet." My heart thumped. "We don't know what kind of stories we'll find on the road. Or if we'll capture usable video."

"Time to stop dicking around with perfection," Pete said. "Remember what a great drug adrenalin is, *compadre*? Let's publish as we go."

"We need a great product when we meet with HOPE next week." *Publish as we go* jacked my pulse into heart-attack rates.

Pete waved my concern aside. "You nailed that in the storyboards, *caballero*. You long for this. Working in the moment."

I wanted to agree, but failed to squeak out an answer.

"OK, boss." Pete pounded my shoulder. "We can do this. Everyone involved knows their business." Pete crawled into his wearable-camera-laden leather jacket. That idea—*Publish as we go*—seemed to calm him.

"We just need to beat the clock." That's all I came up with.

Pete opened the dining room door. "Tadeusz." He called three times before Tadeusz removed his headphones. "We're publishing every day. A web episode at eight o'clock Pacific time. Every night after our day's ride. What's missing to make that happen?"

Tadeusz's face brightened, as if this idea was even better than the pain meds.

"I have the video channel ready. The art and animation elements are all queued. You just need to feed me still and video images. Each day's audio narrative. And any story changes."

"That's all you need?" I didn't mean to sound incredulous—as I always say, Tadeusz is a genius.

He nodded. "That, and Jason Taylor needs to tell me how to match music clips with the storyboard." Tadeusz stopped midway, seeing Eliot in the doorway. "Hi, I'm Tadeusz. Are you playing me in this movie? You're too tall for the role."

She crossed the room to shake his hand, all earnest and friendly. "I'm sorry you can't make this trip. I'm not happy to earn my pay off your bad luck."

They chatted warmly for a few minutes. He brought up a demo clip on his monitor, to show how he creates mashups of live video, still images, and animation.

"Your work is beautiful," she said. Tadeusz beamed, like everyone does who's blessed with her kindness.

"So are we riding now?" I asked, zipping up my jacket, as if I were the one who had my shit together.

■ ■ ■

We hit the interstate—I-5 South—at about half past ten o'clock, so Step One in the plan began more or less as intended. I rode at the end of the line, Eliot's black-leather form in front of me, just like that first journey.

Which didn't help generate the Zen-like meditation that I'd planned for this trip.

On the road, dreams become memories that in turn ignite creative thought. I wanted a trip back to the well, to sip the waters where I first learned to force "inspiration" to work for me upon command.

The original Journey, which gave life to my manga incarnation of Impious Aeneas, was from Dante's ranch, up the Great Basin and across Canada. The precise *where-ness* doesn't matter, just the barren *what-ness* of landscape. Memories of that journey informed the principal sensibility of the Impious Aeneas series.

On that journey, Eliot said, "Stop searching for childish magic and ghosts. The animating force is in the rocks, the rushing water, the shape of the clouds."

I listened to her wisdom then because of what we shared. Like me, she too had lost a mother who followed spirit-guides into the night and then died. Soon after that journey, I learned to animate the force of story with images from nature. It's the living color and shape of the mountains that Impious Aeneas climbs that awaken your sensibilities, preparing you to defeat the White-Bone Demon.

Yet once again Eliot rides in front of me, master of the road with her perfect posture, her ease in handling the curves, the climbs, the unexpected dangers of the road. An unplanned stimulus.

Maybe, on the other side of the Cascades, we'll ride fast. I'll climb out of my head. That figure riding in front won't disturb me.

The Desert Crucible
Why We Ride

[Tadeusz: This is the voice-over for the countdown, to go behind the art+video that shows the title. It's the only narrative that will use my voice. After Jason hears it, he can choose music to roll for the start. He promised an overall plan. Talk soon. —Sean]

I don't want to diminish experiences flowing out of the bottomless traditions of the Dharma, but for me there's this *kensho* thing with riding.

Heaven and earth fall away.

Unity with whatever is at the moment: No discrimination between me and the bike and the surroundings and the thrum of the engine, the wind, the delicate sensitivity in the way the bike lightly dances and wants to gallop.

Ride pony ride. I am the passing surroundings. The surroundings caress the bike as we pass.

There is a Zen saying, "The sun shines on everything." Let go of the discriminating mind. I am exactly where I am supposed to be when I am out on the continent riding all day, every day, for days and days. This is the ground from which one-pointed peaceful exhilaration springs. The sensation of the bike being "other" from my body dissolves.

Thousands of miles, no separation between me and the bike. Riding for riding's sake. For that unity. That sensuality.

But I have to be careful here, because once you say it, once you describe it, you've missed it. I've said too much already.

∞

5.
Black Diamond

Each has his past shut in him like the leaves of a book
known to him by heart and his friends can only read the title.
—Virginia Woolf

LEAVING THE FREEWAY, ELIOT BRAKED hard to avoid the updraft when a semi pulled in front of her.

Labor Day weekend is a big time for riders, with many large parties on State Route 5 around Mt. Rainier. Eliot waved, as motorcyclists do, at each bike passing in the other direction. Older couples on full-dress touring bikes were out, and a few solitary riders on sport bikes jetted past, crouched low over the seat, flying. On her own side of the highway the truckers were considerate, even jovial; no passenger cars pulled into her lane or blocked her passage. Perfect reverie-riding conditions, her body moving through space, as effortless as flying.

In a marsh alongside the road, red-winged blackbirds played, not the hideous starlings that squawked around her shop on Limberlost. Later in the trip, when they reached the Colorado Plateau, solitary ravens would soar overhead instead of the crows that attacked her garden. When they got to Dante's ranch, there'd be white-winged doves and Inca doves, not city pigeons and seagulls, like on the streets of Limberlost Village. For a decade, from when Eliot was sixteen until she returned to Seattle to tend her father, going home meant the hot, dusty ride down the all-weather road under the power lines, then dipping into the cool shade of hackberry, palo verde, and mesquite trees at Dante's ranch.

Few people know that Eliot had been a terror twenty years before, when her preacher-father despaired of her—*"You're as bad as your mother!"*—and shipped her to a boarding school in Arizona, as far from civilization as he could afford. When the police picked her up, a runaway on a stolen motorcycle, Eliot called Dante, her mother's last lover; her brother's father.

"Come live with me," Dante said, after he untangled her from juvenile court. "Work on the ranch."

"Ranch" was a distorted description. Dante first kept the place as a summer home and studio when his art began to sell in New York. When his wife—not Eliot's and Pete's mother—took a teaching position in Massachusetts, Dante became a permanent resident at the ranch, with a half-dozen apprentices drifting through each season. Eliot's first job: repair the fences to keep out the neighbors' cattle. She tore out the palms and oleander, and restored native desert plants. Midway through her effort to turn outbuildings into student bunk houses, Dante asked her help with metalwork for his sculptures, sending her off to community college night school to learn welding.

At Dante's ranch, she and Pete first became close friends. She was eight years older and they weren't raised together as children, scarcely knew each other until Pete was also sent to Arizona for trouble he raised in Washington State. They played old blues as background music in the garage while fixing broken machines; they hiked the desert, giving each other advice about stupid love affairs. The summer Pete turned sixteen—when he visited during college breaks—he shambled onto the verandah one night when one of Dante's sophisticated visitors, with two decades' more experience, was feeding Eliot wine and pretending to misunderstand what "no" means. Pete, his Innocence mask in place, slumped beside the guy on the verandah and said, "Eliot? I need advice."

"Yes?" she said, disentangling herself as Pete leaned across that guy to talk to her.

"Should I rebuild the Triumph I wrecked? Or sell it as parts and buy a better bike?"

They debated his quandary until her pursuer left, and for years they used that question to disentangle each other from unwanted conversations: "Should I rebuild that wreck or part it out at the junk yard? What's your advice?"

This many years down the road, she had no better partner to hit the road with than her own brother. As unpredictable as Pete typically proved to be.

It wasn't lack of work that ripped Eliot up by the roots from the Sonoran desert for transplant in the Puget Sound wetlands.

Now here she was, back on the highway, riding toward Dante's ranch. Only because the problems she had to resolve required more cash than a craftsperson who drifts from job to job can accumulate. If a trip to the ranch manifested the necessary funds, then she'd buck up her courage and ride there.

■ ■ ■

The roads from Black Diamond to Yakima were familiar from summer rides, easy foreplay for the long trip, just fooling around until they reached the desert. The land rolled here, farmers' fields dipping down to where creeks ran through alder and big-leaf maple. Each dip in the road opened its own micro-climate, with enough temperature change that smelling the air was like awaking to a new day. In each roadside ditch, summer sun had burned the grass and invasive weeds down to their early autumnal essence.

Autumn?

Eliot discarded that idea. It was only the fourth of September. The calendar alone promised another three weeks of summer, and they rode for the Sonoran desert. She didn't hate autumn, though she was always reluctant to let summer go. The burned-dust smell of toasted curly dock and seed-sprung hay sent memories of past Septembers up her nose, awakening thoughts of—

She refused to indulge in nostalgia, or regret, stirred up by the odor of plant life that had run its course, flowered, burst its seed pods for next year's life to be dispersed by the wind or birds or small field-dwelling mammals. She denied what lay ahead: November storms, a moldering blanket of leaves, maybe snow, plants decaying, to live again as compost for the next generation come—

A dip with a ten-degree change in temperature shook her out of autumnal reverie. Time to climb up the Chinook Pass Highway, into the Cascades. Loving the flow through the mountain turns, Eliot again passed Pete, who lagged behind to let his camera capture details, and then passed Sean, who was exercising that flashy toy, testing its balance in turns and then speeding on the straightaways.

She didn't approve of the bike, but it wasn't her business.

He'd offered a finer profile on that old thumper Triumph back when—

Riding ahead, she put that red bike and its rider out of mind as the highway twisted up to higher elevations. She used the stretches with passing lanes to check how her wearable cameras performed. The front-mounted camera on the bike gave her no concern—she'd placed that mounting herself, and had captured digital shots with it for the past two years. That camera would perform exactly as she intended, unless the bike was hit by a Mack truck. The wearables stayed in place. She'd check at the first rest stop to ensure that timers and other settings behaved themselves. Utterly unfair of Pete to ask this much, and not give her time to select cameras herself, although the jacket fit well, so she wasn't starting the trip by quarreling with her gear.

Outside of Yakima, they paused to debate a plan. Pete and Eliot had passed through this territory enough that they had an agenda for the first meal on the road.

"Chinese and then the campground in Oregon?" Pete asked.

Eliot said, "If you mean where we ate last May, yes."

"My mind was on food the whole morning," Pete said. "I need fuel after a late night and long ride."

"Eat all you want," Eliot said, "but we camp before dark. I hate pitching a tent with only the bike's headlamp for light."

Riding into Yakima, Eliot lagged behind and missed one traffic light, then accidentally on purpose went straight ahead instead of turning left, which bought her several more minutes alone to convince herself she could float down America's highways with Pete and Sean and maintain an even keel.

Outside the restaurant, Pete's K1200RS sat on its center stand in the parking lot, but Sean's Kawasaki leaned on its kickstand, propped up like a target for a squirrelly teenage cruiser. Shaking her head over his careless parking, she backed her own bike up against the curb and carried her helmet inside.

Fishing out her phone, Eliot found only a text from Roz:

Destiny is a superstar. Promised not to say more.

"Your table will be ready shortly," the hostess said when Eliot inquired after Pete and Sean. "Please join your party in the bar."

She pointed to the beaded doorway under a green ceramic dragon whose glass eyes watched from across the restaurant. Music wafted past the curtain, a voice singing of passion and loss, the vibrato of unhappiness ringing as Eliot jangled through the hanging beads to find only Sean, his thin body hunched over the ornately carved bar, his jacket and helmet dropped carelessly at his feet.

The bartender, a tiny man of about forty, spoke in Chinese, excited and laughing. He gestured and thumped his hand again on the paper he'd laid on the bar. Sean's open and encouraging grin, which skewed the symmetry of his otherwise ordinary face, always forced an answering smile when he talked to strangers. His hazel eyes—reflected in the mirror at the back of the bar—probed innocently, unchallenging. The bartender noticed Eliot and moved to offer service.

"Eliot!" Sean said when he noticed her beside him. "This is Frank Chung. Frank, this is Eliot Arden."

The bartender nodded a greeting without meeting her eyes. Instead he glanced down; Pete's camera sat on the bar, taping every word spoken.

"Guess what? Frank comes from a neighborhood near where one of Laconia's partners has offices in Taipei," Sean said. "Isn't it wonderful how small the world is?"

Frank smiled shyly now, not enthusiastically as he had before Eliot arrived.

"It is nice to talk to you," Frank said carefully, picking up the photo he'd shown Sean of a family standing outside a small bungalow. He tucked it away, retreating into his bartender's role.

"What can I get for your wife?" he asked Sean.

"She's not my wife, Frank, only my friend." He faced Eliot. "Pete will be back in a minute. Can I talk you into drinking plum wine with me?"

"Not when I'm riding," she blurted, then flushed, embarrassed about upbraiding him in front of the bartender, who waited to take her order. "Nothing, Frank, thank you."

Sean and his new friend resumed their conversation, subdued, talking about how Frank ended up bartending for his uncle in Yakima. Standing too close to Sean, Eliot shuffled from one foot to another, then excused herself abruptly.

He smelled the same.

Funny how it's possible to block memories for a decade, and then your nose betrays you.

Fortunately, the women's room at the restaurant reeked of hot sesame oil and air freshener. Eliot pretended to fix her hair. A tsunami of regret washed over her as she stared in the mirror, hearing again what Sean's sister Sophy had said ten years before.

> He's East Coast, you're West Coast. It's like miscegenation. He's headed for great things.

Maybe two centuries ago, in a Regency romance, a woman might maintain affection over a decade. But it's not possible now. Your friends don't want to hear about it. For eighteen months, perhaps two years, you can remain true to a lost love. Then unrequited love becomes tedious. You stop crying and get on with life. Every good carpenter knows to clean a wound quickly and dress it properly to prevent infection. And then gets back to work.

Another woman came in, wearing an expensive emerald-green dress with too much jewelry. Drunk, she brushed past Eliot to find an empty stall. Eliot washed her hands and splashed water on her face, wanting to rinse away any memory-triggering essence of Sean and return to the present moment.

Where she was a temp worker being paid decent money to ride across the desert in support of one of Sean's great things.

■ ■ ■

Eliot stepped away to let the tipsy woman use the sink. Coming out of the women's room, Eliot ran into Pete and followed him to the table where the hostess left them with menus and a promise to find Sean in the bar. Pete kept asking what it was they'd eaten last spring that was so good. Eliot, pondering the kung pao chicken, murmured thank-you when the waiter brought their tea.

Sean slumped into the booth and whipped out his pad. He chatted with Pete while they uploaded files for Tadeusz and waited for food to come. Hunched in a hoodie that used to be black, Sean held his pen in that crabbed way he always did, guarding and shepherding it across the page. Except now: a stylus on a touch screen.

Deep in conversation with Pete, Sean pushed at the bridge of his hawk's-beak nose, as if pushing up his glasses, except today he wore contacts. He still had that lost expression while thinking, as if he observed another scene overlaid between him and whatever real people acted out before him.

He tugged at the neck of his t-shirt, just like he used to, so it's ragged only days after it comes from the store. He'd already worried a hole between the collar and his heart, the same as every other t-shirt he'd ever worn. The first day they worked together that summer, he'd stripped off his ragged t-shirt, distracting her attention as sweat trickled down his neck, across his chest, lost in the hair on his belly. She'd violated the spirit of their ditch-digging conversation then, focusing on his body instead of the higher mystical connections they explored.

"Garlic green beans?" Pete elbowed her to get her attention. "Focus on vegetables?"

"I need protein," Sean said. "Remember what Dante claimed when he kept vegetarian at the ranch? That it was a religious obligation to the universe, like keeping kosher?"

Pete said, "I remember calling it bullshit. And Dante should know. He's full of it."

Eliot let Pete order and then flipped through the images on her cameras, deleting the unusable ones before handing the cameras' memory cards to Pete, who gave her back another set of cards to reload her cameras.

...

Remember what Dante said? She stirred her portion of tofu in black bean sauce, wincing at one particular memory, when Dante offered her advice like he gave in critique sessions with untalented apprentices: *"Don't make me be brutal, sweetheart. You're merely practical and good with your hands. The work you do isn't art."*

"Practical?" She repeated the word, puzzled at the insult.

"That's what we pay you for," Pete said. He offered her the last bits of Buddhists Delight.

6.
Yakima

I ADMIRE HOW PETE GETS people to open up, talks them into signing a release for permission to use their image and voice, and then keeps them relaxed while he records. He snagged great material from Frank in about three hundred seconds, including time spent getting him to sign the consent-to-release form.

After we stuffed ourselves with black mushrooms and vegetables, got all sticky with sweet pepper sauce and delirious with garlic tofu in black bean sauce, I sat back, satiated, feeling more like myself after a few hours' bike ride than I had in months. Pete finished off the mushrooms and bamboo floating in hot sugar sauce. Eliot ate half as much as Pete or me, but studied it harder. She was more ordinary than I remembered, her hair less desert-blond, but just as tightly braided.

"Your shots of Mount Rainier over the bike's fairing are fantastic," I said. "The images of farm buildings outside Enumclaw have the moody lighting and evocative framing that we hoped for."

"Thank you," she said, so quietly that the words disappeared. The waiter came by to ask what more we needed. I asked for green tea and the check.

"Pete's spurring me to take risks," I said, "but your work is so good, Eliot, that it keeps me well within a zone of comfort."

Over Eliot's shoulder, in the next booth, a boy in a green t-shirt read manga while his father prodded him to eat almond chicken. Issue #7: *Impious Aeneas Vanquishes the Overlords of Famine*. One of my favorites. His little sister hopped up and down on the bench, not once persuaded to sit and eat. She wore a blue shirt with a fuzzy applique Monkey King, whose plastic eyes rolled with each hop, always staring at me. My first view of FAIL Studios' licensed merchandise in the wild.

Pete pushed back his plate. "That meal did well by me. I might now have the strength to go on." He explained to Eliot that we'd been up since dawn, setting up computer workstations for Tadeusz.

Given her quiet reserve, I couldn't discern what it was about her that once consumed me. Yes, she drove me out of my mind in bed, but when I ponder the past, I see us sitting by a river in the Canadian Rockies, scratching mosquito bites and avoiding the midday sun. She told stories she'd made up as a kid, about being a Swan Maiden who drank dragon's blood and gambled with knuckle bones to settle the fate of humans. For years I've mostly remembered the ice-slapped-on-the-balls goodbye, rather than that summer's heat.

■ ■ ■

It started with me standing naked on the Sonoran desert early one morning, begging a shy wild-child to come back to bed with me. That whole scene was ridiculous in any modern context. And ultimately, a colossal fail: Eliot curled back inside herself before we rode together as far as October.

We bonded over our mothers, who died young, leaving lonely children behind.

"Freyja, my mother, disappeared into her own spiritual dreams, as if she walked down a hall and a curtain fell behind her." I shared with Eliot what I'd never talked about with anyone before. "They say she died of a stroke, but I found her journal, saying she hoped to join her spirit friends in the other world."

"No! Who let you read that?" Her dismay warmed me. No one had ever understood in the way that Eliot did. She said, "My mother called out to the spirits in rocks and trees, too, but learned weird prayers from Sedona shamans. Who knows what she really believed. In the middle of a fight with Dante, she said she'd take it up with God. Then got in a car, drove away, and died."

This talk occurred over that damn ditch we dug at Dante's ranch. We took a break, passing the water jug between us.

"For years I had nightmares that my mother's spirit-friends called to me," I said. "When I told my dad, he sent me to a psycho-doctor so I wouldn't flip like Freyja did. Then somehow I ended up living with my sister in Amherst, ripped out of Seattle by the roots. My work is how I made friends with the nightmares."

"Is that why you're different from the other artists here?" she asked. "Instead of hanging out on the verandah drinking, you spend all your time in the studio."

"Maybe my real work is still in the future. I haven't figured out the precise details yet."

"Your future? It's here now," she said, grabbing her shovel, as if to step back from plunging too deeply into my life. "Your future is ditch-digging. If you make an effort, we'll be done in an hour."

On the first day of August, Eliot and I left Arizona together, riding up into the Rockies to escape summer heat, then even farther north into the Canadian Rockies, as far as Banff. Mosquitoes and horseflies chased us east to the Atlantic coast, where we ended up at my sister Sophy's in Amherst, where the heat we'd outrun caught up with us.

After forty days of riding and adventure with Eliot, then two weeks of domestic bliss in Sophy's haven, I was on fire to work, but still waiting for the vision to cohere. I read *The Golden Bough* and Chinese folk tales and sketched furiously, waiting for night when I could get Eliot alone and drown for an hour inside of her, wake in the morning to drink more of her essence, buzz around her during the day, smelling her funk on my fingers, tasting the salty sweet honey left there from the last moment alone with her, more in love than I've ever been in my life. Yet also lost in working toward what would become my incarnation of Impious Aeneas and his heroic companions.

Then her father parted us.

Coincidentally, my father Robert visited the day before, taking us out for a disastrous, overpriced lunch. After that hellacious, awkward meal, Eliot left us alone. I chatted with Robert in Sophy's library, the room prickly with Indian-summer heat. Having drunk most of the too-expensive wine my father ordered at lunch, I didn't understand at first what he said in a long sermon about God and remorse. Instead, I saw a doppelganger of myself at age seventy, a stringy old man with a scarecrow frame. That would be my boney hand and long fingers, my own hawk's nose and cheekbones covered in parchment instead of young skin.

"Don't think I'm meddling," Robert said. "But I just bought a small media company in London. When I showed the production manager your drawings and the catalog from your New York show, Tadeusz begged me to get you to come work with him."

"You saw my New York show?" I woke up, startled. My father had insisted for years that I forget art as a career.

"Come to London for six months and work with Tadeusz. I'll put you up in my apartment."

"Just like that? Pack up and leave the country?"

Robert struggled to control a gentle, puzzling smile that finally got the better of him. "Would coming to London right now interfere with other plans?"

I'd definitely given no impression other than idleness in our conversation.

"Think about it. I have to catch a plane for London tonight," Robert said. "Call my office if you decide to join me. They'll make all the arrangements."

Later, I found Eliot asleep, curled into a tight ball. I fell asleep fully dressed, thinking how we might try London for just a while, dreaming that we rode there on our motorcycles.

Summer ended during the night, and a desultory autumn rain began. Eliot woke sullen. Before I could talk to her about London, she announced that she was leaving.

"I'm out of money," she said. She stood when I wanted to lay my head in her lap. "I have to find work. And my father is ill and needs me in Seattle."

Just like that, she walked away. Rode away on her bike.

I went to London both excited and broken-hearted. The new work helped me get over that chafing loss. Tadeusz and I laid the business foundation for what became Laconia Media. When alone over long nights in London, I still had the private pleasure of combining paints on a real palette.

■ ■ ■

While drinking tea in Yakima, we uploaded the images. I added my first pad drawing. Thinking of David Hockney's daily fingerpaints on his iPhone, I wanted to try finger-on-glass as a medium.

Tadeusz flooded Pete and me with a wave of texts, frustrated because Jason hadn't returned his calls. He had no problems with the mess of files that Pete and I sent him, but Tadeusz complained about the lack of artistic direction for syncing music with images.

"You have more talent for that than you give yourself credit," I said, calling Tadeusz on my cell instead of trading more text messages. I made suggestions about how my painting fit with Eliot's still shots of Rainier.

"OK," Tadeusz said, "I'm syncing all that material with the song Jason labeled 'Synchronicity.'"

"Is it like a mountain folk song?" My pad-painting evoked a daydream, with Rainier as a mythic force in the background.

"More like Icelandic psychedelics," Tadeusz said.

Pete took the phone from me. "Please post by eight o'clock, Tadeusz. We won't be online again until after then." Pause. "No, Sean doesn't need to approve the final. He trusts you. You know how to assert the new brand."

I grabbed my phone back. "It's art, not branded content."

Pete jabbed a finger at me, laughing. "In your dreams."

A woman in a bright green dress stumbled as she passed our table, too drunk to be staggering unescorted in a nice restaurant. I smelled gin when the woman put her hand out to steady herself, touching Eliot's shoulder by accident.

"Sorry, dearie."

Eliot flinched and moved closer to Pete as the woman lurched toward the front of the restaurant.

"We better get moving," Eliot said after a moment. "We'll need a flashlight to find a campground as it is."

"Ready!" Pete said, closing his laptop. "But Sean might not be able to move after the last few hours on that bike."

I laughed, because it was a joke. I wasn't about to admit how stiff that ride left me. "I'm ready to go now. I could ride all night."

One thing I had to admit: the maritime climate did well by Eliot—her nose wasn't burned and peeling like it always was in the desert. The mild northern sun only bleached out the tiny hairs on her face and arms, leaving her steel-grey eyes as shaded and secretive as ever.

"You're well equipped?" Eliot asked, making an effort to speak to me. "Did you bring rain gear?"

"Pete promised no rain," I said. She wasn't as tall as I remembered. Somehow, she'd taken on mythic proportions in my mind.

"But it always rains when you ride with Pete," she said.

"Rain is statistically improbable for early September," Pete said. The waiter appeared with the check.

"Let's go," I said, fishing for my wallet. "I'll get this."

Pete said, "I'm calling Tadeusz to make sure the last upload is OK. I'll be quick."

Eliot bolted ahead of us. I took an extra-long stride to catch up.

"It'll be fun to work together," I said, walking beside her.

She smiled, as if struggling to keep her manners. Then her cell buzzed and she ducked into a hall off the foyer to answer it.

Left alone in the foyer, waiting for Pete, I found a text message on my phone from Milo:

"YR ON!!!"

I punched his flash-call number. No answer.

"What do you suppose this means?" I asked Pete, showing him the text when he came into the foyer.

"That was fast," Pete said. "Guess the bet is on."

"What bet?" Foreboding trickled down my spine.

"I bet Milo that you produce better new product in a week and attract a bigger audience than Laconia can in the same timeframe."

"What do I lose?"

"Nothing. You only win. You get back rights to all your early Impious Aeneas work."

"Dammit, Pete. What do I risk if we lose?"

"Oh I like hearing that. Sean Wentworth thinks he's taking a risk." Pete rubbed his hands together. "You're already hanging your neck out, publishing live every day while we ride."

"Milo would never take that bet."

"I'm persuasive. So we ride—and seven days from now, you'll have your rights back for Impious Aeneas. Plus a new audience and a concept that HOPE will green-light."

"Wow. Milo agreed to this?"

Pete said, "Is Milo going to drive Laconia guys to produce more footage than God could draw? Yeah, he is."

"This isn't a deal. I didn't sign anything—"

"My former friends," Pete paused. "They promise to ensure that Milo respects the results. It's all good."

"There's no way Milo would take a bet with so little at stake."

Pete shrugged, a gesture that alarms anyone who knows him. "He gets my services for twelve months if we blow it. But, c'mon boss, how could we blow this? Unless we get crushed by a truck on the Interstate. Then it wouldn't matter if we lose the bet."

• • •

Eliot waited outside the door, taking jittery dancing steps in her motorcycle boots.

"Destiny sold it!" She hugged Pete, then lifted and spun him around. "My welded Motorhorse piece. Destiny got full price at the Saturday market, after you put that outrageous ticket on it in July. The buyer didn't even want to haggle."

"I told you it was worth two more zeroes." Pete twitched a smile, happy for his sister. As soon as she let go, Pete whipped up his video cam and began shooting our bikes, which stood in a line: beasts of the road, loaded with baggage like crusaders' palfreys of yore. He captured Eliot's audio, though I don't think Eliot noticed in the midst of her rapture.

"But Destiny is the one who sold it! Do you know what this does for her confidence? We'll have to talk the girl down off the moon after this."

I tapped her shoulder for attention.

"You sold wh—"

That toddler in the Monkey King shirt burst through the restaurant door ahead of her parents, hopping two-footed down the steps, then pausing an infant's moment to stare at the bikes. Monkey King shifted his eyes to gaze back at me. The little girl pointed to the sticker on the Kawasaki and shouted, "Monkey King!" as she ran toward my bike.

Afterwards, the multidimensionality and simultaneity of action made it difficult to explain to the officer what I'd seen:

The child cried out.

Eliot shoved me, as if for leverage, and leaped down five steps.

The woman behind me shrieked, a sound I'd never heard from a human throat.

Eliot wrapped arms around the child and rolled onto the curb.

Our bikes fell slowly, like dominos.

Only then did I see the white Chrysler LeBaron, its brake-and-backup taillights flashing on and off, and the car lumbering up the parking lot, careening against a Jeep parked at the end of the row, the Jeep's homemade bumper gouging a deep, dark scar into the slow-moving Chrysler.

"I lifted the bike off her," I told the officer. Though I'd mostly been a member of the audience, my fingers still tingled from the scare. I hadn't even noticed the weight of her R100RS when I lifted it for the second time that day. "The bike only trapped her boot. She could have pushed it off on her own, but she was all wrapped up around the little girl."

Pete, who'd copied his memory card before the police arrived, handed it over and signed an evidence sheet, insisting that all card content was copyrighted and not to be used for any purpose other than evidence. When he finished, Pete began to pick up our bikes, taking pictures of the damage.

Calm as Artemis through the commotion, Eliot talked with a second officer while huddling with the little girl's parents, the child now sheltered in her mother's arms. The blond imp buried her head whenever Eliot or the cop smiled or spoke to her, too shy to greet her superhero rescuer.

When the officer let me go, I joined Eliot with the parents.

"She knows better," the mother was saying. "Too much excitement, I guess."

"Monkey King distracted her," I said, feeling guilty. I offered the little girl a Monkey King sticker from my pocket. She hid her head again, so her father took the sticker and thanked me.

The officer listened to his shoulder radio. He said, "They picked up the driver. So no one else is in danger."

Eliot, after brief goodbyes to that family, joined Pete to inspect her bike.

"Lucky you," Pete said. "Not one scratch on your bike. Just this nick of red paint where your handlebar scratched Sean's bike."

Still rattled, I didn't give a damn about the bike. It wasn't till I'd kicked it into gear that I noticed the crack in my mirror. Neatly down the middle.

I called to Eliot over the sound of the bikes as she adjusted her mirror and checked her gear. "Are you OK?"

Her fingers had to tingle much more than mine did from the scare. She'd taken action. She'd saved everything.

But Eliot merely nodded. "We have to ride like hell if we're going to make the campground tonight." She kicked her bike into gear and smoothly pulled away, headed for Highway 97.

Pete said, "This is just what Milo would do. As soon as he took that bet, he started cheating."

"Paranoia isn't your style," I said, ready to ride. "He doesn't even know where we are. It's just fate. Or coincidence."

"I thought we didn't believe in fate." Pete had his head down, sending a set of accident images to Tadeusz. "And Milo connived on shit like this even before he met my Eastern European friends."

The Desert Crucible Episode I
Mountain Roads

[Tadeusz: Use the image list from the 2pm email. Match it with whatever strum-and-thunder music Jason provided. Looped sound might also work well here. —Pete]

Days after I've been riding, it echoes in my head and inner visions. The mountains, rushing rivers everywhere, riding in the snow.

The best? Diving headlong at impossible speeds into an endless succession of curves and turns. Testing the bleeding edge of tire adhesion. Just barely kissing the pavement with sparking metal, this side, now that side, now this side. Stand on the brakes at the last second, flame up the gas early and out.

At least double the speed marked for curves. 25 mph –> 55 mph. 40 mph –> 85 mph. Sweepers at 100 mph –> 125 mph. Hell yeah! Truth be told, all riding on straight roads is on the way to this.

Thrilling, laser-pointed focus, sharpening attention to a razor's edge. It is all-consuming, athletic, challenging, precise, skill testing. I'm never happier than when I am leaned over, feeling for the pavement with my toe just before metal, full hard on the gas in the turn. Heaven on fire!

All this, just riding a piece of cold machinery? Yes: the superb beauty of controlled motion from the chaos of all other possible motions. Dancing with the machine, with perfection impossible, but nearby— if I tighten my focus, time my body more finely to the machine's nuances and rushing road. Brake a little later.

This is what I'm living for.

The world drops away.

Flying into impossible roads with no-mind.

∞

7.

Tumalo

The past is not a package one can lay away.
—Emily Dickinson

ELIOT
Sunday

SOUTH OF MOUNT HOOD, ELIOT led them off Highway 97 to one of her favorite rides, down well-paved, empty logging roads that traced the spine of the Cascades, offering spectacular vistas and long empty miles with sweet curves and dips. The best kind of riding, sunlight flashing between tall trees as they traveled.

By the time they returned to Highway 97, clouds drifted east across the mountains, gathered and lowered over the Central Oregon desert just as the sun hid behind the Cascades.

A downpour started while they were setting up camp at Tumalo Falls and continued through the night. Tired, eager to get out of the rain, Pete and Sean dived into one tent, while Eliot crept into her tiny dome, undressing in the dark while rain pounded the tent. She lay close to the other tent, listening to Pete and Sean, who posted on a blog and on Twitter in between phone calls to that other guy—Tadeusz?—to discuss preparations for the next day.

"Far freaking out!" Pete shouted. "Two hours live and six zeroes in the number of views! Oh fuck a duck. You win the goddam Internet, boss."

"Hey asshole!" a voice shouted from elsewhere in the campground. "Shut the ever-loving fuck up."

Pete's voice dropped. "What the hell are you doing, Sean? Don't read the comments."

"I'll skip the troll stuff and the acid reflux beeswax," Sean said. "Here's what I wanted to see. Geezus. Look."

"'Sean Wentworth is working ten levels beyond everything he did before,'" Pete said. "OK, boss, you're smiling. You like that. Here's a good one. 'This washed away the grit in my eyes from that FAIL preview trailer for the Monkey King movie.'"

Sean laughed—no, giggled—as Pete read web comments.

"We have to post several times a day, you and I," Pete said. "And we need to start answering questions tonight."

"No way."

"Yes, way. If we're going to be doing a live journal, we have to answer audience questions."

"OK, I'll put an Askmonkey invitation on Twitter. We'll do it in five minutes."

"Bite me, Milo Speiser," Pete said.

While Pete and Sean worked, Eliot texted congratulations to Destiny for her market success.

Des: I sold $1040 worth of clocks too. Enuf to buy my aunt's house?

If only. Eliot sent comfort back, since Destiny really asked a bigger question.

Eliot: I'm working on it. Roz too.

Ten minutes later, Destiny had another message.

Des: The guy knew you. Who bought the Motorhorse sculpture.

Eliot: Who?

Des: Can't remember. Roz has all the credit card stuff.

Eliot: What did he look like?

Des: My rich grandfather. Found me at last. Rescuing his princess.

After an exchange of emoticons, Eliot clicked off. *Rich grandfather, found me at last.* What Destiny always said when they discussed tactical options for keeping her out of foster care.

Pete and Sean talked past midnight and then, it seemed, went to sleep. After fretting for hours, Eliot managed to leave consciousness behind. She woke once, her legs and hips cold because the earth had sucked away her body heat. She put on her shirt and long johns to keep warm, and then sought sleep again.

In the morning, though, it still rained. Eliot listened for sounds from the other tent that signaled time to get up. The torrent drumming on the tent's rainfly set a hypnotic beat, leaving her lost in a road-dream where she wandered through a parking lot in a strange town. Two drunken men in a white car shouted belligerently at passersby. She ran into a Laundromat. Sean was in the back, loading wet clothes into the dryer.

"You should be careful of them!" she called. "They want to pick a fight."

She fumbled in her pockets for change to call the police, finding only a nickel and a penny. She pressed buttons for 9-1-1, but got nothing except her nickel back. She tried again. Again.

The men came in. She jumped back to warn her brother, but he'd disappeared. She ran out the back door, grabbing a wooden stake from a pile in the yard.

"Stay away from me!" she warned. She swung the stake as a sword, leaped over the stack of wood, and ran. Rounding the corner of the building, she smashed up against a dead-end where a wire fence surrounded a yard full of mean dogs. If she got past the dogs, she'd be able to scale the wall on the other side. She thought for a moment, foolishly, that because she was a good person, the dogs wouldn't hassle her and would instead go after those men. But she knew that wasn't right. She crossed the first wire fence and perched on the second, her leg over, ready to jump into the dogs rather than let those men touch her. An angry collie took her leg into his jaws. The larger man had his hand on her shoulder, trying to wrest her out of the dog's jaws.

A thin, bedraggled old woman stood in the doorway of the house, fiercely angry.

"What are you doing to my dog?" the old woman scolded the man, as though he were baiting the dog with Eliot.

"But it was Sean in the Laundromat, not my brother," Eliot said, straddling the wire fence, wishing the dog would let go, then aware that she dreamed.

She struggled to wake up, too hot, sweating in her long johns.

The rustling outside sounded like camp being dismantled. She scrambled into jeans and boots, and stuffed her sweat-drenched sleeping bag into its sack. As she crawled out of the tent, the pool of water that had collected on the rainfly flooded down her neck.

■ ■ ■

"Welcome to the desert," Sean said, his hair matted, rain running in rivulets down his face. "Help me fold this tent, then I'll help with yours."

"Where's Pete?"

"He went to find a Laundromat to dry our sleeping bags. We couldn't rouse you, so I stayed behind. Let's get out of here before we drown."

Grit, water, and leaves ended up stuffed into the sacks with the tents, while they got drenched struggling to break camp. They escaped the campground to follow Highway 97.

Where every truck they passed on the highway doused them with a swoosh of water.

Eliot and Sean found the Laundromat and Pete, who pointed them toward a café across the street for breakfast. Eliot used the women's room to wash her face and rebraid damp hair. When she emerged, Pete came into the café dangling a power strip, striking up a conversation with the waitress and making her laugh. Then he joined Sean and Eliot.

"She doesn't think it weird that we need to recharge a dozen devices."

They plugged in phones, laptops, and camera battery chargers. Sean immersed himself in his tethered pad, tapping messages, occasionally making that motion to push up his glasses. Pete stressed over food options. Sean decided on pancakes and eggs. Eliot chose bacon with hers and drowned it all in that god-awful institutional syrup from plastic tubs with peel-back foil lids.

"The coffee tastes like floor cleaner," she said, hoping to make benign conversation.

"I always drink tea when I travel," Sean said. "It's safer."

He fished the teabag from his cup and set it aside. He seemed lost in thought. Before cutting into his eggs, he propped his pad against the sugar dispenser to fiddle with it while he ate. After a few bites, he began drawing with a stylus.

Pete had on headphones, listening to whatever played on his laptop while typing like a madman. Since both guys were lost in that world, Eliot crossed the café and bought a Portland newspaper. Not that the news interested her, but she had nothing else to hide behind, having left her paperback in the fairing pocket of her bike.

While Eliot read, Sean went to the restroom, leaving his pad open before her, tilted her way so that she couldn't help but see. The same blue palette. Even so, it's immoral to pry. Or at least improper. Eliot read her newspaper.

The Prussian blue beguiled. She looked.

And saw all that breathtaking power again, but new this time. Merely figures in a landscape, like years ago, yet the color, the movement, the story that Sean drew in each character's face. Like when you have to bite your lip not to cry.

To avoid looking at the drawing, she read the text. Sean's meticulous, tiny handwriting was woven into the sketch:

> At one time we were famous lovers
> at the foot of Cold Mountain.
> You carved the wooden beams for farmers' lodges,
> burnt with charcoal and hacked with adze.
> I spun wool into soft yarn and wove blankets
> that captured the mountain's beauty.
> In later centuries we hunted together
> as brothers near Two Grey Hills.
> The corn we ate was winnowed and milled
> And cooked by our wives who—

"Eliot, you shouldn't peek yet. It's just my crappy doodling," Sean said, dropping into his chair at the table.

"Sorry. I didn't mean to snoop."

"It's just so bad." He shook his head. "Let me show you the drawings when they're ready."

Having humiliated herself, Eliot returned to reading lovelorn advice in the *Oregonian* while the guys finished their eggs. If she had to smell him, hear his voice, study his drawings, it would mean—

Eliot went to the counter to ask for a second cup of the dreadfully acidic, burnt coffee. The clock over the cash register read 9:30, which was as good a time as any to call Cora on Limberlost Island. Eliot stepped outside the café, standing under the overhang as rain beat down.

"I'm so relieved you called," Cora said right after hello. "I went to the evening service last night. I put a billet in with questions for you. And Sarah Johns—you remember her? She's the clairvoyant. A wreck of metal came to Sarah in a vision. I've been so afraid for you, I couldn't sleep last night."

Cora faithfully attended services at the Limberlost Church of Pure Manifestations in Christ Consciousness, a tiny sect of faith healers. She crowded her house with crystals for healing, pots of herbs for teas and remedies, paintings of saints in their ecstasies, and Pre-Raphaelite women communing with God. She papered her kitchen wall with magazine clippings of the Divine Masters, an eclectic ménage that included Meher Baba, Krishnamurti, Muktananda, and Martin Luther King, Jr.

"It wasn't me in her vision." Eliot hated to feed into Cora's superstitions. She didn't believe Sarah Johns had any special powers except a unique ability to play on people's fears.

"I'm glad you're safe, sweetheart. It's good that your friends are taking care of you."

Eliot tried to change the subject. "Are you well?"

"Of course I'm fine, dear. Just a little dizzy spell yesterday. People were so kind to pray for me last night."

"Did you call the doctor?"

"I'm trying. But doctors only see a meal ticket when you show your Medicare card."

"Not all doctors," Eliot said, seeking to stop the flow of words. "You need to go to the doctor I found for you. Promise you'll go as soon as Roz can take you." When she got a modest positive reply, Eliot hated to ask the next question, because business seems so crass between friends. "Has my real estate agent called you?"

"Not yet. But my agent says that she has an offer to show me. Full price."

"Wait, don't take it!" Eliot's heart hit hard against her ribs. She didn't mean to say it aloud. Cora needed to sell that land.

"I know you want to be our neighbor, dear. And we need you here with us. But this is so much money."

"Let me make a counter offer. I'll call my agent now. Please wait, Mrs. W."

"We will, honey. But don't you fret. It always works out right in the end if you have faith."

Eliot didn't believe that—chances are mostly fifty-fifty.

She left voice messages for her agent with instructions to make the best possible offer, knowing she'd have to swallow pride and ask her sister for help to match a full-price offer.

Pete was drinking tea with Sean when she came back from the phone call.

"What's the word?" Pete removed his headphones. "Did you sleep? We got so frigging hot that the sleeping bags ended up as wet inside as the tent got outside."

"I'm OK," she said, not hearing it in her own voice.

"You just get whomped with a misery stick?" Pete's examination made her squirm.

"Thanks. I called Mrs. Waddington. She's not well."

"Wow. Someone needs care and you're not available? Who'd believe it?" Pete said. That wasn't a real question, and she wasn't about to discuss her disappointing call. Nothing to be gained by brooding over a problem she couldn't act on.

"It's time to hit the highway," Sean said, switching off his pad and zipping his pack closed.

"I have to go to the john first," Eliot said. She wanted to brush her teeth before zooming into the rain again. "I'll meet you in the parking lot."

"Take your time. I'll check the oil level on the bike," Pete said.

As the restroom door closed behind her, Sean's voice rumbled, deep, distant.

"Is Eliot still doing everyone else's karma?"

. . .

On Highway 97, the rain haze lifted oil from the pavement so it floated as a thin film, leaving the highway slick and treacherous on the ride from Bend to the Klamath Basin. The road dipped down from the high Oregon desert to emerald grassland farms and swamps filled with tule rushes. Sean raced ahead on the straight highway. What she noticed as he passed: he was still too tall, his torso too long, his jacket barely covering his belt.

Years before, that same narrow torso distracted her at the ranch, when Sean hung over the fence watching her work on Dante's new cistern. She'd paid a dude with a ditch-witch to dig the trench, who made a pig's breakfast of the job and then left town till October. So she tackled the ditch with a shovel, distracted by Sean, who persuaded her to let him help dig. The dark hair on his arms and belly got sweaty while he worked, which made it hard for her to concentrate. When he took a break, he splashed water down his front, promising not to bathe during the drought days if she'd let him be wet now. She considered firing him because his long, narrow torso drew attention to skinny hips emerging from the top of his jeans. She had to force herself to keep her eyes on her work.

Then, two hot humans breathing in her dark adobe shack. After all their jesting and jostling over work, she let him inside. In her shack's dim light, he moved gently, spoke softly. Not like the visiting artists who pursued her as part of their total desert experience.

When he first touched her, tracing the cupped U of her thumb and index finger like the drawings you make in the second grade, he talked about his vision for new work that, he said, began to emerge while digging that ditch.

His lips were cool, so her own lips must be hot, betraying her. She bit his lip and coaxed his tongue to follow hers; still, only his long fingers rested across her hand on the table top. She touched the arch of triceps on his upper arms, drifting to stroke the coarse black hair across his belly.

In her loft, he wanted to go slow, but she climbed on top in the narrow bed, licking and fondling him into an excruciating frenzy. Then she pretended to cuddle and purr, but soon tortured him into fond excesses. She thought she'd proved how wild she liked it, so that he'd understand how daring and intrepid she was.

But moments after they both caught their breath, his baritone voice vibrated through her spine, into her chest.

"I don't want to hurt you. Ever."

So, why had she let him?

...

They rode fast after they left Klamath Falls. The damp day and Pete's desire to reach Winnemucca to gamble pushed them down the road. However, an ill-favored wind locked on their trail and pursued them as they cruised through Klamath Falls, seeking the road to Nevada. They took Highway 140 where the Cascades separate the Klamath Basin from the interior plateau, crossing Bly Mountain Pass at five thousand feet, riding full speed through rugged ponderosa pine country into Arctic air.

By the time they reached the town of Bly, Eliot hoped that Pete or Sean would stop because of the cold. But they rode on, slowing only for the through-town speed limit. She snapped photos of the movie theater, closed decades earlier, now revived as a feed-and-hardware store, and framed more snaps of the abandoned logging equipment on what was once the Twiling Brothers lot, unmoved for many seasons, rusting and half-buried in dirt, like dinosaurs sinking into a primordial pit. Eliot repressed the desire to investigate any salvage potential, which she usually did at abandoned homesteader outbuildings in the Cascades. Likely antique pickers had long ago gleaned all that history and sold it to interior designers to decorate rustic cafes.

Snow glowed in the sky to the north and east. The air smelled of frozen water. The road climbed for fifteen miles until they reached Quartz Mountain Pass. At the sign for the summit, with no shelter in sight, huge hailstones pelted down. The bikes squirmed at each slickened curve of the road. Eliot tucked in her arms to let the fairing shield her, so hail hammered only her knees. Unprotected by the small fairing on that Kawasaki café racer, Sean was pounded by hail, yet he barely slowed up though the ice fell fast and hard.

Where the highway dropped down onto the plains after Drew's Gap, the hail stopped and the wind eased enough to allow a pleasant ride through the farmland. Except Eliot couldn't get warm. She concentrated on wiggling her toes in her boots as she snapped flicks of grazing cattle that stared dumbly as the riders passed. Or maybe they stared at dumb riders.

At Lakeview, they stopped for gas.

"We need dinner," Pete called across the pump island to Sean. "It's still a long way to Nevada."

Eliot didn't wait to hear Sean's answer. She carried her helmet across Highway 395 to the café on the opposite corner. Pete hadn't asked her opinion, but she needed to warm up before getting back on the bike. She hoped like hell they'd stop at the next campground. Yet she wasn't about to be the first to chicken out.

Another bike stood in front of the café, a restored BMW R75 laden with long-distance traveling gear. Inside, she nodded at the rider who sat at the front counter, dressed like an Alaskan fisherman in an all-weather suit and showing no signs of suffering. The rest of the café—ranchers, guessing from their well-worn Carhartt pants and jackets—stared as she set her helmet on a table and crossed the café. In the women's room, she rubbed her hands in a stream of hot water to thaw out. She stayed in the hot washroom, combing her hair and scrubbing her face until the frozen red glow of her cheeks subsided to a normal color.

Back in the café, Pete sat with the R75 rider at the counter, drinking coffee and talking. At the table where Eliot had left her helmet, Sean drew on his pad, stopping to stare out at the ice-grey clouds shrouding the eastern horizon.

She joined Pete at the counter.

"It's more'n likely you'll see some snow," the R75 guy drawled. "You going up Highway 395?"

"No," Pete said. "Highway 140. Winnemucca-to-the-Sea."

"I got some snow on the ride down from Pasco. Thought I'd go to California."

"We'd hoped to find more summer here in the desert," Pete said.

"Seems like it's raining everywhere," the man said. "I'm fine though." He tugged at his all-weathers. "I got wool underwear and thermal pants."

And he used duct tape to seal the cuff of his all-weather suit over his boots.

"Nice bike," Pete said, which is the equivalent of a Miss Manners greeting for bike riders.

"Very nice rebuild. Your work?" Eliot said, which prompted a story from the R75 rider about his efforts. Eliot congratulated him, and never breathed any hint that the cheap fairing detracted from the BMW's style, though she gave him a card, encouraging him to drop by her shop if he was ever on Limberlost Island. Pete got the guy to pose with him by the bike while Eliot snapped flicks.

As they waved farewell to the R75 rider headed down the road, Pete said, "You're always shy. And here you are, touting your own business, which I've never seen before."

"I'll give the guy a free fairing if he comes by my shop," she said. "That after-market crap plastic should be illegal."

When they rejoined Sean, Pete related what he'd learned: snow lay ahead.

Sean didn't glance up from his pad. "I can't think until I'm warm," he said.

"Here," Pete said, tossing a key on the table. "You left this in your bike."

The waitress took orders from Sean and Eliot for barbecued beef and from Pete for mashed potatoes, a fried egg sandwich, and a side order of vegetables. Waiting for food, they made abysmal jokes to cheer up, not yet debating what to do. Eliot again deleted unusable photos and traded memory cards with Pete, who uploaded the hailstorm still-shots for Tadeusz, plus footage he'd captured during the R75 conversation. Hungry, they fell silent when their orders arrived, but the food tasted foul, and the coffee and deep-fat-fried vegetables burned their stomachs. Eliot ate while trying to read Sean's notebook upside down.

> Once you were a master smith
> who made treasure
> out of dust and stone.
> I was your unhappy wife …

Sean laid his napkin on the notebook screen when the waitress brought the check. Eliot glanced up to find Pete watching her read.

"Are we heading further down the road?" Sean asked.

"I froze my frigging nuts off," Pete said, with a note of finality in his voice. "Any possibility of genetic reproduction of my line was reduced by at least eighty percent today."

"My sleeping bag is still damp. The tents are wet," Sean said.

"We should spend the night here to dry out," she said.

"No one so practical, so capable as Eliot Arden," Sean said, smiling, apparently meaning to offer a compliment.

8.
Lakeview

The past is a foreign country; they do things differently there.
— Lesley P. Hartley, *The Go-Between*

ELIOT
Sunday Night

THE CASHIER AT THE CAFÉ pointed them to a motel, a U-shaped compound of concrete blocks stacked up in the Sixties and painted turquoise. Eliot parked her bike and bounded through the rain to the motel office. The young woman at the desk set aside her nail polish when Eliot dashed through the door.

"Brr," the woman said. Her nail color matched her peach lipstick. She wore shimmer-black eyeliner. Her straightened hair was a flashback from a *Friends* TV episode. "You must be freezin'. They was sayin' on the radio that there'd be snow in the passes."

"I thought it was still summer," Eliot said, offering friendly West Coast weather humor.

"We never ever get weather like this till October," the woman said, trying to avoid smudging wet polish as she passed over a registration form. "We got all kinds of people wanting to get off the road 'afore the weather starts tonight. What can I do for you?"

The woman gazed past Eliot to smile a much warmer welcome for Sean as he came through the door with Pete.

"I'd like a single," Eliot said, laying down her charge card.

"We each need one," Sean said. "I'll pay for all three rooms."

"All I got left are two rooms with a double bed in each. You guys'll have to bunk up together."

Sean stepped out to check his bike because he didn't know its license number yet. The motel registrar chatted while Eliot signed forms.

"We had a retired couple in here last week who was pullin' a trailer with their bike all the way from Florida. The stories they told, you wouldn't believe. Ten years of history with their motorcycle travels."

Eliot, tired beyond words, smiled goodbye to the woman and went to fetch her gear, not staying for the end of the trailer story.

"Ugh," Sean groaned outside the office. "A night with Pete in close quarters. He does this sit-up-and-preach-in-his-sleep thing that scares the hell of out me."

"Wait till he finds out you take all the covers," Eliot said, unthinking. She unhooked the Krauser bag that held her gear and tugged her sleeping bag free from its tie-downs.

In her room, Eliot cranked up the thermostat and stood for half an hour in the shower. After, she padded around in her underwear and t-shirt, hanging the damp sleeping bag in the closet and laying out her storm suit and leathers to dry. She hung socks from the edge of her boots to air them out enough to survive another day's wear without laundry. After combing and braiding her wet hair, Eliot crawled under the blanket to nap, lulled by the peaceful thrum of the heater fan.

Then her peace was interrupted by people making love in the room next door. The woman seemed inarticulate for all the noise she made. Eliot hated to be judgmental, but it sounded more like puppies wrestling and squawking than real lovemaking.

It ended quickly and, due to the motel's no-smoking rules, there weren't after-sex cigarettes; they immediately switched on the TV, loud, to an early-evening cartoon show. Eliot flicked the remote to find news on her own TV, covering the noise of the neighbors' SpongeBob reruns.

A car bomb destroys a wedding in Mesopotamia.

An heir to British royalty commits an extraordinarily mundane, human act.

Lions cuddle like lambs on a new heated rock at the zoo in—

In the bathroom for a drink of water, Eliot poked open the window, which overlooked a deserted lot covered with a ratty tangle of buckbrush. In the center of the lot, a solitary wizened apple tree, the hope of a pioneer several generations earlier, now hunched in the high desert, its tiny apples withering yellow, unpicked, on leafless branches.

The beginning of the end of that star-crossed season long ago smelled of apples left on the tree.

She and Sean had crossed the continent, up through the Great Basin, over the Canadian Rockies and across the Great Plains of Alberta and beyond, crossing the St. Lawrence and ambling through New England, talking endlessly. Books. Memories. Shooting photos (Eliot), sketching in oils or charcoal (Sean). Making love. Counting stars and then telling their dreams in the morning.

Then foundering in the shoals of star-crossed love—well, class-crossed, as Eliot now viewed those dark end-days.

From the moment they arrived at Sophy's, August having given itself up to September, the smell of overripe apples and the barking dog behind the neighbor's fence drove her crazy.

"It's immoral," she complained, "letting a dog bark like that. Letting apples fall to the ground and rot."

"Forget it, Eliot. We don't need any scabby apples."

"I'm going to ask to pick them."

She knocked on the neighbor's front door to offer her assistance. No answer.

"He's a recluse," Sean called. "He hasn't spoken in years. The apples rot every September, and the bees get them."

Over the next week, she proposed ideas for getting the apples.

"Maybe we should ask for the dog, too. It's not happy there. He stops barking when he hears my voice."

"You can't take a dog on your bike," Sean said. "You'd have to say goodbye before you even began."

At the end, he said goodbye after they'd barely begun. They parted in Salt Lake City. Eliot rode to Seattle to care for her father; Sean rode back to the ranch to pack up and join his true love.

Painting. The bitch Muse that stole him.

And to join his father, who offered that special gift: *the chance to do your heart's work.*

In the sodden rain of Seattle, caring for her relentlessly unhappy father, Eliot congratulated herself on her life's greatest success:

letting Sean go with no recriminations, no clinging. She gave up the only love she'd known and commenced an ordinary, everyday life.

■ ■ ■

Eliot tried to doze in the Lakeview Motel, longing to abandon consciousness, her head under the blanket. Avoiding thoughts of lost desire on Limberlost with memories of lost—what?

She needed to concentrate on the alternate plans she'd worked through with Roslyn, to keep from losing Destiny to the system. If someone else bought Cora's land, she needed to refocus the mission: keep Destiny and Cora safe, find new shelter for them.

And she needed to stop revisiting why she'd let Sean go.

When that loss occurred only because you just can't always get what you want.

Under the heat of the scratchy motel blanket, Eliot resolved to never again give up. She'd seize control of more than just small things in life. She'd no longer meekly accept disappointment when the universe refused to accommodate her larger desires.

Propelled from bed, energy pulsing, Eliot yanked on her nearly-dry jeans and slipped into tennis shoes. She put on her happy, everyday self, and went to knock on Pete's and Sean's door, just for the sake of their company. As she passed the neighbors' window, the open curtain revealed the young couple in bed watching the overhead blue flicker of SpongeBob's undersea world. The woman had a Dr. Pepper while the guy sucked on a Coors Lite. He smirked when he saw Eliot. The girl jerked a blanket over her head.

Sean and Pete, munching chips and watching the last few minutes of a Seattle-Patriots football game, had started a party without her. Pete, buried in his laptop, also had Tadeusz on speakerphone. It was a working party.

"Seahawks are creaming the Patriots," Pete said as Eliot walked in the door. "Six seconds left. They were three points down at the quarter, then Seattle scored on this incredible pass."

"They have God on their side," Sean said solemnly. He was immersed in his pad, stopping to punch text on his cellphone, not watching the television.

"Naw," Pete said, "it's not God. It's all the frigging fumbles. Seattle has scored on three of them since the half. C'mon, Eliot. Aren't you excited?"

"Nothing has roused passion in my heart since the Sonics left Seattle." She sat beside him, passing over the memory cards from her cameras.

"There is that." Pete appeared pensive. Fake pensive. He began loading the contents of her memory cards onto his laptop. "You want a beer, Eliot? Or some of this?" He waved a flask, which she knew contained Glenmorangie, since she knew Pete.

"I found ice downstairs," Sean said. He took the flask from Pete and poured amber liquid into a bathroom drinking glass.

"Heathen!" Pete said, glancing up from his work. "Machine-ice in fifteen-year-old scotch?"

Sean poured her an ounce of alcohol. She declined the ice. He sipped his drink, chasing it with long swigs from a carton of milk. Under the dim motel-lamplight, Eliot noticed for the first time the silver hairs salted among his short-cropped dark curls. Tiny crows-feet around his eyes, lines of determination around his mouth. Not comfortable studying him full on, she snatched glances, taking in pieces as she waited out the end of the football game. Long and lean, but gym-rat basketball thin, not muscled like he'd been that summer. His clothes, maybe not even as expensive as he'd worn then, hung from his frame; he still cared nothing about how he appeared. He might pass for a common Microsoft geek.

The only part unchanged: long, strong fingers, now grasping a stylus as he worked on his notebook pad. Fingers that were made to paint.

■ ■ ■

At the end of the game, Pete finished uploading files from his laptop and threw Eliot out of the only chair so he could oil his leathers, forcing her onto the bed beside Sean, who'd surfed though shopping channels and settled on an old Jim Jarmusch film.

"I saw this last winter," Eliot said. "But I missed the opening that time, too."

Unused to drinking and failing to pace herself, Eliot got a little bit drunk too fast, making it difficult to sit next to Sean and not fall into their old posture for hanging out together.

Pete finished with his leathers and checked his laptop, frowning. He reached for his cellphone. He jabbed at the screen, switching to speakerphone.

"Tadeusz, are you seeing files come over? This is taking four times as long as it should."

"I'm seeing about a megabyte a minute," Tadeusz said, his voice as clear as if he were in the room with them. "This batch won't make tonight's post. Which is already waiting. Except—"

"Yeah, yeah, Jason Taylor hasn't called." Pete frowned at his laptop again. "I haven't raised him either. His phone just goes to voice mail and—"

"And his voice mail is full," Tadeusz said. "With me begging him to call. Did you see Boing Boing today?"

While the guys talked about audience response to their media project, Eliot ran water from the bath tap over a cup of ice. No more alcohol.

Hunched over his laptop, Pete ended the call with Tadeusz and punched another number, then clicked speakerphone and laid the phone on the desk while he typed.

"What?" It was their sister Sam, who still hadn't forgiven Pete all his trespasses against her.

"Sam, that laptop you told me to use—"

"The grey one, right? Not the black one? And you reformatted it?" Her voice pitched high with that arch annoyance of a sibling who doesn't trust her brother to get one damn thing right.

"Yes. I followed every step to wipe the disk and reimage the operating system. Yesterday, it seemed fine. Tonight it's taking ten times as long to upload files."

"Let me guess," Sam said. "You're in a motel with a lousy Wi-Fi connection."

"No, I'm using my own cellular node, just like last night. And I'm not that stupid."

Sam sighed the sigh of the put-upon sister, forever cleaning up after her little brother. "Send me a remote invitation, like we always do, so I can fix it."

Pete did as instructed, muttering first to Sam, then to himself after she hung up, that he'd planned all the networking too well for this to be his fault.

At the movie's commercial break, Pete went to fetch more ice. Sean headed to the bathroom, once more leaving his pad open to current drawings and notes.

> For my own secret,
> I wished to cut my dreams in mother-of-pearl,
> to be allowed to tend the fire and to hold the sack
> while you seek gems in the dust. I want your fingers
> to trace the golden rod of my spine again,
> like a thousand springs ago.

Sean returned just as she read the last lines.

"How lovely," Eliot said. "Is this one of your video characters?"

"It's several stories," he said, taking away his pad. "In this one, I want to give voice to a woman who feels she's never heard. It's not ready yet."

"Sorry to snoop." She handed back the pad. "But how do you give voice to someone? Don't you just listen?"

He was already lost in his drawing again and didn't seem to hear. She reached out to trace Sean's spine, but Pete came back, groceries in his arms, collapsing into the armchair.

"Here we go, kids. We can party now," he said. He opened a bag of sour cream-and-onion potato chips and poured another finger of scotch. "And, Sean, here's the goddamn key to your bike again. Some kid's going to thank you for a free ride if you don't change your reckless ways."

Eliot pretended to choke to keep from laughing. Pete scolding and indignant: hilarious. She sipped her ice water, wanting to dull the itch of fingers that needed to reach out. Pete poured chips on the table for himself and tossed the open bag to Sean, who failed to catch it, spilling the whole bag over Eliot.

"My bed!" Sean exclaimed. "Chips in my bed!" Trying to retrieve the chips, he spilled scotch over Eliot's shirt.

"OK, you guys have had enough," Pete said. "You're as bad as the Patriots' wide receiver."

"You expected me to catch a lousy pass like that?" Sean said, still fumbling with the bag. He scooped chips off Eliot's chest and belly, dropping them back into the bag, making her laugh because the situation was ridiculous and the chips tickled. Crumbs fell down the top of her t-shirt. She wanted his hand to stay on her breast, where it belonged.

"This is what passes for a party in our old age? You have to sleep on that side of the bed with the crumbs." Pete shook his head just as his cell rang. It took both Pete and Sean to find it and turn on speakerphone.

"Pete?" The level of irritation in Sam's voice was as high as the phone's volume. "What the ever-loving heck did you install on that machine?"

"Nothing. I'm just using it to transfer files and send email."

"It's broadcasting everything three times. That's why your file transfer takes so long."

"What did I do wrong?" Pete said. "I didn't do anything."

"Let me run diagnostics overnight," Sam said. "Can you set it so your laptop won't go to sleep?"

"Sure," Pete said. "Since it's taking so long to transfer files, it'll be running till breakfast anyway."

Just before she hung up, Sam said, "Did you see that squabble on Gawker over Milo Speiser's video posts?"

● ● ●

Prime example of why Eliot stayed off social media, only lurking in a few corners of the swamp on rare occasions.

Pete sputtered a stream of invectives.

Sean slapped him twice on the back of the head — a sort of fake jock move — to keep Pete from posting a single word on line.

Their friend Milo had visited Dante's ranch at midday, a camera mounted on the dash of a white truck captured the familiar dip down to Dante's sanctuary, but before a decent focus was pulled,

Dante appeared: shirtless, his long white hair a dandelion's mane framing his gaunt face, a shotgun in hand.

The dialog began with the cameraman-driver's voice-over:

"You invited us. We're here for art. So you can show off the birthplace of the Impious Aeneas heroes. You said you had old video to share."

Most of Dante's portion of the conversation was garbled, as if recorded underwater, since the cameraman declined to exit his SUV. The few clearly heard words:

"Art and theft are not the same. What's here belongs to my son. Haul your thieving ass out of here."

That line shut Pete up for thirty seconds, until he watched further: a collusion between Milo and the FAIL movie people had created a collage of Sean's old art with pre-production cuts from the unfinished Monkey King movie. Milo's web posts referred to Sean as the artistic son of Dante—the Old Master he'd just made to look like a whack job.

Sean flicked Pete's laptop so that the Gawker window closed.

"Milo just lost his bet, Pete. All by himself."

Eliot, who'd kept quiet through the viewing of the debacle, now said, "Dante looks ill."

Pete glanced her way, still ashen from watching the show. "What to do?"

"Nothing," Sean said. "Did you read the comments? People are reaming Milo. Instead of an exposé, they see aggressive trespass, an attempt to stake a claim on another artist's work. Milo blew it, posting that."

"I'm calling Dante," Pete said, once more seeking his phone.

"It's late," Eliot said.

"He doesn't have to answer." But when Pete got a hello from Dante immediately, he flicked to speakerphone.

"Peter? God, I'm glad you called. Did you hear?"

"Just now. What should I do?"

Dante sighed. Or perhaps it was a sob. "Don't know that you can do a thing. She's gone."

"What? I meant—"

"Claudia says nothing will bring her back."

"Dante, I called about the cameraman."

"What cameraman? When will you get here, Peter?"

Eliot found Sean staring at her. With a finger pointed to the door, he indicated that they needed to leave Pete alone to finish the phone call.

• • •

She didn't remember stumbling back to her room. Once during the night Eliot woke up to stop dreaming that she was back in Seattle seeking another road to the desert, fighting wind and cold and rain, failing to get her bag packed, failing to choose clothes to take, while everyone waited impatiently for her to be ready.

Emergency. And failure. But only a dream.

After stopping that frustration dream, her fingers traced the V down Sean's sternum, tickling the hair on his chest. So familiar: waking in the warmth beside him, his hand touching hers where it lay above her head. She still slept that way, on her back with her hand flung behind her head as though fallen in a swoon, and he still lay on his stomach, his hand across hers. When he rolled over in his sleep, how easily she inched up against him, and he never moved away, just pulled her closer, tugged her arm up around his chest when she laid it lightly on his waist. The tight mound of his buttock muscles pressed against her belly.

The warmth, the lovely warmth. She kissed that knob, his cervical vertebra. He dragged her thigh up over his and held her hand there. She smelled eucalyptus from the Dr. Bronner's soap he still used to wash his hair.

Pete pounded on her motel door.

"Eliot, get up! Time to hit the road!"

She woke from that dream, dismayed. Alone.

"Come on, before the clouds fall again." Pete's voice rang out loud enough to wake the whole motel and half the dead. "Sean's already packed and waiting."

The Desert Crucible Episode II
The Land-locked Rose Spirit

[Tadeusz: Here's the voice-over audio. Use the Image list from my 10pm email; find whether Jason uploaded any twangy rockabilly to match this woman's voice. —Pete]

They brought my great-great-grandmother here in a box from the Old Country. She watched all her children die, her spirit never crossing the boundary to another place. My mother ran away, but this place reeled her back. Because my great-grandmother was buried here, too, we can never leave. The Old Spirits need us, since they were carried here, like our ancestors, taken away from their Old-World stones.

We knit and sew and glue them into our stories, and they put fruit on the trees come fall.

I can't leave—the family leading strings always pull us back. But you have to understand that we're not trapped. It's how we keep the land alive.

At Christmas, I'm going to marry my step-sister's cousin. The brides-maids will wear blood-red velvet and each will carry a green wreath with a single white rose. Cool, huh? And I'll wear a Santa Lucia crown. No, we aren't going to light the candles. That would be silly. And dangerous.

He's totally into it—staying here in Lakeview, I mean. He gets it, why we stay. It isn't inertia. Is that the word? We live here where I can talk with my grandmother since her spirit is in that rose garden you see across the highway. And she's still here because her grandmother brought the rose's root stock over the Applegate Trail, all the way from Tennessee.

So please understand, we're not landlocked. We're not stuck. We're just waiting for the wheel to turn. It's like waiting for the weather to change.

∞

9.
Denio

SEAN
Monday a.m.

SLEEP ABANDONED ME BEFORE DAWN. I sat on the little balcony outside our room, watching cirrus clouds gathering as the sky gradually lightened, amazed at what the change in scenery, sound, and sensation had done for my psyche, evoking memories for which I had no creative use. Perhaps it came from the different quality of light and from cleaner air than I breathed in London.

Yet that wouldn't account for how much Eliot disturbed my equilibrium. I've wasted too much time quarrelling in my head with Milo, like Monkey with the White-Bone Demon. But twisted memories of Eliot also did not feed the meditative head time I'd hoped for this journey. I wasn't sure how to survive this trip, barely hearing my own thoughts over the blood pounding. No more alcohol, for one. I'd drunk more in the past three days than over the last three years. Bad enough dealing with road food without insulting my own injuries.

Attending to morning business, I brushed my teeth and packed, and then—as if my notes reflected profound insight—I posted on the *Desert Crucible* blog, and dreamed up a couple of arty poetic lines to tweet on social sites. **#TheDesertCrucible** was trending.

After Pete woke and dressed, he went to fetch Eliot. Just as I tucked my phone into my jacket, Milo called.

"Sean." Instead of hello. "Can we get together today?"

"No. I'm in Hell-And-Gone, Oregon, soon to be in Back-of-Beyond, Nevada."

"Are you safe? I'm worried about you. Riding with that riff-raff."

Riff-raff meant Pete.

"We're often cold and wet," I said. "But we're fine. We're having a great time."

"You must be exhausted."

His concern grated, shredding my damp, hung-over mood into frost crystals.

"You don't give a rip, Milo. Why did you call?"

"We're working on contract details this week. I'd like to plan a special project for you. One that makes you happy."

"Don't patronize, Milo. We've talked the details to death. My participation in Laconia is over."

"But Sean—"

"I saw your colossal mistake with Dante. Do what you will with Monkey King and my other heroes. But leave Dante alone."

"That was just a timing thing. We need you—"

"Sorry. Can't hear you over this connection," I said, lying. "Talk to you in a couple of weeks."

I was downstairs with a headache, hitching gear to my bike when my partners appeared. Eliot, more chipper than should be possible after the scotch-and-TV excesses from the night before, must have slept a hell of lot better than I did, what with Pete thrashing, spilled scotch and potato chip litter, and my stomach churning on alcohol. She pointed past the mistaken diner of the previous night to a pancake house farther up the street.

Slumped in the booth at the restaurant, I read the social feed on my phone to avoid real personal interaction and to nurse my aching head. When the woman appeared with her order pad and poised pencil, I asked for a single pancake, an egg, and hot chocolate, deciding to forego even tea.

"That sounds good," Eliot said. "Sean's got the right idea."

"I need coffee," Pete said. "I'm not a kick-start model."

"Me too—if it's really coffee," Eliot said. "But since we crossed the Cascades, every cup of coffee results in a stomach ache. Sean is our worthy leader. We should follow."

She handed out compliments with one hand and poked me in the ribs with the other. Feeling ill, I made for easy prey.

The morning light slanted through the café window, turning her grey eyes silver and lighting her face like a portrait of Jane Burden by Rossetti or some other Pre-Raphaelite. That quiet smile didn't incarnate criticism or challenge. Years earlier, I'd called her Artemis, the goddess of the wildland. When she deserted me that autumn, I'd privately cursed her as Kali incarnate—neither apotheosis fair to the real Eliot. I've been too busy projecting my internal turmoil, perpetually defensive, as if everyone were as combative as Milo Speiser.

The whole ride so far, and especially last night, proved that Eliot meant just what she said back then: *We'll always be friends.*

I handed my phone to Pete when he begged for the weather report. The waitress brought our food, and I started on my pancake and egg, hoping that road food might provide enough calories to bring my weight back up. Eliot seemed vibrant, the clover-honey colors in her hair glowing.

After breakfast, out in the restaurant parking lot, Eliot sparked to life while she tugged her storm suit over leather jeans and helped Pete secure equipment to his bike, as animated as in the old days, making up a dumb story.

"The Mummy People froze in an ice fall twenty-five thousand years ago while hunting mastodons," she said, her voice ringing across the parking lot. "Discovered and thawed by a National Geographic team, they now travel through Arctic weather in pursuit of the cosmic experience."

"What can we learn from them?" I mused as I tied a second scarf around my neck to cut out more wind.

"We can't. The Mummy People haven't evolved enough to be human," she said. She fired up her bike and pulled on insulated gloves. "Their skulls are small, which means limited brain capacity. They never know they're cold."

"What is this cosmic experience of which you speak?" Pete asked. He buckled his helmet.

"Like us, they're sure they'll know one when they see it."

Pete switched on his bike and let it purr to warm up. "What if the local cowboys mistake the Mummy People for ninjas?"

"It will be war!" Eliot yelled over the noise of the bikes. She mounted her bike, kicked it into gear, and pulled out onto the highway.

Behold the warrior Eliot, former wild-child. How had I ever charmed her out of her shell back then?

· · ·

When we picked up speed at the edge of town, the blast of cold air shocked me into wakefulness. Steam rose in the fields around the little geyser outside Lakeview, as inviting as a Japanese bath, but the bank of clouds to the north held December weather.

We traveled only a few miles on Highway 395 before turning east and climbing a thousand feet to Warner Pass on Highway 140, riding into the desert through a devastatingly beautiful canyon where sagebrush displaced sugar pines. Clouds threatened adverse weather on all sides, but the sun shone. Wind numbed my face and chest, but I came alive in ways I'd missed for too long.

Only one thing distracted from the thrill of pure, exhilarating life: Eliot riding in front of me. She still had the perfect rider's ass, as beautiful as any Pre-Raphaelite might draw.

Not good for achieving the proper meditative road state.

I passed Pete where the road dipped near Adel, the blacktop straight and clear before us. Eliot waved as I passed her, that warm, amused smile visible through her face shield. Or perhaps I imagined it. She and Pete reveled in the fun of the ride. Although the morning remained freezing and harsh, like last winter's solstice in Reykjavik, I found the best ride yet on this trip, pushing that bike to the max for twenty miles. Twice I cut speed for pairs of calves who strayed onto the road. When the little ones heard the bikes, they ran back to their mothers and stared as I passed, their white faces as startled and attentive as wistful children. I remembered that open range requires caution; but visibility was good that morning. And I was so damned tired of caution in life.

The road curved up toward Blizzard Gap, where a parade of cattle came down the highway and met the bikes. I cut my speed to a crawl. Pete and Eliot were soon close behind me. Rather than a few calves scampering for their mothers, several hundred cows migrated down the roadway. Calves ran from one side to the other when they discovered their mothers missing and our bikes too close. Those that scrambled over to my side hauled up short, bellowing because the road's shoulder dropped steeply into a canyon. Three times we passed huge black bulls. Pete pulled out in front of me, then stopped dead at one point to capture video of the cows and the staring calves bewitched by the bikes. I stalled my bike behind Pete's, not fond of cows at close quarters.

Eliot waved at the last bull lumbering down the highway shoulder. Near the top of the Gap, we passed four mounted cowboys holding the line at the end of the herd.

"Cold frigging day, eh?" Pete yelled at them.

The cowboys grinned, each waving a PBR can in greeting.

The cattle gone, though the noise of their bellowing still echoed in the canyon, we pulled over for a moment.

"I was sure that second bull mistook my bike for a hot cow," Pete said. "His cock was so long, it about dragged on the ground. Did you see it? My heart was pounding."

"I'd defend your virtue," Eliot said. "It's probably one of ten mistakes you haven't yet made."

"Let's go," I said, anxious to ride fast again. "That was an unplanned half hour."

"We have cow breaks," Pete said, "instead of coffee."

"Watch out for the cow-pies," Eliot called as I rode away.

After Blizzard Gap, we reached empty sage prairies. No towns, no ranches, no highway rest stops. A few miles later we crossed into Nevada, though the sagebrush didn't change in the new jurisdiction. Two miles over the state line, though, rain caught us again. Brusque wind flung tiny stinging drops, too big to be mist, cold enough to be ice. This was antelope country, and I wanted images, but the gamin beasts must be hidden under a large sagebrush with the birds, of which I'd also seen no signs.

But then, any living creature with any sense would not be out in this weather.

Forty-five miles into Nevada, I switched the fuel tank to reserve and then motioned Pete to turn off at Denio Junction, the only stop between nowhere and Winnemucca. Three miles down that side road, we came to a small huddle of aluminum trailer houses and a gas station, where a sign hung on the door: *Closed today for the funeral.*

Pete pulled up beside me where the road changed from pavement to all-weather. "What do you think?" Pete asked, staring off at nothing, which seemed to be the town of Denio.

Eliot came to a stop and lifted her helmet's face shield. "Why'd you pass the Chevron station at the junction? I gotta pee."

Ignominy. I wheeled the bike around to speed back to the highway. Just as I kicked into high gear, a white pickup rolled onto the roadway from an unmarked side road. I braked hard, the bike shimmying under my hands. The driver, lumbering onto the road at twenty miles an hour, sped up to thirty, never giving any indication of having seen me, though I rode in full sight of his left rearview mirror.

■ ■ ■

At Denio Junction, Pete and I filled our gas tanks. Eliot, faster with simple chores than we were, went into the café. I fumbled with the gas cap, my fingers too cold to function well.

"Let's stop for a while," I begged.

"I have to," Pete said. "My butt's froze."

A young man ambled over to take our money for the gasoline. "Not much a day for riding."

"Actually, we get paid to freeze our fannies," Pete said from across the driveway, leaving me to settle the bill for all of us. "It's a tough job, but someone has to do it."

"What else can I get you for?" the man said, taking my credit card to write up a slip.

"We thought we'd do some Christmas shopping, since the big day must be just around the corner, judging from the weather."

The man chuckled. "Maybe you need a couple of burgers to warm up with. Fresh off the hoof."

As I crossed to the café, the man called out, "It's never this cold so early in September."

Inside, most of the room was paneled with photographic fake wood, the kind tacked up over most of America in the Sixties. One side, though, held an immense oak bar from an Old West saloon, with a thousand business cards stapled to the low ceiling. A couple of locals sat at one table chatting with a woman in an apron, their elbows propped on the plastic table cover as they sipped coffee from disposable cups stuck in plastic holders.

The woman glanced over when I came in, checking whether I wanted service. Pete and Eliot apparently decided against food. They stood by the bar reading the overhead business cards.

"May I have a hot chocolate?" I smiled at the woman. Everything else on the menu would kick back farther down the road.

"Sure thing, sir. I'll bring it to you."

The man from the gas pumps let himself in behind the bar.

"Get you anything? Coffee?"

"Naw, I gave it up," Pete said, inspecting the bar stock.

"I know what you mean," the fellow said. "I haven't had a decent cup since I left Berkeley."

I checked him more closely—about thirty, the man resembled a Sixties-era Tab Hunter, and I'd pegged him for a back-country Mormon ensconced in the desert, avoiding the larger world. A hasty, erroneous judgment. After he listened to our plans for the night in Winnemucca, he told stories while heating glasses of brandy for Pete and Eliot.

"I grew up in Lakeview. My dad and my uncle bought me and my cousin Jack a trip to Winnemucca when we turned eighteen. They wanted us to sow our oats out of town. My uncle said he lost his cherry in a whorehouse in Winnemucca. And what was good enough for him—"

The man poured brandy in the glasses.

"A pinch of sugar?" he asked Eliot and Pete.

"No way," Eliot said.

"Glad to hear it," the man said. "Most people out here think white sugar's what God laid out for the Israelites when they starved in the desert. I always figured manna tasted more like Styrofoam, since God wouldn't want them getting too comfortable."

Pete had warmed to the man while his brandy steamed, and they talked world events, trading preposterous interpretations of the current presidential administration. Eliot read a paperback novel. The woman came with my cocoa. I conducted the morning's Internet business. Pete joined us, buried in his own laptop. He had a three-way session going with Tadeusz and me in just seconds.

. . .

Pete: OH FKME. The original lighting plan for the entire video requires bright sunshine.

Sean: We have worse conditions than the real Aeneas ever endured when he fled Troy. I had a few old drawings without either Impious Aeneas or Monkey King. But they can't be used. The light's wrong.

Pete: Never was a possibility. Not about the light.

Sean: I hope the new drawings fit with the video.

Pete: Voice, vid, and still are all up on the server. This shit takes forever to upload.

TadNow: Are you reading comments from the first posts?

Sean: Never read the comments

Pete: NEVER READ THE COMMENTS!!!

TadNow: OK maybe you wise guys should read the numbers. Two posts and we're trending in the top 10 views.

Pete: You should see the look on Sean's face right now.

TadNow: Laconia called everyone back from vacation.

Pete: Heh.

TadNow: So I don't open their email. No return-bit-to-sender to let them know I'm online. Milo's calls go to voicemail. He's truly pissed & wants to know where everyone is.

Sean: is everything OK with our people?

TadNow: We're doing like you said, boss. No one resigns till you have a new contract. But we be dancing to Jason's music & ready to leave the Dragon Master behind.

Sean: And Jason? I can't get him on the phone.

TadNow: Still absent, I'm nervous, choosing the music. But it's working ok so far.

...

"Milo called me this morning."

I hadn't yet mentioned that conversation to Pete.

"Bet his pants are on fire." Pete didn't seem concerned.

"He wants me to come back to Laconia."

"I bet he has the sads, now that you aren't his Monkey tool." Pete buried his face in his laptop. I suspected that, despite his warning, he was reading the comments.

I began drawing on my pad, brushing Eliot's elbow when I reached for my cocoa. She'd seen the drawings the night before, so she knew that I work on more than animation. I bumped her again as I doodled words when I hadn't yet determined what the next image would be.

> The soft rasp and whisper of our fingers
> say all that is needed
> beyond the rattle of our children at play in the arroyo.
> A flock of swallows was seen today.
> The clouds are high in the sky.

Pete dropped coins in the slot machines, but came up empty. "You can't win on nickel machines," he said. "We get to Winnemucca, then we play for real. Blackjack. I can win at blackjack. Are you gambling with me tonight, Eliot?"

"No. I need my money for an even rainier day than today."

"I'll stake you," Pete said.

"I have no desire to flush anyone's money down the toilet— mine or yours."

A couple came in, neither of whom was much over twenty-one, with two little kids in tow. While the guy played slots, the woman ordered food and set Cokes in front of her kids, then started plugging quarters in the poker slot machine. When six quarters came back on a good hand, she went over to eat with the kids, warning them repeatedly to sit down, shut up, and eat. When the man won, the quarters all went back into the machine, his muscles bulging below his t-shirt sleeves as he mechanically dropped coins in the slot. He played as if a monkey on his back drove him to it. His wife watched intently when she too wasn't plugging quarters. The only thing that broke their concentration was the kids, who couldn't sit still. Eliot watched them, her mouth compressed into a thin line when the four-year-old's rear got spanked for standing up in her chair.

Eliot flipped open her novel, as if trying to ignore everything in the café, including my open pad on the table by her.

My hand, drawing on the pad, wouldn't obey my brain, a residual effect of vibrating for over a hundred miles. The quality of the sketches didn't matter though, because I needed only a representation of the hyper-aware sensations while riding. I'd catalog dream images to put into the next story, scenes that followed two people through a series of incarnations over several centuries, what I hoped would be a story worth pitching to HOPE. I doodled more images, but the story remained too picaresque. It needed a controlling myth to give it shape.

Laughing, Eliot knocked my right hand down, which I leaned on while I drew, so that my face fell onto my pad. Eliot and Pete shared a joke that I'd missed while musing.

"You ready to go?" she asked. "We uploaded all our photos and video to Tadeusz. Now we need to examine more highway."

"Sure." I got out my wallet to settle the cocoa bill.

"Allow me," Eliot said with exaggerated largesse, laying down a five and some change. "Anything else you need? A candy bar for energy to battle the Arctic winds?"

The bartender-manager said, "I got some cayenne pepper you can put in your socks. Keep your toes warm."

"I'm OK," I said. "After you shiver for twenty miles, you think you're warm."

"You be careful." The man waved.

At the bikes, while we all bundled up, Pete stood staring at his phone. He shoved it over for me to read.

Samlam: a bug in your bios sends every byte to my former clients

Pete texted back rude words.

"What?" Eliot asked.

"Our sister's screwed-up life is making our work complicated," Pete said.

"Isn't it the other way around?" She buckled her jacket.

"Not this time." Pete jammed the phone into his tank bag.

"Who are her clients?" I'd missed the details of the Byron family drama. "If they're getting our raw feeds, we have copyright problems. We should call Karl to—"

"There aren't copyright issues," Pete said. "Some poor quant in a cubicle somewhere is studying *The Desert Crucible* raw material, trying to find a threat to national security."

"That's novel," Eliot said. "Too bad they can't compare still shots from the first journey to find hidden meanings."

Pete laughed. "All Sean's real secrets are analog."

I followed Eliot back to the highway. The drizzle and fog lifted, revealing sage and rabbit brush extending to the horizon.

Now I perceived where we went wrong. What I learned through my father's beneficence: it's about building and enabling a team, so that together we do our best work. When Tadeusz and I first built the Laconia team, I didn't follow my instincts: I didn't call Eliot and beg her to join us.

Our new team is what's making *The Desert Crucible* work so well. That's what Tadeusz and others from Laconia wanted most: a chance to work well on a team. This trip needed an additional artistic goal: to bring Eliot onto the creative team as more than a hired hand. She needs the chance to work on a project greater than what a single person can achieve.

The Desert Crucible Episode III
#1: Regenerated Demigods

[Tadeusz: Sync this with the still-images/vid from this morning's ride. Find the most minor-key music you can in Jason's tracks. Since this is truly bad poetry, you should read it because you have the best voice if we can't find Jason. The fucker. —Sean]

Once you were a master smith who made treasure
out of dust and stone.
I was your unhappy wife,
dissatisfied with my stick while turning the garden.
And dissatisfied with the single loutish son
you got on me one night a thousand springs ago.

I was dissatisfied with your gifts,
like the squash blossom necklace meant to appease me,
because I was so unhappy with Silence
as you laid turquoise in a silver eagle,
no dust to disturb the smooth beauty while I scold.
In your secret heart you cannot find the anger to beat me.

For my own secret, I wished to cut my dreams
in mother-of-pearl,
to be allowed to tend the fire and to hold the sack
while you seek gems in the dust. I want your fingers
to trace the golden rod of my spine again,
like a thousand springs ago.
When we knew our thoughts without
the waste of words to shatter the silence.

I will grind corn this winter day
while you carve masks for the festival.
The soft rasp and whisper of our fingers say all that is needed
beyond the rattle of children at play in the arroyo.
A flock of swallows was seen today.
The clouds are high in the sky.

∞

10.
Winnemucca

SEAN
Monday Night

FIFTY SMOOTH, FAST MILES DOWN the road, my bike cut out just as a cold mist caught up with us again. I pulled over where a dirt road took off through the sagebrush. A white pickup zoomed past, its wake rocking me and the bike as I put my foot down. When I lifted my face shield, the smell of wet silver sage and damp desert soil washed over me, releasing a spring-tide flood of memories. I'd forgotten about rain and sage.

"*Que pasa, amigo*?" Pete pulled up alongside. Eliot slipped off her bike, pulled it up on its center stand, and joined me on the shoulder.

"My bike stopped," I said. "Like it's not getting gas."

"Did you flood it when you tried to start it?" Pete asked.

"I don't smell gas," Eliot said. "That's not it."

"Give it a minute," I said. "I'll try again."

Pete went behind the nearby sage for a comfort break, and Eliot walked off into the alkaline wilderness, kicking at rocks, drifting far away from us.

I scanned the horizon for signs of life. The only evidence was Pete crunching over the sandy ground behind me.

"I'm not finding the spiritual experience I hope for," I said.

"You could always try acid."

"No harsh chemicals," I said. "This divine experience was supposed to flow organically."

"Maybe you haven't taken a big enough risk yet," Pete said.

"Maybe it's too damn cold and raining."

Pete studied his map through the plastic window of his tank bag. "It's a little more than an hour to Winnemucca—maybe less the way you ride. Want to call it a day there?"

I nodded. "I'm done in by the cold."

"No shit, Sherlock. Look, the map says that mountain is called King Lear. Craggy and bearded, don't you think?"

"Poetic name," I said. "Perfect for a wilderness formed specially for poets and artists."

"Where?" Eliot said, coming up behind us, shading her eyes to scan the horizon. "Can we get away before the poets find us?"

"OK, insult or jive? Which is it this time?" I said.

"Always both, my brother," Pete said.

"I found these jackrabbit bones," Eliot said, holding out a pile of tiny shards. "A femur and a few rib bones, don't you think? Wonder what I can make them into?"

"Can we ride yet?" Pete asked.

My bike started on the first try. I raced away into the mist.

■ ■ ■

At Winnemucca, off the freeway and out of the wind, we cruised through town at the posted twenty-miles-an-hour speed. The sky began to clear. A hint of a gentle September day drifted on the air.

"Maybe we should keep going." I'd followed Pete into the lot at the Shady Court Motel, nestled in the shade of the Interstate 80 embankment. Eliot parked beside us.

Pete switched off his bike and jerked it up on its stand. "No way. Let's go conquer the town."

"Nix on town conquering," Eliot said. "I need to rest. Then I'm going to find real food. But I refuse to look at the highway until tomorrow."

After unloading the bikes and fetching the camera memory cards from Eliot, Pete bunked up for a few winks. I dropped my bags in our room, and emptied my pockets on the table with Pete's stuff, looking for my bike key. I returned to my bike, where I'd stupidly left the key again, and dicked around at figuring out what was wrong. Reluctantly, I knocked on Eliot's door for suggestions.

She called to come in, then held up a finger while she spoke on the phone. I stayed near the door, waiting.

"I think your doctor is right," she was saying. "Get all the shots and medications they recommend. You always tell me to be extra safe." She paused. "Do not leave early. They didn't put you in the hospital to steal your Medicare."

After a few more admonishments and best wishes, Eliot hung up, letting free a stream of exclamations.

"That woman can be so exasperating. Mrs. Waddington went with Roslyn to the doctor, who put her in the hospital overnight for hypertension. She thinks it's a major insult to her faith."

"Is she Christian Scientist? Or Jehovah's Witness? I met two missionaries in Taiwan last spring. I'd forgotten about that sort of thinking."

"No. She's one of those people like my mother. She believes any crazy idea from anyone who says they talk with spirits."

"You once agreed with me," I tried to make my voice sound normal, "that both our fathers dealt inappropriately with our mothers' visions."

She bit at her lip. "I worry that people take advantage of Mrs. Waddington. She needs whatever modern medicine can provide. It's only September and she's already sick. What happens when winter comes?"

"She must be important to you."

I tried to coax more from her. She'd just spoken a hundred more words in succession than she'd uttered since we said hello in Seattle. Eliot's Northwest life sounded similar to her chores at the ranch, serving as others' vassal.

"You're laughing at me," Eliot said, her shoulders lifting turtle-like around her ears. I so much wanted to overcome that shell of defense.

"No," I said. "I thought you meant to be funny."

"Mrs. Waddington and her niece are good friends. Even if she believes we're spirits from outer space, come to save the world. People like that are the real Communion of Saints my father prattled on about." She turtled up again. "Don't laugh."

"Never," I said. "I know what you mean. I found that connection with my friends at work. If you could—" I stopped myself from saying more. The stars still weren't right. "I came to ask for more ideas about what might be wrong with my bike."

"Did you check to see if the hole in the gas cap is plugged?"

"Yes. I worried that the tank bag blocked it. But I don't think that's it."

"The fuel valve and the filter?"

"Checked 'em. The needle valve isn't stuck. But maybe the fuel float isn't adjusted right. If you get a minute, can you check it?"

"There's lots of daylight left. I'll take a look before dinner."

She dismissed me. I walked back to the other room, and fished in my pocket for the key. But now I had only the bike key. Pete slept too deeply to hear me knock.

"I'm locked out," I said when Eliot answered her door, again with one finger in the air while she spoke on the phone.

"You need to be in school tomorrow," she said, sounding like my sister used to, when I resisted the daily grind. "But do not stay out on Lost Point alone. Can you sleep at Roslyn's house?" She listened. "OK. Bunk in my shop till I get home. It's just a walk up the street to school." More listening. "I'm serious as death. You have to be in school. Tell me you'll do the right thing."

She finally clicked off her phone, annoyed—sunk so far in her own thoughts that I didn't dare ask.

"Pete locked me out," I said. "I'll be quiet if you let me stay here until dinner."

"Come in. I'm done for, but make yourself at home."

• • •

She was asleep before I had my pad in hand to draw.

I kicked off my boots and rolled up two notches on the baseboard controls. Then I posted more inanities in the guise of creative insights on the *Desert Crucible* blog and social feeds. But I couldn't get warm till I crept my toes under the bedspread where Eliot lay sleeping, her eyes flitting behind their lids, watching a dream movie. Her hair fell out of its confining braid and wreathed her face in a honey fringe, her skin ethereal in the dim light. Her hand, thrown behind her head in the way she always slept, betrayed a vulnerability that strangers never perceive.

She's the same after ten years, as if carved from alabaster stone, slightly touched by weather. The blanket rose softly as she breathed, the only movement in the room.

OK, Pete's right: I romanticize women too much; I don't give them room to be real. I found my stylus to make notes on the day's events and to sketch those cows headed for lower elevations. We'd seen no large birds, no real wildlife. In the project plan, I counted on animals to appear in the desert, like spirit-guides in a dream. We needed more wildlife in this landscape to set fire to the *Desert Crucible* animation. Betrayed by unseasonal weather, I'd unearthed only a plague of pointless memories.

I nodded off in the chair, then jarred myself awake, and so crawled under the bedspread, leaving the blanket in place, taking only a corner of the bed. I wasn't asleep, merely thinking deeply with my eyes closed. About Eliot on the ranch, planting a garden, fixing broken-down outbuildings. Dante must appear incompetent out there in the wilderness, lacking his acolyte to keep the home-stead in order. Back then, when apprentices read the *Book of the Hopi* and speculated on Anasazi spirituality, Eliot read about their irri-gation systems, then dug trenches to grow more vegetables without depleting the ranch's water supply. In the fall she sealed the work-shop's windows and taught people how to start a fire in a tin jenny. Snowed in at Christmas, artists required Eliot's help to put chains on their cars when they needed to escape into town.

Deep in my heart of hearts, I knew that I should never have come to Seattle, but it was too cold everywhere else. I went into a bookstore, so that Eliot wouldn't think I followed her. Bolts of exquisite resist-dyed cottons stood against the bookstore's back wall. Louisa, Milo's assistant, fingered silk with the same blues that both Hiroshige and Turner used to paint the night sky. A clerk ap-proached me with a may-I-help-you expression. Behind her, I spied Eliot with a docent from the museum. She'd think I followed her after all.

"What would you like?" asked the clerk, who was lovely.

"About six meters of this cotton."

"I'm sorry, I only speak English."

"I am speaking English. I want six meters," I repeated.

"Are you making fun of me? That doesn't even sound like a language."

"I'm speaking English."

Annoyed, as if I were rude, the clerk glanced around, desperate for help in dealing with a crazy man. What had I come to Seattle for anyway? Eliot came over to ask the clerk a question. She'd see me. And then she'd know.

"Sean, what are you doing?"

Eliot shook me awake.

"You're grinding your teeth and pushing me out of bed."

I stumbled into the bathroom to splash water on my face. Pete thundered into the room just after I flipped off the water faucet.

"I need dinner," Pete said. "My rumbling stomach woke me."

"Let's go to the hotel," Eliot said. "Nothing else popped out when we came into town."

"What hotel?" I asked. "I only saw casinos. One had a Rib Roast Special for dinner tonight."

"Naw," Pete said. "We're here for Basque food."

"I need a dinner that will help me sleep," Eliot said. "I keep dreaming I'm back in Seattle, trying to pack warm clothes and find a dry road out of town."

"Everyone has that dream," Pete said.

■ ■ ■

"Just a mineral water." I refused the offer of alcohol.

Looking like a spirit guide we'd created for *The Desert Crucible*, the bartender at the Winnemucca Hotel had massive, muscle-knotted forearms and a burly barrel-chested torso that made Zorba the Greek seem infirm. Snagging a green bottle from the cooler, he popped the metal cap with an opener chained to the cash register, and set it before me with a glass and ice.

"What a beautiful bar," I tried to engage the man.

He scarcely acknowledged my compliment. His bushy black-and-white brows met over the bridge of his beaked nose. A dusky, sullen-looking younger woman came in from the kitchen to harangue Zorba in Basque while he rang up our drink orders. When the woman returned to the kitchen and the register drawer closed, the man seemed to forget her and went back to reading his newspaper, ignoring my feeble attempts at conversation as easily as he did the young woman.

Two old men at the end of the room craned their necks to watch TV, one leaning on a cane. A rerun of *Hogan's Heroes* played, a favorite with the family that lived in the flat next door to me in London, who raised the volume every night just as I sat down to dinner. Hearing the canned laugh track made me hungry, but dinner wasn't served for another fifteen minutes. Pete played the nickel slots, no more inclined to conversation than the bartender. Eliot read the signs and clippings on the barroom walls, oblivious to the world around her. The bartender disappeared into the kitchen just as Eliot came back from cruising the bar's literature.

"What did Erskine Caldwell write?" she asked Pete. "There's a review posted on the wall that he wrote of this place in 1962. Did he write mysteries?"

"I don't know," Pete said, popping a nickel into a slot. Two lemons and an orange. "I didn't read books in 1962."

"I'm walking down to that drugstore while we wait," she said. "I'll be back."

"Tobacco Road," I said. The door had already swung closed behind her. I cruised the barroom walls, too, pushing my glasses up the bridge of my nose to read the newspaper articles. I'd given up on wearing contacts. Wasn't happening in the desert. "How come I'm invisible?"

"Eliot has a permanent hard-on for you," Pete said, drinking his piñon punch, a weird concoction the bartender talked him into.

"Whatever happened between us died years ago. Any sign of life is actually *Night of the Living Dead*."

"Ask Eliot. She wants you." Pete threw back the rest of the piñon punch, wiping his lips with his fingertips.

Eliot came back in five minutes, wearing that sweet, satisfied smile she had at the end of a long day's work, tucking her cellphone into a pocket.

"Is it dinner yet?" she asked the bartender. "I'll be gnawing on your bar if I have to wait much longer."

"The table's set and the soup's on." The bartender grinned at her eagerness. "I'll give you another drink, too. OK?"

"No, thank you," she said. "I'm ready for food."

"Lead the way," Pete said.

We followed Zorba to a dining room painted a turquoise that hurt my eyes. Long tables covered by red-checkered cloths filled the room wall to wall.

"Oh too wonderful!" Eliot said. "It's like the basement at my father's old church. They even have an upright piano. We just need a warbling soprano to sing 'Nearer My God to Thee.'"

Her hand brushed my thigh as we scooted straight-backed chairs under the table. When she stretched to glance around the room, her knee rested against mine, where she left it when she smiled at the waitress and refused coffee.

"Look!" She nudged me. "Matching pictures of the Blue Boy and the Pink Girl. And the Praying Indian Brave. This is like a time machine. Don't you feel right at home?"

"Nope," Pete said. "Not a known experience in my life."

"You came on the scene too late for the church potlucks every fourth Sunday. Also, wrong father."

"I can thank Dante for that at least," Pete said. "I didn't have to eat in the most world's most bizarre room."

"Shh," Eliot whispered. "A room like this means real food. Suppers at Mrs. Waddington's church are wonderful, and their basement is only painted sea-green with gold-flecked ceiling tiles."

The thin, grim-faced young woman who'd argued with the bartender earlier brought platters of salad and homemade bread, then returned carrying a tureen. She ladled out an aromatic beef broth with onions, tomatoes, and carrots. The woman, her face chiseled from sienna onyx and her hair tied back tightly, reminded me of a Spiritist friend of my mother's, who also never smiled.

Pete stared down at the soup, his spoon poised.

"When you visit other cultures," Eliot said, "you have to try the local food as courtesy."

Any suspicions about the food proved groundless. We each moaned with delight over the chicken with rice pasta, the clam spaghetti, and beef in a tomato sauce.

An old man took the chair by Pete, asked us to call him Jack and reached over in a friendly and familiar way to dish his soup and take a piece of bread. He ate with the gusto of a much younger man. Answering Eliot's questions, the old man said, "I've ate at this hotel for fifty years, since before Nevada took to living off cards and dice."

I listened to Jack's story as he dished more chicken-and-rice onto his plate. I've made friends with bartenders, teahouse attendants, and elderly shopkeepers on three continents, but Eliot was more naturally at home here. Pete took over, having a great time talking to Jack about food. Eliot's knee still pressed into mine as the closely placed straight-backed chairs crushed us against one another. Each time she moved, her arm brushed mine. She flirted boldly with old Jack and talked with Pete about the mileage he got on the BMW. I might as well be invisible or asleep, dreaming that dream about being awake.

To finish the carnivores' orgy, that grim woman brought platters of steaks, sliding a huge piece of beef onto each plate.

Then Eliot dropped her napkin and reached down for it, her hair brushing my leg. My cock gave a start as she fell into my lap. I wanted to put my arm around her, press her against my thigh, unknot her hair and—

"Here," Pete said to Eliot, watching me the whole time. "Have another napkin. There's a whole dispenser."

She said, "I can't eat much steak but, lord, this is the best food I've encountered in some time."

After I settled the bill and we walked out into the Winnemucca night, Eliot danced on the sidewalk—which she managed with grace, even in riding boots. Pete tramped along behind her.

"If free Basques can manifest such wonders as that meal, then we must support their struggle for independence in Spain," Pete proclaimed.

"Your usual self-centered politics. Piss-poor radical that you are. But that soup? Unbelievable!" Eliot said. Music drifted from a nearby house. Paul McCartney sang "Maybe I'm Amazed," nudging free a sense of regret and loss.

"Don't you agree, Sean?" She tapped my shoulder.

I jerked awake, surprised that she spoke to me.

"Yes, it was good," I said.

"Did you see that waitress? Do you think she's Basque or Native American?" Eliot spoke close by my ear, like in earlier times. "I've never seen a face like hers. Her expression never changed."

"She was beautiful though," Pete said, "in an eerie way."

I slowed, lagging a half-pace behind. We came to the casino Pete had nominated for his night's playtime.

"Is this your stop?" Eliot asked. "You going in to gamble? Or do you want to just leave your money at the door and walk back to the motel with us?"

· · ·

Pete stayed, making a deal out of giving me my room key, which I'd left on the table when I emptied my pockets earlier.

Eliot and I wandered down side streets to the Shady Court Motel. I counted the number of moments we'd had alone together since leaving Seattle, wanting the chance to say something real.

"Stars!" Eliot exclaimed. "Clear skies tomorrow."

"But clouds on the horizon," I said, regretting it immediately, since I wanted to be buoyed aloft when her spirit soared like this.

A black-and-white shepherd rushed at us, barking. I jumped, grabbing her arm. The dog stopped at the property edge.

"Take it easy," Eliot said. "He won't get you."

"It just startled me. The night's so quiet, I forgot where I was."

Dogs up and down the street answered the shepherd's alarm, their voices echoing among trees and houses. Eliot touched my hand, then danced away from me, skipping onto the curb and then into the middle of the deserted street.

"I long to hear a coyote," she said. "If we sneak under the freeway and up into the hills, will we hear one?"

"Maybe. But later, when we camp—"

"Yeah. No use wandering into unknown country in the dark."

We walked on, not speaking. Trucks rumbled along the nearby freeway. Stars glimmered. Crickets chirped.

"Are you eager for new adventure?" Eliot said.

"Pete's right. It's best that we stop instead of freezing for another hundred miles. That's hell, not adventure," I said.

"I don't mean today. I mean in life. You must be restless after years working at the same thing."

"*The Desert Crucible* is brand new," I said. "That's the purpose of this trip."

"I'm sorry." She stopped so suddenly I bump into her. "It's just—you used to say you had to explore new mysteries in your work. This is just more video, isn't it? I thought—"

"Maybe I stick with things longer now. Though I hope our work this week is the foundation of a significant change."

"Long ago," she said, "I didn't understand your work. Please forgive me."

Just like that, on a side street in a desert town, freeway rumbling behind us, stars overhead.

"I don't remember anything to forgive," I said, lying.

"Did you make peace with your father?" Her voice promised that warmth and care that I once basked in.

"We've become good friends. He's a much different person than I thought," I said. "He's an incredible man. I wasted my adolescence, blaming him for my mother's tragedy. If only—"

I stopped, feeling too much, saying too much. A coyote cried on the dark hillside beyond the freeway.

"There's Coyote. The Old Trickster." She touched my hand, again for only a second, standing still to listen. Then she walked on, me trailing her.

"It's too easy to misunderstand people," she said. "I didn't recognize the actual depth of my father's pain for too long."

"Pete says you were an angel, taking care of your father."

"No, no angel. I got mad and yelled at him. Walter—my father—made hard work out of dying, for both of us. He struggled with God, became more rigid and unhappy each day. None of us would be angels if we endured pain like his."

"How very sad," I said, unable to say more.

"Yes. If my father were Job, then his God lost the bet. He tortured the faithful man too long. You're lucky with your father."

"Lucky? Yes, I am. I learned a lot from Robert. How to work hard. How to be honorable. Other people depend on me now. I work for my team, not just for myself."

"I understand," she said. "I'm about to take the biggest risk of my life and I'm scared. But it's Destiny. At least this time I'm taking a risk for love, instead of doing what other people want."

"That's great," I mumbled, confused, thinking she described an impending marriage.

"I admire your work," she said. Her breath brushed my neck.

"Thanks." Childish embarrassment rose at that compliment. Again the coyote howled above the din of nearby freeway traffic.

At that tender moment, my cell rang. I'd have ignored it, but the ID said it was my sister Sophy. She and I shared the same father, but little else. She's an archeologist, East Coast, and twenty years older than me. When my mother died, she ripped me out of Seattle to live with her in Amherst. And she's—she's not a warm person. Sophy hated that I'd abandoned the academic life she wanted for me. This time, her call interrupted the moment. I listened to what Sophy had to say, reported my own plans, and got off the phone as fast as possible, wanting more time alone with Eliot.

"That was Sophy," I said. Of course Eliot didn't ask. She shrank back into her shell while I was on the phone. "She's working a Basketmaker site in northern Arizona and wants to meet us at the Grand Canyon."

"Your sister?"

"Yes. She's eager to see you again," I said.

"That's nice," she said. Then more stony Eliot-silence.

"She's moving to the West Coast, since Robert and I are both settling in Seattle. Of course, she's still pushing me to return to academia." I tried once more to pull Eliot back into intimate conversation. "Nothing that either Robert or I tell her about the thrills of business life will ever convince her that I'm not a heretic."

"Look, here we are," she said, stepping away from me as we came to the Shady Court. "And here's your bike that I forgot to check this afternoon."

"That's OK," I said, coming back to earth. One minute so close, the next she was gone, inaccessible. "You'll get another chance if it doesn't fix itself."

She smiled, murmured a good-night, and fished in her jeans pocket for her room key. Then her door closed and I was alone.

■ ■ ■

I fumbled with my key in the room door lock, plagued by that whisper of her breath on my neck, the rush when she fell into my lap at dinner. I never let myself remember how her touch set me on fire. How that scaredy-cat girl once became my personal succubus.

I switched on a lamp and got to work on my notebook pad, uploading files for Tadeusz, finishing my social media chores, and then returning to sketch on glass. My hands no longer trembled from the day's bike ride. I was able to answer a text from Robert without having to re-tap words due to shaky fingers.

> Robert: You couldn't find time to write and tell me you stole the Internet? I have to learn about it on The Guardian newsfeed?
>
> Sean: My hands have been full.
>
> Robert: This is what you and Tadeusz holed up doing all last year?
>
> Sean: You don't like it?
>
> Robert: I don't know what the hell it is. But it must be art because I can't tell whether to laugh or cry. I admire your genius.

I wasted my adolescence hating Robert for a laundry list of sins: for not noticing soon enough that my mother was ill, for not doing the right things for her (though I never could determine what that was), for going away to London after my mother died. Those were the early sins, but I added to the list every year, bitter because Robert didn't acknowledge the value of my work, kept pestering me to come to work for him instead of wasting my time drawing pictures. Back then, in my mind, Robert's biggest sin was pretending that we were a family, with him playing patriarch.

Maybe I'm not the only person who was a giant effing asshole as an adolescent, or who stayed that stupid for too long into adulthood. When I joined Robert in London that year, I entered another universe, where Robert turned out to be the father I always wanted. No, more than that: the best man that I know. He ran a principled business, treating people around him with enormous personal respect. That first year, I came to know him as a real person who possesses a deep intellect and questing spirit. Over the ten years we lived together, he changed from a seeker to an adept. Two years ago, he had a tussle with pneumonia that sucked away his energy. Already past retirement age—Robert was in his forties when I was born—he wanted out of the business. He'd more than earned his freedom, and it was past time for me to step up. I promised to buy out his share of Laconia, to aid Robert's exit from business.

That's how I ended up in bed with Milo Speiser. Great business instincts, huh? Unfortunately, I didn't inherit one of Robert's key personal attributes.

I fell into an uncomfortable reverie, staring at the motel wall. I think I knew I was asleep when that woman came to me: the dark woman from the hotel dining room with her thin, angular frame and solemn, unexpressive eyes. Her face was now shrouded in a purple-and-gold scarf. She beckoned with her finger—not to follow her, but to go where she pointed, down a dark hallway.

Pete saved me from that miserable road-dream when he returned from the casino, knocking over a Krauser bag and spilling his shaving kit on the floor, then noisily phoning Milo Speiser and leaving a message.

"Just won two hundred dollars at the craps table. Having a wonderful time."

I watched Tadeusz's video post for the day, since a conversation between one sober and one inebriated person has small chance of success. Tadeusz's post for that day proved to be better than the original storyboard; the still shots amped up the visuals as if they'd been designed purposefully to fit with the animation.

As if Eliot read my mind, having never seen the storyboards.

Pete, however, hung over my shoulder, literally breathing down my neck.

"Holy shit, brother!"

He pointed to the number of views in the thirty minutes since Tadeusz had posted.

"People seem to like it," I said.

"Foolish of HOPE Productions to wait another week to green-light your work." Pete yawned mightily. "Check your voicemail in the morning. They'll be begging you."

"Pete," I paused the playback of the video stream, "I'm not wild about this video of Eliot."

"It's just another travel shot, boss," he said, again peering over my shoulder. "I had Tadeusz braid these into the story. It's a sort of leitmotif. It's supposed to evoke the image of hobbits on their single-file journey."

"You always shoot Eliot from the back. It sexualizes her, turns her into an object."

"It's just a person on a motorcycle. Wearing, I might add, enough clothes to resemble a Federation storm trooper in a high-tech snow suit."

The graceful curve of her buttocks where flesh meets saddle. One of Nature's most aesthetic forms.

"And the music!" I complained. "Whatever Tadeusz chose, it's like Easy Rider swamp-rock whenever the camera shows Eliot."

Pete dropped onto the bed beside my chair, reclining fully dressed, boots on the bedspread. "Perhaps sexual objectification is in the eye of the beholder."

"You need more neutral shots, my brother," I insisted.

"Ah, yes. Brothers. Union. Sharing of life." Pete smiled, staring at the ceiling, his hands folded over his chest.

"Even if we don't share DNA." I scanned the comments, then closed the video. "You and Eliot are more family than—"

Pete sat up suddenly.

"Eliot is a woman, dimwit. She doesn't need brotherly love."

"It's not like you said. I talked to her tonight."

"Did you talk about love?" Pete stood, tripping on the bike luggage again. He stuffed the spilled clothing and shoes back into the case. "You guys are just Echo and Narcissus all over again."

"We understand each other," I said, not liking the "narcissist" association, and also not remembering the details of that myth.

"She's never found her own voice. Do you really know what she thinks? Or are you projecting your own thoughts?"

Pete knocked his running shoe out from under the baseboard heater, kicking it into my shin.

"Three points!"

The Desert Crucible Episode III
#2: Jack of Hearts

[Tadeusz: Use this voice track with the interior shots plus wide-open space shots. The Mountain is King Lear so if you can hang any ideas off that, go for it. Find music from Jason that calls up fate and chance, but make sure it's just a single, simple guitar. —Pete]

Came to Nevada in Fifty-nine to herd sheep, but hated it. Biting the balls off little lambs with bare teeth might come natural to lotsa sheep men, but I'm not one. Great Basin oysters raw? No thank you, ma'am.

As soon as card houses came to the region, with everything drifting up from Reno, I switched to dealing blackjack. Name's Jack so black-jack suits me, like a leather glove in winter, a French glove come spring time.

See, I got the knack that lets me keep a place in the best house, and move easily when a house starts to boil too hard behind a bad task master. A poker player, he's got to read your tells, know when to bluff or fold. Me, I only got to attend to your bad habits. No, not like your maiden aunt, slappin' your elbow off the table. I can see in your eyes if you're counting cards. Your lips twitch. You blink in time with the cards. You can't keep a good conversation. I save my boss plenty, just seeing who can't count without blinking as he counts.

And the drink. I got a better Breathalyzer in my nose than a Nevada state trooper. I know when you're getting too rowdy about the number of chips flowing my way. You're the one that's losing. I'm just doing my job. So when ol' Demon Rum gets you to start accusing me, I scratch my ear and the floor guys'll be over to walk you out the door. I'm better than your mother-in-law, knowing when you're finishing the drink that's too far over the line.

You come to my table when you want to play with Fate. You got anything else you're playing, then I just scratch my ear.

∞

11.
Battle Mountain

SEAN
Tuesday a.m.

SOUTH OF BATTLE MOUNTAIN, AN HOUR after dawn in Nevada, wildlife finally appeared: a Red-tailed Hawk soared above us. Inspired by the hawk and the beauty of the desert, I accelerated hard, as if the force might lift me off the seat and into the air with the Red-tail. Seventy miles of dry, straight, cold road stretched out, seldom patrolled by state troopers. Turnoff signs pointed down gravel roads to ranches, not cities.

I opened the throttle, feeling the g-force of speed, as if my body might break all physical barriers, soaring on freedom I'd missed for the past decade. No thought beyond the hum of the bike, the white lines passing like dots.

From nowhere, one of those huge diesel farm trucks was on my tail, taking its half of the road out of the middle, too close for comfort. I added speed. The monster truck still filled my cracked rearview mirror. Then, with an extended blast of its horn, the truck passed me, so close that I could reach out and touch it.

If I weren't holding onto the bike for my life.

The white truck cut back into the lane so abruptly that I put everything into braking without flipping or skidding the bike.

Another blast of its horn, and the white truck sped ahead, leaving only its diesel stink and fear inside my helmet.

After my fingers stopped tingling, I twisted on more speed again. But now my eyes darted over the highway before and behind me, checking my mirror, covering three hundred sixty degrees for traffic and side road entries.

Peace and speed for forty miles at ninety miles per hour.

Then the bike lost power again, choked, and died.

I cursed my bad luck, not wanting to spend time practicing patience again. I'd struggled with that for years in London. Pete and Eliot lagged a minute behind. When I tried the ignition again after they stopped alongside me, my bike fired up immediately.

Eliot flipped up her face shield.

"Same problem?"

Her friendly concern should have warmed my heart, but here, vulnerable with a stalled bike, I defended myself against her charity in an evil impulse.

"Yes," I said, "but this seems to be a self-healing bike."

"Want me to check it?"

"No, let's get some more miles down."

■ ■ ■

Ten minutes later, the clouds closed in again. We climbed in elevation, headed straight for an ominous but beautiful purple veil drifting across the mountains. It was impossible to avoid the inevitable—another lesson from this trip—and the rain came down hard as we passed the Pioneer Cemetery outside Austin, Nevada, though the sun still shone brightly in the valley below. As we rode up the hill to the town, cold, painful rain drenched us. With no place dry to park, we left the dripping bikes and scrambled inside the first café we found, to eat breakfast and get warm.

"Switch bikes with me, Sean," Eliot said. We chose a booth that let us watch our bikes out the window. "Maybe if I can feel what your bike is doing, I can tell what's wrong."

"I'll tell you what's wrong," Pete said. "It's a disposable bike. Five thousand miles and it seeks the elephants' graveyard."

It was Pete's leased bike, but my problem. "The bike is fine most of the time, Eliot. But I'd appreciate your insight."

She'd switched her attention from my bike to the café's wall art: motorcycle silhouettes cut from old saw blades; crumpled fenders and dented tanks painted over with Grandma Moses-style pictures of abandoned pickups outside old barns.

Pete yawned and held out his cup to the woman who came by with a pot of coffee, a round, rose-colored woman past social security age, with a broad smile for us and a name tag pinned to her sweater.

"Earlene, may I have some cream, please?" Pete started the conversation that would lead to a signed release agreement and new video footage. Pete had already set one of his cameras to shoot the café's motorcycle art.

"Of course, dearie," Earlene said. "We'll get the fire going in here so you can warm up."

"Thanks," Eliot said, "but we like being cold."

The woman laughed, a sweet girlish chirp. "I never knew bikers was such liars."

"We like the weather you got here, too," Pete said. "Why'd the pioneers build this town under a waterfall?"

Again, the tinkling laughter. "They built the town here 'cause of the mines. Biggest turquoise mine in the world. Did you see it on t'other side of the pass?"

"No," Eliot said. "We came up from the north. Did you know, it's sunny and nice down by the cemetery?"

Earlene said, "It's like that a lot here. We sit under a cloud and a mile away the sun's bright and shiny. Makes you think that the Rain King lives under this here mountain."

Earlene fluttered away, chipper as a house finch, to place our orders and start the fire.

"Makes you think those pioneers should have built the town where they buried their dead," Pete said. He cupped his hands around the coffee, as if to warm his fingers. I longed for the hot chocolate I'd ordered. My hands still shook from cold and the long morning ride. Eliot sat by me, so near that her knee rested against mine. Pete watched her, so I checked, too, for the signs of affection that Pete misread. But Eliot offered only her clear-eyed, friendliest self. One thing I hoped for seemed to be happening: a crack in the wall between us.

Earlene lit a fire in an old potbellied cast-iron stove, expertly coaxing heat from the black monster. Pete, still seeking cream, started sipping his coffee black. He scowled.

"This is just like Tajikistan."

"Exotic?" Eliot asked.

"No. All the coffee I got in Tajikistan was instant Nescafe in lukewarm water."

"Your fingers must have sucked all the heat out," she said.

Still grousing, Pete accepted Eliot's memory cards with that morning's camera work and began uploading them for Tadeusz. I wondered, but decided to check later when we were warm, whether either Pete or Eliot had caught on camera that white truck that tried to run me off the road.

"Did Sam fix that bug on your laptop?" Eliot asked.

"Twice so far," Pete muttered.

Eliot was inserting fresh memory cards and checking settings on all her cameras when her cellphone buzzed. She studied it and then began to answer messages.

"Pete." I had to nudge him to get his attention. "Tell Tadeusz to change up the music for—"

My own cell phone, set to vibrate, jumped on the table, skittering toward Pete, who grabbed it, checked the ID, and handed it over.

It was Karl, our attorney.

"Hey, buddy! How's the road?"

"Cold and wet," I said. When there isn't a planned meeting, a surprise call from an attorney can't be good news. "What's up?"

"My office received a follow-up over that estoppel they handed you on Friday."

"I haven't said a thing, good or bad." I'd been scrupulous on social media: *The Desert Crucible* only. Not a word about Monkey.

"It seems FAIL expected you as part of their deal with Milo to acquire all of Laconia," Karl said.

"Their disappointment saddens me." When I said this, Pete glanced up from his laptop, then closed the lid and watched me as I talked with Karl.

"Yeah, buddy?" Karl said. "They intend to motivate you. FAIL found out about your option with HOPE. I have another estoppel for you. FAIL claims that *The Desert Crucible* is a Laconia work product. They want your concession in writing this afternoon."

"Or what?" My voice rose too loud for the room, then broke.

Pete took the phone. "Karl? Sean can't speak at the moment." He listened at length, his expression unchanging. "Karl, I gave you a kill switch for this kind of thing. Go use it. Yes, now."

He handed me back the phone.

"OK, but atom bombs aren't usually my way," Karl was saying, as if he still had Pete on the line.

"What bomb?" I asked.

"Ask Pete. I'll get back to you when I learn more," Karl said. When I started with more questions, Karl said, "I gotta go. Just learned that Jason Taylor is in jail. Have to go bail him out."

Pete was back on his laptop, seemingly oblivious to the world, and Eliot was still busy texting on her own phone.

I said, "Karl found Jason. He's in jail."

Pete raised his hands, questioning the heavens. "Mr. Clean? Mr. I Don't Drink, I Don't Do That Shit? What could Jason get arrested for? Washing his hands too much in public? Skateboarding in the University parking garage, like when he was thirteen?"

"No idea," I said.

"It's got to be that witch wife of his." Pete began tapping texts on his phone.

"What kill switch?" I asked, all the while knowing that Pete would stonewall me. "Who dies?"

"Milo just loses any hold on you," he said.

Eliot glanced up then, listening.

"What did you do?" I asked.

"Just shared some crap with Karl that I had on hand," Pete said. "Don't worry about it, boss. Seriously, it's fine. Worry about things worth worrying about. Like Jason Taylor."

...

Earlene, the waitress, returned with my cocoa and Pete's cream.

"You must be reading my mind," I said as she set a little shaker of cinnamon down with the steaming cocoa. "That's just what I dreamed of."

"I'm a champion mind reader. Where do you think I get the great stories I tell?" she said.

"You're reading his mind and you're not slapping his face?" Pete said. "You should have seen how he watched you bending over to make that fire. You can't trust him."

"Well, he's got to clean up his act if he's going to stay here." Her eyes twinkled and she tottered away to fetch plates of eggs and potatoes. Earlene's peppery spirits spiced the meals enough to make rubbery eggs and soggy hash browns palatable. After breakfast, we stood by the fire to get toasty before departing. With no other customers to serve, Earlene pulled up a chair to join us.

Eliot asked about the metal motorcycle cutouts.

"My Ray does those," Earlene said. "Some like to work wood. He likes the feel of metal."

"I agree with that view," Eliot said. "He's asking a modest price. You only sell from the café here?"

"My son put some up on eBay for him."

"Good source for that work. You might try Etsy and Pinterest, too. I've had luck there. Here, take a look at mine."

Eliot and Earlene bent over her cellphone, pointing to pictures.

"You make nice things," Earlene said. I yearned to pull that phone my way, to see the images. "I put some of my knit things up for sale a few times a year. I never thought to put Ray's doo-hickeys up there. You make good money on this?"

"Some," Eliot said. "I do better at street fairs and Saturday markets. Though, truthfully, I don't see much chance of that for you in Austin."

"My sister down in Vegas puts things out for us at the swap meet," Earlene said. "Them pennies add up, if you're careful."

"Don't you know it," Eliot said. She put her cell away. No luck for me to catch a glance. "Care counts."

"Where you folks headed?" Earlene asked, bringing Pete and me back into the conversation. "How long you been on the road?"

"We started in Seattle four days ago," Eliot said. "We were headed for Arizona. But the rain gods built a wall of water between us and the Colorado Plateau."

"Lord, I know what that's like," Earlene said. "We used to dry-roast here all summer until the day my old man got a vacation from the mines. When we climbed on his bike, that's when the rain started."

"You ride, ma'am?" I asked. I stayed with the conversation to keep my mind from wandering back to the phone call from Karl.

"Oh my, yes. Ray, my husband, rode home on an old Indian after Nam—he was in that one early. 'Earlene,' he yelled from the street, 'get your ass out here. Let's go.'" She smiled at Eliot. "That was our honeymoon, on account of we got married when he was drafted and didn't have a chance then for a honeymoon. We rode together for years. Ray's last bike was a BMW all got up for touring. I have to say, that was my favorite."

"I have an old R100RS," Eliot said. "Best ride ever."

"You lucky thing. My old man's tough, but I thought he'd about like to cry when he had to sell that old Beemer."

"Is your husband gone now?" Pete asked.

"No, Ray's in the kitchen cooking. He quit the mines years ago. For a long time, every place we thought of, we rode there. A couple years ago his eyes got so bad, he can't ride no more."

"That's a shame." Eliot said.

"Poor guy," Earlene said, shaking her head. "When Ray goes to his VFW meetings or plays poker on Saturdays, my son comes up from Tonopah and takes me riding with him. He's a good boy. We don't tell Ray, 'cause it would just be mean."

"I hope my son is good to me when I get old," Pete said.

"You have some foundation work to do there, little brother," Eliot said.

"You got kids, honey?" Earlene asked.

"No, not me." Eliot smiled.

"You better get started," Earlene said, slapping my knee. "You got to plan for your wife's future. Life insurance ain't going to take care of these things for you."

The front door banged open and a loud, laughing knot of older men tramped in just as Eliot started to set Earlene straight.

"Earlene!" one man shouted. "What's for lunch? I could even eat your gut-burning chili today, I'm so hungry."

"Where's Ray?" another called out. "I want to show him my new hunting knife."

"I gotta go, kids," Earlene said, jumping up. "You have fun and be careful. Rain or no, I wish I was out there with you."

We started gathering up our electronic gear, sorting whose scarf belonged where, crawling back into layers of clothes. Most of our gear was stashed, and we prepared to face the facts: that this was the day the earth would end in Ice, not Fire this time.

Pete picked up his phone, checking one last message, then frowning handed it to Eliot, who kindly passed the handset on to me. From Dante:

Water for her horses. Claudia only ever wanted water rights from me. Fuck me with a laaawyyer

Eliot thumped Pete with a forefinger on his wrist, a comfort gesture. "We're out in the middle of nowhere. If we can't fix a problem over the phone, we'll just handle it when we get there."

Pete nodded, yet he seemed to be staring into the abyss, instead of just reading a text message.

• • •

Outside, the rain had worn itself out, leaving only a fine mist.

"Damn!" Eliot exclaimed, punching my arm as I wiped the bike's rain-drenched seat with an oil rag. "How come we didn't get Ray and Earlene for our parents?"

"You'd have to grow up in Austin, Nevada," Pete said.

"A small price to pay," Eliot said. She waved at Earlene, who stood in the café window for a quick goodbye. "Don't you wish you had a place in the world to be happy like Earlene?"

My knees and thighs still warm from the wood stove, I prepared to ride, pulling up the hood of my sweatshirt as a barrier against the wet helmet liner. I found the key in my bike's ignition again, this time before Pete chided me.

"Let me take a quick look," Eliot said. She'd started her bike, but left it purring to stand by me. "Open the gas tank. Let's see."

I didn't get a chance.

A white double-cab pickup—the same one that cut me off?— roared up beside us, screeching to a halt, then made a quick, jarring three-point turn.

Metal screeched on pavement. The diesel truck roared as it accelerated, speeding out of town, having clipped Eliot's bike. Her bike, still purring, lay crumpled like a wounded animal, its fairing shattered and the front-end a mangled mess.

"No!" Eliot cried.

I put my hands out to steady her, but she stepped away, running to switch off the bike.

Pete stood quivering, a hair's breadth from the bike that lay at his feet, now dead. "I didn't have my camera."

Eliot clenched him in a hard embrace. "My god, an inch more and it would have been you. Are you OK?"

"I didn't have my camera."

People tramped out from the café and crossed the street from nearby. Eliot still hugged Pete and didn't seem to hear anything others said. Her eyes glistened, the nearest to crying I'd ever seen. Pete wiggled out of her grasp, repeating that he was OK, turning on his camera to capture the crowd reporting what they'd all just seen. I watched Eliot rather than the crowd.

"Happened just like that."

"Amazing no one was killed."

"Driving like the devil."

What no one had seen: the license plate of that truck. But everyone described the model in detail.

"Dodge Ram," one man said. His service shirt had the name Bob embroidered in red script. "Can't miss that grille in a lineup."

"The 3500," a second said. He was as tall as me, but even slimmer and more than forty years older. "This year's model."

"Yep. Turbo Diesel, for sure," an edgy, sunburned teen guy said. He stood near Bob, his face too similar not to be related. "Can't miss that rumble."

"It's in that six-ton class," Bob said. "Could crush a herd of motorbikes with that one.

Slim old guy said, "I'm betting it's a few hundred pounds short. And no real load in the back."

Eliot held Pete's free hand, the one without the camera. He didn't wiggle free. But he still wasn't answering anyone with more than a single word. Or even showing the standard Pete resentment at being asked repeatedly about his wellbeing.

...

While waiting for the state police, Eliot listened to Pete's suggestions. I didn't have one to offer. The wrecker arrived before the police, idling patiently while the cops did their business. The state police took less time than at the scene in Yakima. In this case, no one had anything useful to report other than a description of the most common truck in the west. The crowd concurred on the make and model and that it was white. Not red or black. Or silver.

While Eliot was busy with the state patrol, I paid the wrecker. Pete now denied that he'd been shaken. All he wanted was whatever footage he could capture, plus conversation with the locals. Later, when Pete flipped off his video and said goodbye to one of his new best friends, he ended up beside me.

I said, "I think that same pickup tried to run me off the road near Battle Mountain, just before my bike died this morning."

Pete watched the wrecker guy finish his task. "Should we consider sabotage by our competitors?"

"I can't believe that," I said. "We're in the middle of nowhere. We don't know where we'll be from one half of the day to the next. No one could find us unless they made a pact with the devil."

"Or the Furies," Pete said. "However, with so much at stake, it's not paranoid to think—"

"Yeah, it is. We've already won. We've got miles of video and a bigger audience than we dreamed of. All that's left is Dante Gawain and the ranch. What's to sabotage?"

"Outside of the legal attack Karl called about?" Pete laughed. "That won't work. But Milo has a personal preference for sabotage."

"You've been saying that about Milo since college."

"And you've been making excuses for that shark since college. He wants your balls on a platter, *compadre*. However, even if Milo's trying sabotage, stop worrying. What worse can happen?"

...

The police left and the wrecker carted away the carcass of Eliot's bike. The crowd dissipated quickly, there being no drama left to entertain them.

"Should we rebuild that wreck or part it out at the junk yard? What's your advice?" Pete said. He'd recovered—no longer ghostly pale as he'd been just after the crash. Once the crowd departed, Pete began persuading Eliot of a silver lining.

She punched him. "Just shut up, Pete."

"It's a workplace accident," Pete said, rubbing where she'd punched him. "So Sean has to pay for it. He's our employer."

"I have insurance," Eliot said. Ice must flow in her veins, given how coolly she handled catastrophe.

"We'll have to double up," Pete said. "Nothing else to do."

"Not in this ghost town," Earlene said, having comforted us with more hot chocolate and another chunk of wood in the stove. "But all that gear won't fit on two bikes."

Earlene fetched boxes from the kitchen, promising to ship whatever got left behind. We made quick work of combining our gear, leaving extra clothes, Eliot's tent, and more behind. Pete boxed up the Krauser bags from her bike, which were scarcely scratched. Eliot was on her cell much of the time, standing off in the corner so that only snatches of her conversation carried to where we packed.

"Me again. Who has power of attorney? Someone has to ..." ... "Did you submit an offer?" ... "I can't make a live meeting for a few more days." ... "Can you write a letter or ..."

When she rejoined us, Eliot printed her address in block letters on the ragged spiral notepad Earlene offered. I insisted on leaving all my paper money with Earlene, to cover shipping costs.

"Neighbor problems at home?" Pete asked.

"It's handled," Eliot said. She brushed her hand over Pete's head, a move so unlike her. "I'm so glad you weren't hurt."

Pete twitched where she rested her hand on his shoulder. She punched him, shaking the camera he'd focused on Earlene.

"Let's hit the road," she said.

The Desert Crucible Episode IV
#1: In Spider Grandmother's Home

*[Tadeusz: Link with the roll of the café interior, exploring art on the walls;
use the most country-fried music Jason left you. That hellhound loser has
been no help because he was in jail. —Pete]*

I lodge where the Spider Grandmother once did.

Please, I did not steal this home from her. That happened before
I came to this country. Having come here, was I to leave this lair to
live in a cave with mice and burrowing owls, because Spider had
been evicted? She pursued her people to different lands—fruitless
plains and sandy earth traps. It's true that she was pushed out. But
not by me. I'm merely re-inhabiting, rebuilding.

It's not as though she'd woven this land into paradise before giving
it up. This is hard country that's never seen heaven. When I first
came, I bought a straw broom from the True Value store and swept
away the dust left after Spider Grandmother deserted this home. I
began to knit to make the place livable. And don't go making jokes,
implying that I crochet Budweiser cans into fishing caps. In this land,
Spider Grandmother wove beautiful rugs from the wool of her own
sheep. Sure, we have a few more generations to catch up and craft
our own culture here. But it's not like Spider's people sprung fully
formed from the soil, whatever their stories claim. They migrated,
too, displacing others who left to avoid them. Or heard that life was
better South of here. Or West of here. Or who chose to go back
North where they came from.

We'll get around to creating beauty one day, those of us who chose
to stay in Spider Grandmother's old home. I knit pieces, thinking my
own grandmother once made an orange afghan—crazy enough
that a pioneer's daughter chose a pattern named for another high-
desert tribe from two oceans away.

My own tribe has the Internet to find and pass on new traditions. I
knit. My old man, like the Thunder god, carves motorcycle totems,
finding the spirit left in discarded iron, freeing it to live again.

∞

12.
Austin Summit

These people inhabit a magical world,
but must save each other without magic.
—E.A. Stewart

ELIOT
Tuesday Midday

OUTSIDE THE CAFÉ, ELIOT AVOIDED the shards of broken headlight left on the street, making herself not see Pete standing there, making herself remember Roz's text from that morning: *"Cora seems better; watching out for Destiny. Don't worry."*

Eliot called to Pete. "Let's get going."

"Ride with me," Sean said. "I'd be glad to have you."

Pete said, "You're lying, *compadre*. You been hanging off the side like Kenny Roberts at Laguna Seca. Eliot will be in your way."

Surprisingly, Sean pressed for Eliot to ride with him. Before she agreed, her cell phone rang. It was Destiny.

"Hold on. Destiny calls." She gave a wait sign and stepped back up to the café porch to listen.

"Are you in school? How's Cora?" Eliot said instead of hello.

"Yes. She's fine, I think. A rich woman bought our house."

"No, wait."

"Yeah. I just called Aunt Cora to make sure she's OK."

Destiny blurted details: an offer fifteen percent beyond anything Eliot could ever gather, all the waterfront parcels included so the neighborhood wouldn't be ruined by developers. "The agent came to the hospital this morning to get her to sign. Now we're freaking homeless."

"No, you're not." While a wave of disappointment washed over her, Eliot rushed to reassure Destiny. "This stabilizes your aunt's finances. You'll still have a home on Limberlost."

"Don't patronize me." Destiny repeated the pet phrase she'd used over the first few months of their friendship. "Cora's old. She's in the hospital. This whole scene is falling apart."

Eliot, forlorn at her own lost dream, hunched up on the café porch, now unable to stop staring at the taillight pieces littering the pavement. What she did next was what Roz had warned her not to do. Eliot stood there on the café porch, making a promise with no guarantee that she could keep it.

"Listen, Destiny. I'll make this right. I promise. Roslyn already started the process to make me your guardian."

"Really?" The word broke into several syllables as Destiny squeaked and hiccupped in answer. A bell sounded. "I have to get to class. Call me tonight. I love you!"

Hanging up, Eliot found Pete waiting and Sean tapping texts on his own cell, seemingly oblivious to all but his own world.

"Trouble on Limberlost?" Pete asked.

"Destiny. Life as a soap opera. Stay tuned tomorrow," Eliot said, pretending that her secret desire hadn't just been dashed on the rocks of commerce, like her bike trashed on the street. She buckled up her jacket and pulled on her helmet.

"I bet it's random assaults by the universe," Pete said. "We control fate. It's not destiny."

"Yeah, that's it," Eliot said, the words echoing inside her helmet, "random assaults."

"It's like playing pachinko," Pete said, employing his favorite Japanese pinball metaphor. "It's all in how you seize control of the random and make it work for you."

"Who has control?" Sean asked as he clicked off his phone. He tucked it into the tank bag and prepared to ride.

Eliot climbed on behind him, her long legs curving up around his thighs as she tucked her feet onto the foot pegs. She clenched the back rail of the seat, knowing this ride would kill her knees as well as her ass. The placement of the foot pegs bent her knees at an angle

guaranteed to induce cramps after fifty miles. The seat wasn't con-
toured for anyone larger than a ten-year-old. She thought about her
knees. The weather. She wiggled to make sure the wearable cameras
adapted to passenger position.

This bike roared. It didn't putter *Limberlost-Limberlost-Limberlost*
like hers did. Her crushed bike. Which was just a bike.

There'd be another bike.

And there was other land to find on Limberlost. She'd shake off
that temporary, selfish desire immediately, and instead focus on the
next step for stabilizing Destiny's life, which meant finding housing
for the three of them so that Cora, as well as Destiny, had care and
supervision. Cora and Destiny both needed to be in town anyway,
not at the farthest end of Lost Point Road, too far from services and
school. She'd take the money already socked away and use it to
remodel her shop into three bedrooms.

Leaving Austin behind, Sean accelerated gradually on the wet
road, obviously checking how the bike handled with the addition of
a passenger. Eliot knew he'd find this bike less squirrelly on the
curves, offering less punch on the straightaway. Maybe he'd take
fewer risks.

In the first few miles, she repeatedly slid up the seat and collided with him. She failed to lift off the seat the first time they crossed
railroad tracks, her clattering teeth unpleasantly reminding her to
relax with the bike. Clinging lightly at first, she wrapped more
tightly so she melded with Sean as he managed the curves of the
road. Jammed against him on this ride, there was no respark of the
old electricity. They were merely miserable and cold. The tiny café-
style fairing on Sean's bike offered no protection for either of them.

Up the Austin summit, and then down the southeast side and
around the corner. Where snow found the riders.

More random assault by the universe.

Eliot hugged Sean as ice crystals blew into them, her thighs
pressed tightly against his, her arms wrapped around his waist. The
bike skittered across the road when the crosswind hit, as though a
fine coat of Vaseline covered the pavement. They could ride far
enough through this weather to get away from it, though she

wished the silver sage grew tall enough to shelter bikes and people so they could just wait it out.

Sean kept the bike steady in the wind, yet Eliot felt his muscles tighten like steel bands around his chest and shoulders with the strain of the task. She wasn't comfortable letting go to wipe snow off her face shield, so it must be worse for him, since he needed a tight grip on the handlebars: no free hand to clean his face shield. She sought to anticipate and match every move Sean made, neither of them able to predict whether the wind would next blow the front or rear wheel out of control.

The ice-wind penetrated her all-weathers and the leathers and long johns she wore underneath, freezing her chest and knees. The thin slice between her front and his back offered the only warmth on the bike. Eliot hugged him closer.

She'd need a zoning exception from the Village council if she was going to remodel her shop into a living space. Who knew how to help with that? She considered every friend on Limberlost, thinking of who best to call, easing away from shock and wild thoughts to create a backup plan. What you have to do when the universe's fifty-fifty odds don't break your way.

The rear wheel skittered left, but Sean accelerated out of it, as if he felt the road before the bike did.

13.
Round Mountain

SEAN
Tuesday p.m.

BY THE TIME WE DESCENDED to the Highway 376 junction, the snow stopped, the wind died, and the sun threatened to break through. We paused to stare back up at the treacherous passage. Eliot on the bike didn't leave room for me to shake out tension and change positions, but I stretched my shoulders and hands. The clock on the instrument panel said that the eons we'd endured lasted only twenty-five minutes.

"How's your bike?" Pete asked when he arrived.

"No problems," Eliot said before I could answer. "I'm guessing it has to get hot at high speeds. Ask again in fifty miles."

Pete pulled back onto the highway and sped away.

"Hey, Eliot! You OK back there?"

"Yes. And I believe we have escaped the gates of hell." She closed her face shield and wiggled to find a comfortable seat.

Between the Toiyabe and Toquima mountain ranges, the road traced a long narrow valley where sage had been ploughed up for dryland wheat farming and cattle grazing. The sun, already angling to the west, broke through to shine on the eastern range. Clouds played cat-and-mouse with the sun. Occasionally dark veils cut across the highway, often drifting away before we encountered moisture, but sometimes dropping rain and hail before we escaped to dry road again. I watched with trepidation as snow descended from the tops of the Toiyabe mountains, but the Toiyabe peaks caught those clouds and held them, shaking snow onto the pines and firs that covered the canyon sides. The mountains accepted the ice veil with grace, their elegant geniality reminding me that mountains live and breathe, the same sense that overwhelmed me during those summers in Arizona, when I'd sit on the canyon rim above the ranch, watching mountains age under sun and desert storms.

The Toiyabe mountains hampered the wind, so the rain seemed mild. I relaxed to enjoy the ride, not having to force the bike through unreasonably severe elements.

Eliot's thighs pressed against mine, her breasts against my back. Dust-devils whirled in fields where rain had dampened the thin topsoil and released the heavenly incense of sage and summer storm. I hadn't experienced that sense of belonging to the earth since leaving the States.

Eliot tightened around me. The bike died.

As though she sensed it before it happened.

I stopped on the shoulder. She jumped off and unbuckled her helmet. The bike's instruments showed no sign of overheating; but, as Eliot predicted, exactly fifty miles had passed since our last stop.

"You want to take off the tank bag?"

I complied. She unscrewed the gas cap.

"Hear that?"

"No. My head is still roaring from the road."

"That suck of air as the vacuum broke. You've got a clog or a kink in the breather hose."

Pete pulled up beside us. Eliot explained the problem.

"Well, doctor," she said, smiling at me, like how the sun broke through the clouds, "we'll have to operate at the next stop. But I think we can save the patient."

Once again the bike started easily after sitting still for a few moments.

Just like she seemed to restart easily after that catastrophe in Austin. How did she do it?

■ ■ ■

A small town, Round Mountain, appeared not far down the road, guarding the world's largest open-pit gold mine. We stopped at a service station, one of the few commercial buildings in town.

Immediately busy at the repair tasks, Eliot fetched the tools she needed from Pete's saddlebag. When I took off my jacket and rolled up my sleeves to help, the corners of her mouth twitched as she struggled to be polite. She said, gently, "I can tell you how to do this yourself if you want."

"You do it. We don't need to take any longer than necessary."

She picked up a wrench to start work, then paused. "It looks bad out here in cowboy country, me doing it."

"I don't care about that," I said, with more hope than truth.

Pete reappeared from taking a leak. "What are you guys fighting about?"

"We're not fighting," Eliot said. "We're negotiating how to fix Sean's bike."

"If you're worried about hurting his ego, forget it," Pete said.

"I don't give a fig about my ego," I said, but not convincingly.

I pushed my last two dollars in coins into the soda machine, masking embarrassment over my mechanical incompetence. Pete followed and bought a Coke. While Eliot worked, we made small talk with the service station attendant, a kid who didn't fit the local desert farmer mold, though his rolled-up jacket sleeve revealed knots of muscle, probably from bucking hay bales. He wore jeans rolled up to just below his knees, showing skinny calves above mock-Beatle boots. An angel-wings patch spanned the back of his jeans jacket, except black as a raven; a heavy chain anchored his wallet. Sigur Rós played ethereal Icelandic rock, loudly, from his office-shed.

More than one cultural generation had passed through America since I last travelled this landscape. I remembered the landforms, yet this was an unfamiliar country where I didn't know the language, the cultural norms, or the hopes and wishes of the inhabitants. I was a stranger in a strange land.

The kid—his name was Zack—answered Pete's inquiries about the road ahead. His attention seemed to be diverted by Eliot's ass bent over my bike.

"She your wife?" Zack asked Pete.

"No, my sister."

The kid flinched, but Pete laughed and offered a high-five in a gesture of forgiveness.

"You her old man?" Zack next asked me.

"No, she's her own woman."

Zack studied my bike and its mechanic. He pointed to the Monkey King sticker.

"Cute. Did you borrow your kid's motorbike?"

Without waiting for an answer, he drifted away to hover near Eliot, not hearing Pete's question about what people did for fun around here. The sound of Zack's conversation with Eliot got lost as a diesel pickup rumbled past on the highway while Pete and I studied the map to decide how far we might make it that day. Then Zack's voice drifted back to us.

"You a hard-core feminist?" he asked, flirting, not trying to hassle her.

"No, I don't go to church," Eliot said. "They tried to raise me Four Square, but I fell away."

Their voices fell away on a desert breeze, then rose again.

"Northern Arizona. NAU," Zack said.

"Nice town." Eliot's favorite tone of encouragement, Key of G. For Generous. "What are you studying?"

"Art history."

"No way!"

"Yes, way. My way. Everyone's already told me there's no future in it." Zack, animated, shook both hands to emphasize his point. "But I love art. And I'm not going to commercial art school. I want to study the masters."

"You'll hate those people." More pure Eliot sounds. Key of E, Earnest, with five cents' free advice.

"Not news. I get that lecture from my uncle all the time. Can't be any worse than high school." Zack pronounced it *hyskooool*.

"Yes, it is," Eliot said. "You're real people. You can't imagine the cultural shock. And it won't be about whether you know Renaissance painters' techniques."

The wind carried their voices back out to the desert again. She didn't glance my way while she dispensed advice about careers in art. I know lots about brush techniques from both early and high Renaissance, but she didn't seek my input.

She finished work on the bike and asked where she could wash her hands, seeming to enjoy Zack's flirting, though he was more than fifteen years younger than her. After some coy wrangling, Zack sent her to a trailer house on the next lot over, with instructions to knock on the door and say Zack sent her.

When she was gone, Zack laughed, throwing his head back. "I'd be out of my mind if she was sitting behind me on a bike. How do you stand it?"

"Umm —" I was out of my mind.

Pete said, "That's a question modern psychiatry can't answer."

"You don't see that every day," Zack said. "A cute ass who's not a smart ass. And she's got enough brains, she can blow her own nose without help."

Eliot ambled back across the lot toward the bikes. I flushed, embarrassed to be joking with a kid who coveted her. She buckled her helmet, snapped her jacket shut, and pulled on gloves, waving goodbye to the ardent admirer circumnavigating her as she prepared to ride again. A 4WD Ford Ranger pulled up for service and diverted the kid's attention.

"You got a new boyfriend, Eliot," Pete said.

"He must like the dipstick lipstick I use." The face shield muffled her voice and veiled her expression.

"He likes your fine buns," Pete said.

She got on behind Pete, kicking down the foot pegs and making herself comfortable. "These buns don't feel very fine after a hundred miles on Sean's bike."

I'd assumed that she'd ride with me.

Not ready to go when Pete took to the highway, I stood in the middle of a potholed gravel lot near the world's largest gold mine, realizing that she was still my Artemis.

Zak with the neo-Beatle boots was free again.

"Did Pete record your story?" I asked as I checked my bike, knowing full well Eliot had checked every damn thing.

"No, your friend started talking to me about videotaping, but I had customers before we did anything."

I offered him my personal card. "When you're browsing tonight, will you check out *The Desert Crucible*? Then write to me. I want to hear what you think of it."

Zack glanced at the card, then at the sticker on my bike.

"Shee-it, man." He held out his hand to shake.

"Seriously. Write me. Do you have any of your work here? I'd like to see it."

"My notebook's in the shack."

Inside, I got a signed release like Pete does, and then I recorded what Zack said as I snapped his artwork, all the while worried that I'd fail to get the proper focus. Zack's work—already beyond juvenilia—was too influenced by fantasy sci-fi tropes for my personal tastes, but filled with an energy that would soon break free of such restrictions.

"Since I've been out of academia so long, I don't know what advice they give at North Arizona," I said. "But I wish you'd choose the future of art instead of its history."

"I'm not destined to be a great artist," Zack said. "That's why I chose art history."

"Don't even think about how great you are—or aren't—for a decade. Just sign up to work with every possible teacher, and listen to the ones that make you work your ass off."

Fortunately Pete had assigned me the fast bike, which allowed me to catch up after staying back so long.

The Desert Crucible Episode IV
#2: Raven

[Tadeusz: I shot this so it needs a lot of cleanup work. I fully trust that you can make better decisions than me with material like this. If you can't find still/vid shots with birds, go with just this art. —Sean]

The desert made me what I am. Rotted sand fills the pattern of my Vibram soles, but doesn't weigh me down so much that the ancient gravel stops my soul from flying over this land.

I know every arroyo within a day's flight. I know every stand of rabbit brush sturdy enough that I can alight to watch the shadows of clouds flit over the mountain. I know every fold in the lower hills, and I can find my way in those valleys at night, when the moon defeats the sun.

I know the lighting of this landscape across four seasons, and the transitions in between. I'm a plein air painter, using the tip of my own wing feather, capturing how on a clear winter day the sun glints off the window of a miner's rusted hut in that gully. With the soft down from my breast, I can shade chalk and charcoal to describe the physics of heat rising from pavement when summer sun parches this landscape.

I know the limits of my domain.

I can fly. I soar. But migrate I cannot do.

∞

14.
Caliente

SEAN
Tuesday Night

MONKEY RODE MY BACK FOR the next hundred miles across Nevada, not as a companion on pilgrimage nor to whisper instructive stories in my ear. Rather, Monkey wrapped his arms around my head and clung on tight, generating a headache. Then he covered my eyes with his paws, playing hide-and-seek when I needed to see the road. Instead of helping Impious Aeneas combat demons, Monkey carelessly swung his iron cudgel, the whir ringing in my ears.

To drown out the sound of the Monkey King's harangue, I made up a song, humming it at the same pitch as the bike's engine. But I couldn't get beyond the first few lines.

> My heart, once a placid lake,
> Now ruffled by winds of desire,
> Oh, Artemis, goddess of the wildland
> Listen to the cries of man—

Then—what? What would I beg for? Was the goddess Artemis ever inclined to accept supplication? And don't songs have rhymes?

I was fine when I got out of bed this morning. The legal assault from Milo didn't faze me (I'm trusting Pete, like he insisted). Karl hadn't sent an update about Jason, but there wasn't any action I could take to help. Eliot lost her bike, but she was dealing with it like a champ. Other than those blips, *The Desert Crucible* was progressing. Yet instead of a meditative ride, reconnecting with the power of the universe, I'd connected with slick roads, cold, wind, and treacherous drivers. My mind was focused, it's true: on keeping the bike on the road. And not freezing my knees and balls. No room for deep thought other than—

I want Eliot to like me.

In a totally whipped, mind-not-on-business kind of way.

We stopped for gas again in Warm Springs, another clutch of trailers housing a few families who pumped gas and fried burgers for passing truckers and ranchers. Cold, pelting rain, now more familiar than sunshine, burst on us as we pounded up the rickety wood steps into the tin-house café.

Inside, Pete headed for the can; Eliot and I sat in a torn Naugahyde booth and ordered hot drinks and toasted cheese sandwiches. I asked for tea. The woman behind the counter put a cup of water in the microwave. When she served it, the cup wasn't hot enough to warm my hands.

Eliot and I watched two women and a man, apparently locals, shoot pool in the back of the café. Eliot offered to share her potato chips, then touched my hand; it didn't seem to be an accident. When I glanced up, she pointed to the sign over the cash register:

We don't serve women here. You have to bring your own.

"Damn," a woman's voice twanged from the pool game in the back room. "Only one stripe left, and I go and sink the eight ball."

A thin, pale woman, haggard from cigarettes and indoor life, sipped on a light beer and laughed at her poor luck.

"I'll rack up the balls, but you gotta break, Harold," the other woman drawled in that twangy Great Basin accent you hear once you crest the Cascade mountains. "I can't break for shit."

"I gotta be going," Harold said. "Shirley'll be wondering."

He chalked his stick and slammed the cue ball into the stripes and solids at the other end of the table, instantly forgetting Shirley.

Back from the bathroom, Pete scowled at his Nescafe. "Geezus. And there's no TP in the john. Here we are, back in Tajikistan in time for the fall colors."

In spite of tepid beverages, we joked ourselves into a good mood while warming up. Eliot went to make a phone call in the girls' can, and came back elated.

"Damn, Pete, you're right. I called your attorney Karl. He's all over the issues."

"What did I tell you last Friday night? I'm your best hope for escape from catastrophe." Pete folded his hands in mock prayer. "Experience counts."

I laughed. "Yeah, Pete knows most all the paths out of catastrophe, having been there a dozen times."

Eliot, however, paled again. "You could've been killed, Pete. I keep seeing that over again."

Pete coolly sipped his cool Nescafe. "However, as usual, cruel Fate can never access my precise GPS coordinates."

We plugged our electronics into an outlet behind the booth, attracting the usual shifting eyeballs of people wondering what we're up to. Then we sorted through still photos and video, uploading several selections for Tadeusz. I posted adroit comments on all the social boards and, as an extra, posted a couple of the finger paintings I'd done on my pad, with my best guess at intriguing captions.

Billiard balls crashed in the backroom — which I'd been drawing on my pad. Pete, seeing my pad, shook his head.

"They don't realize that Sean Wentworth is about to make this lost highway as famous as Forks, Washington. I should get the sweatshirt franchise going now for Caliente and Warm Springs. Denio sounds best, though, don't you think? As if anything other than weather might occur in—" Pete shifted his voice down a tone, "the Town Called Denio."

Warmed in body and satisfied that *The Desert Crucible* advanced according to plan, my spirits rose on a bubble of confidence.

Then I botched it by stopping in the men's room while Eliot and Pete climbed back into their riding gear. In the mirror, I faced a guy in a black leather jacket and blue jeans, a red bandana tied around his neck, hair long enough to provoke my sister Sophy into commenting on Romantic Artist curls. An aging version of that adolescent who admired Eliot at Round Mountain. Thirty-five years old, Super Geek dressed as James Dean for Halloween.

At my age, real men should—what?

Eliot gracefully mastered the basics of everyday life while I stumbled along with my head in the clouds. In work with my team, I profess to be the master of control. In real life elsewhere, a fundamental difference gaped like a canyon between us: Eliot's serene practicality and my space-case anxiety. No wonder she judged me unacceptable years ago.

Yet what had Pete said? *"Ask her. Ask her how she feels."*

The pool players didn't glance around when I passed, all of them busy racking balls for the next game and enjoying each other's company. Monkey King, riding on my shoulder, laughed at how irrelevant my tumultuous inner world is to actual living people.

Outside, I stopped Eliot before she climbed behind Pete.

"Want to ride with me again?"

She flipped up her face shield. "I don't think my butt can stand it," she said. "Your bike is made for only one person."

"You be the rider. I'll be the passenger," I offered.

That surprised her so much, it embarrassed me. I'd not done enough when her bike got smashed.

I said, "You're so casual about that wreck. Yet you're always so particular about your bike and gear."

"That truck came so close to Pete, it scared the hell out of me. My bike died a hero's death, protecting Pete."

* * *

Several miles as a passenger was good punishment. The café racer seat, not built for a human, offered the same comfort as an upholstered brick. I held the grab rail to stay steady, not wanting to distract Eliot by holding on to her. In spite of Eliot's smooth handling, after about twenty-five miles, my hips and knees hurt like hell. I concentrated on the back of Eliot's helmet, watching the road unfold in the reflection.

South of Warm Springs, the road climbed to higher elevations where the vegetation colors were brighter than just silver sage. The high hills had sharp, weathered faces, with layers of colored rock. On the way up to Coyote Pass, small trees grew among the sage, though I'm not a good enough naturalist to discern demented piñons from dwarfed junipers or deformed cedars. I hoped they might be Joshua trees, regretting how much I'd forgotten about the desert biome.

Because I didn't have control as the passenger, my paranoia reawakened every five minutes. I kept checking the cracked mirror, looking past her shoulder for attacks from the rear, and scanning the roadway for hidden side roads. Then the empty highway lulled me into safety and peace again. I relaxed, releasing the grab rail, resting my hands on my thighs. Passenger, rider, and bike were united as one—until the next sharp curve wakened memories of that 4WD truck running me off the road near Austin.

At one lull, the highway dipped sharply into a tiny valley, launching me up close against Eliot's back. She reached around and tugged my right hand up, so it rested at her waist.

My thighs curved around hers, my crotch at her backside, awaking muscle memory of how we'd lain together for a mystical ninety days, the pace of our breathing matched, floating free together in the universe. The last time I was—

Near Coyote Summit, the road curved around a blind left turn between two hummocks of land that formed a small canyon. When we entered the shadow of the north hill, the air blasted cold just as Eliot veered to avoid a creature in the road. The bike collided with it, jolting hard against my buns as the back tire squirmed on the pavement. She braked with flawless control and kept the bike upright. When the bike was stable, she slowed and wheeled back around.

She let the bike coast to where the collision happened, near a garnet-colored rock overhang. Yet there was no sign of an animal or anything else on the road. The ditch was too shallow and the banks of the hill too high for an injured animal to crawl up.

Eliot flipped open her face shield.

"You want to get off?" she said.

I still clutched her waist, having grabbed onto her when the thirty seconds of crisis began. I dismounted and pulled off my helmet, bewildered, searching up and down the road for signs of a coyote, certain the animal was at least that large.

"Where did it go?" I asked.

"You saw it, too?" she said. "Was it a dog or a coyote? We hit it for sure."

"It was right here." I stomped the pavement. No blood, no sign of anything.

Bemused, Eliot said, "Must be why it's called Coyote Pass."

"Maybe the Trickster got us."

She nodded, as if accepting my guess. "Let's get out of this dark canyon. We'll head to where the sun's shining and wait for Pete. I should be ashamed for going so fast."

Once we left that little canyon, she put the bike up on its kickstand, and we stretched out road kinks. She beat her hands together, complaining about fear needles in her fingers.

"At least," she said, "you didn't have to see me cry about killing a dog. Or a damn coyote."

"And Pete's too far behind to give us a hard time for riding so fast that we see ghosts," I said.

"I can't make your bike go slow," she said. "One of the spirits you talked about last night needs to remind me that only gods and birds fly."

"We're getting close to the Navajo reservation. Maybe some Dineh wolf-spirits wandered out here."

She cocked her head, serious again. "Do you believe that? About spirits coming among people?"

"Yes. I mean, no, not like my mother believed. Just as metaphor. Things I can't explain, ideas that come from nowhere, I call it spirits. But no ghosts or spirit-people talk to me."

She kicked pebbles from the shoulder into the ditch. Behind us, a sharp whistle sounded.

A raven soared overhead. A kingbird flew above its back, harassing the larger bird. The raven cawed and cronked, diving into an arroyo to escape, but the relentless kingbird shrieked *Whit! Whit!* and pursued the raven. We watched until the birds disappeared behind another jagged hill.

Eliot said, "Since we came to sage country again, I understand what I've wrestled with for a long time. The desert forces you to step outside of yourself. You can't be lost in head trips. The heat or the storms—one thing or another demands that you deal with it."

Her grey eyes shined in the light, her face soft and a little grimy from the road, as guileless as ever, leaving me ashamed of how inside myself I've been.

"Say it again, please," I begged. I hadn't heard her words clearly while watching her lips.

"I—I mean," she stuttered, as if I'd criticized her, "that where I live, all the grey days and the wet and the cold keep me inside myself. All winter long, I think too much while I'm working. It's as if I've waited for the weather to break for years."

"I bet you sneak out and build your ideas between the raindrops. A new rabbit hutch, a better compost bin," I teased. "That would be just like you."

She shook her head no, but said, "Yes, except that's everyday and ordinary. I should have achieved more by now. I've been stuck inside my head."

I touched her hand without thinking. "It's like that for me, too. Not just because of the weather. Being a stranger in a strange land kept me inside my head a lot."

Pete came around the corner, his bike not faltering for any ghost-animals on the roadway. Eliot put her helmet back on and tugged on her gloves.

Pete stopped, lifting his face shield. "That bike must be a communicable disease. Anyone who touches it gets speed-fluenza."

Eliot grinned. "I got a cramp in my hand and couldn't let go of the throttle."

"Thanks for waiting for me. It's nice to see my friends every fifty miles or so."

Pete pulled away, and we prepared to follow him. I stepped back to offer the rider's seat again.

"No," she said. "I'll be a passenger until the next stop. I want to sit back and keep my eyes open for Coyote. That old Trickster is following us."

. . .

There was no next stop. Nor any local or migrating birds to divert my attention. Nor any impediments to a speedy, smooth ride. We flew across Nevada, riding fast to escape the clouds, hoping against hope that rain wouldn't pursue us out of the Great Basin onto the Colorado Plateau.

At five o'clock, we passed through Caliente, the prettiest town we'd seen in Nevada. Yet, however tempting it might be to stroll the town's two lovely streets, clouds still loomed in the west. And my sister Sophy was meeting us at the North Rim the next day.

Across the state line in Utah, the road dropped onto another agricultural plain, and we broke through into sunshine. In my rear-view mirror, Pete kicked his feet in a victory dance. On the seat behind me, Eliot raised her arms in joy. When she dropped them, I squeezed her hand and dragged it up to rest on my thigh while we rode. The wind, blowing toward us now, pushed back the ever-threatening rain. The clouds behind us glowed coral with the impending sunset.

The bike hummed between my legs. Eliot pressed against me. Like flying in a dream, once forgotten, now returned. Comfort, at the same beat as the human heart.

Near Newcastle, Utah, I stopped on the highway shoulder and studied the map through the plastic window of my tank bag.

"There's no campground for miles," I said when Pete glided up beside us. My finger hovered over our current location on the map, between the Antelope Range and the Harmony Mountains.

Pete said, "My needs are modest. No more highway, that's all I ask of the universe."

"Fifteen minutes from now, any tent pitching will be in the dark," Eliot said.

"Let's get rooms in Cedar City," I said, guessing what they both wished. "We worked too hard today to camp in the dark and cold."

"It's only Sean's money," Pete said.

"I'm beat," Eliot said. "Though I didn't do anything but sit and watch the white line roll by."

We rode another thirty miles through low mountains covered with cedar and bristlecone pines, taking care as we approached a real city to stay within posted speed limits. A beautiful pink glow followed us, with stars gradually popping through the twilight. Cedar City unfolded on the hills, an orderly, well-planned town with a state college and the usual tidy homes and wide streets of a Utah commerce center. After hours in the empty desert, we passed under Interstate 15 into the bright lights of motels, gas stations, and grocery stores. Back in modern civilization.

Unable to bear the road any longer, I pulled into the first Texaco station. Pete followed. We refueled the bikes and prowled the station's small grocery, reading the jackelope and fur-bearing-trout postcards, buying and gobbling chocolate-coated peanuts, sipping orange juice. No one wanted to get back on the bikes, even to find a motel. I hung by Pete, who struck up a conversation with the service station manager, who was busy monitoring the gas pumps, making change, and processing charge slips.

"Yes, it's a beautiful town," the man replied to Pete's comment. "I came through four years ago and fell in love with the place."

Sid—the name pinned on his uniform—asked about the bike trip and our plans for the coming days. In his mid-fifties, a healthy paunch resting on his belt, a trace of grey beard-shadow glistening along his cheeks, Sid answered Pete's questions about the road between Cedar City and the Grand Canyon. Eliot stood close by me, her breath soft on my neck. Or maybe I imagined it.

"Where are you from?" Eliot asked Sid.

"Bensonville, outside Chicago. A dying town. America is out to do away with the family and small towns." Color rose in Sid's face. "The old man and woman who lived down the street from us—they wasn't married, else the bureaucrats would cut their social security money. That's what government does to families. Living poor isn't bad enough, you got to live in sin, just to stay alive." Sid chewed his lip. "Me, I believe in family. It's the best thing going in life. So I picked up my family and came here. You got kids?"

"Not yet," I said. "Someday."

Sid laid aside his passion and returned to the mundane. "I hope you enjoy your stay. You going up to Zion tomorrow?"

"Yes," Eliot said. She stood so close that I had to resist putting my arm around her as I used to when we traveled together. "Can't wait to see it again. Where's the best place to spend the night?"

"The motel down near the interchange. Under that sign over there. My friends Joe and Thelma run it. They're real good people. Here, let me give you this." Sid filled out a discount coupon for the motel. "I got one here for you and your wife, one for your friend."

Sid handed a coupon to me and another to Pete. I didn't care to disabuse the man of mistaken notions about marriage, so just thanked the guy. I paid for everyone's gas and the postcards Eliot laid on the counter, and we said goodbye, leaving Pete behind to prompt the guy into a longer conversation.

We registered at the motel and then carried the baggage up to our second floor rooms.

"Hope you weren't too uncomfortable riding," I said, still imagining the pressure of her thighs around me from our ride. I set the bag with her gear on the table in her room.

"I'm not complaining," she said. "But you can't make me ride that hard again for days. I might skip dinner. I need a walk."

"I was thinking the same. Maybe find a grocery store for fruit and yogurt instead of another Wild West dinner."

She smiled, but didn't respond.

"Maybe we could walk together," I said. Hoping.

"Sure. I'll get these memory cards ready for Pete and then put on sneakers. Ten minutes?"

"I'll meet you downstairs."

I ran to tell Pete not to wait for dinner. Already free not to wait, Pete had sent a text message:

Going for a burger. Mendicant lovers must find their own way.

The road hadn't damaged any key elements of Pete's inner nature. I texted back that his room key was at the registration desk.

■ ■ ■

Eliot walked with me under the stars, strolling the tree-lined streets past scrupulously neat houses, avoiding dogs.

Eliot tugged my jacket sleeve as we entered a side street. "You remember, don't you, that people don't walk in America? Other than the urban core of some cites?"

"Walking makes us suspects for any recent crime," I said.

Once, in Boise, the police stopped, searched, and questioned us, because we wandered down suburban streets after midnight on foot. Recalling that event unleashed a string of memories and associations for both of us. Telling old stories and trading new ones about the last few years' adventures, we walked for a couple of miles, stopping to buy apples and yogurt to eat while we roamed.

"Tell me about life in Seattle. You live in your father's house?"

Eliot said, "I've been on Limberlost Island since my dad died. Where my life is a firch pile."

"What's firch?"

"Junk you keep in case you need it later. I salvage windows and doors and recycle them for people's remodel jobs. My father's old service garage is full of lumber, metal parts, and people's discards."

"Like your old workshop at the ranch?"

"Better. With twenty dollars in nails, caulk, and galvanized flashing, I could build you a livable shack in a week."

"That's how you make money?"

"Scrounging and cobbling things together? Yeah." Eliot walked beside me in silence for a few minutes. "I tack the pieces of life together from others' castoffs. I work on the edge of things. I'm irrelevant to the greater economy—except maybe for property taxes. Which I can hardly afford."

"No one could believe you're quite so irrelevant," I said.

"I try to be useful. I coach a girls' soccer team and play softball in the spring. But we'll fall asleep from boredom if we talk about my life. Tell me about your glitzy life."

"Glitzy? All I do is work."

"You sit alone and draw all day?"

"No, I do everything with my team." I described life with my old team, how we worked late every night and cruised the streets together on days off, doing what urban people do. "You'd laugh at us, Eliot. At dinner, we eat noodles together and watch three TV programs at once. We call it 'cultural research.' I typically spend eighty hours a week with my team."

"Ick. I'd need more solitude than that. But you must do more than just work."

"I play basketball with some ex-pat Americans."

"Sean, don't you have friends to hang with? Only your team?"

"We are friends. More like a family than anything I grew up with. And Sunday evenings I hang with my father. We watch TV and talk, like Americans. Or we did until he came back to the States. He's one big reason why I'm moving my work to Seattle."

"Who are your U.S. friends?"

"Pete, of course. And Jason Taylor. Tadeusz and some of my old team will be joining me. We're building a new team—"

"Guard me," Eliot said out of the blue. She ran up an alley to deposit our litter in a household garbage can, arousing several dogs. Then, darting away from me, she called, "Let's run for it!"

I followed her down the street as we tagged the long shadows we cast under mercury vapor lights. I stopped in the middle of the road, first because it's hard to run in boots, and second because the streetscape seemed like a hyper-industrial dystopian dream. I fished out my phone to capture the scene, crappy lighting and all.

"What do you see?" Eliot came back, as silent and swift as a dream-spirit.

"Cars everywhere, each bigger than my apartment in London. Mountains of stuff: freestanding swimming pools, giant lawn-mowers, trampolines in every yard. Dog-runs larger than any yard in a London suburb."

She gazed about. "It's just any American city."

"I haven't been here in a while. The wide, wide streets aren't what I'm used to."

"Mormon city fathers built the streets wide enough for a wagon to turn around."

"Thoughtful," I said, ready to walk again. "But why was every-one then always turning around to go back the other way?"

By the time we arrived at the motel, I'd walked and run enough to breathe deeply. And to feel comfortable with her again.

"Good night," she said. She leaned against the door to her room, reaching down into her jacket for the room key. "You sure know how to show a girl a swell time."

"I hope you'll let me take you out again sometime."

"Oh sure. Maybe the prom."

She tossed her head back, pretending to flirt, like she had with that gas jockey at Round Mountain. Under the motel porch light, her grey eyes gleamed, large as an anime heroine's. Her hair, falling out of its braid again, feathered around her face, begging to be untied and set free.

I leaned over to kiss her, then after I touched her lips, I had to grab hold of myself.

"Sorry," I said. A man could write a book about what I tried to read in her expression. "I'll see you in the morning."

In our room, bike junk was strewn everywhere. Pete sat oiling his leathers again, filling the room with the soft odor of mink oil. Scant remains of a take-out burger and fries littered the table top. I crashed on the bed, thinking, *how do you become a lover instead of a friend?* First, it's a certain angle of the hips, then an intriguing hand gesture that's so characteristic of that person, it's part of why she's beloved.

But what starts the shiver from the second chakra up the belly to the solar plexus? Why become conscious of your groin now, when the same person previously stirred only a mild desire for conversation? How does it happen that you become too aware of how another human's jeans fit? How is it that your fingers recall what it's like to unbutton a fly that's not your own?

The TV news announcer said, "A new study indicates that the actual number of homeless people is much higher than the government has claimed."

"Another reward from the government's crusade for self-reliance and justice," Pete said. "How's your search for truth and justice going, boss?"

"Clearly I've been reading the wrong map, making the obvious difficult." I grabbed my pad and returned to knock on Eliot's door. She was once more on the phone, but motioned me in.

"I'm locked out again," I said when she tapped to end the phone call. "You have to let me stay here."

"Sure." She pointed to the sole chair. "Have a seat."

My benign untruths were stupid. Set a bad precedence.

"No," I said. "I'm lying. I'd just rather be here with you."

She tipped her head, studying me. "And I failed to suggest that the manager has an extra key for your room."

The Desert Crucible Episode IV
#3: Horse Woman

[Tadeusz: Sync this with the new canyon shots. Look for a simple 3-note melody for backing music, since Jason's no help. And add back the sounds of pool balls clacking if it didn't come through on my recording. —Pete]

I knew and loved that horse more than the man I live with.

The vet was out this morning—I hoped to turn it all around, but it ended up being time to put the poor beast down.

Colic, like it was a little teeny baby, and not a creature of great beauty, bearing the mark of all God's glory.

I found him at dawn, trying to vomit, then rolling on his back because of the pain. I felt my own insides tangle up in kinks. Not sympathy pains, just wracking myself with disgust, dismay, distress that death stalked my wonderful friend.

What to do after you pay the vet, take care of the business, and it's good-bye, all-over-now for the love of your life?

What could I have done differently? The question busted my gut all morning, but the vet said by the time I was out of bed, it was already too late.

I figured the best thing was to get out with people, maybe shoot some pool in town. If I'm in company, I'll buck up. If I hang around my old man, I might kill him if he says, "You still cryin' over that damn horse?"

I can do this. I can bear it. One screwdriver—the healthful, Vitamin C kind—and I'm about ready to go out. Except I look in the mirror and see sun and cigs did me no favor. I'm still blond—thank you, L'Oreal—but the mineral in the water here is hell on hair. All that crying, I look like the gully around the bend after a bad rain.

He was such a dear friend. He set me in motion, let me ride on my dreams.

∞

15.
Zion

And your very flesh shall be a great poem.
—Walt Whitman

ELIOT
Wednesday a.m.

HER HEART THUMPED LIKE a dropped shoe at the sound of his knock. Her hand on the doorknob burned, mottled white and pink with flustered anticipation. Eliot opened the door for Sean, faking a casual invitation to make himself at home while she finished her phone call. Then she excused herself to take a shower, where she stayed a long time, to calm down. Dressed in t-shirt and sleep-boxers, she dried and brushed her hair, texted reassurances to Destiny, then busily sorted her gear and laid out clean clothes for the morning, while sneaking glances at Sean in the mirror.

He lay on the bed, alternately watching TV and drawing or tapping on his pad, sprawled boyishly, his hips and legs confined in blue jeans. This wasn't a seduction of the innocent, but Eliot used such an obvious ploy—acting as if she had work to do, but in a sleeveless t-shirt and shorts—because she didn't remember how seduction worked. Normal people would laugh to see her trying to make a move. She interrupted her useless tasks several times to watch Sean watching TV before she caught him peeking back. She settled beside him on the bed, Jane Austen novel in hand, and flicked on the reading lamp.

"This won't bother you, will it?" she asked.

He stared at the TV, watching a baseball retrospective.

"Pete Rose has surpassed Ty Cobb's record for base hits," the excited announcer said in a film clip showing the famous hit. "The Cincinnati Reds player-manager singled off Eric Shaw of the San

Diego Padres to earn four thousand one hundred and ninety-two career hits."

"*Sic transit gloria mundi*," Sean said.

"Just plain 'sick,'" Eliot said, flipping to the chapter where she'd lodged a bookmark, her foot accidentally brushing Sean's leg. Pete Rose wept with joy in the next scene.

"I'm a tough SOB, but I couldn't hold it," Pete Rose cried. "I looked up in the sky and saw my father, and Ty Cobb was in back of him. Dad was in the front row. Ty Cobb was a tough, tough man, but my father was a tough, tough, tougher man." In the next replay, Mr. Rose wept with transparent remorse.

"Oh brother." Eliot grabbed the remote from the folds of the bedspread and scrolled to a weather-scan channel with classical background music.

"My father was just a plain SOB," she remarked.

Which was the wrong joke: Sean launched into raptures about his father again. Another time, perhaps she'd listen to the canonization of Robert Wentworth, but not in bed at the Comfort Inn in Cedar City. She revived her resolve to speak her mind.

"Sean, can we talk about this instead?"

She boldly traced his sternum with her fingertips. When he didn't resist, she cupped and rubbed his chest in the way he liked. His eyes flashed, like an animal surprised by headlights in the night. Then he wrapped her in his arms, spawning joy and ecstatic transport that surpassed both her memory and imagination. Fingers and tongue explored parts of him that she'd made herself forget. That pelt of dark hair over his belly. How the muscles of his back and torso came together. Long, hard thighs. The instantly familiar motion, undoing his zipper. The warm, firm handful of his balls.

When she kneeled over him, he lifted off the pillow to press against her. A hand slipped into the back of her boxers. This one time the universe accommodated her desires, and she had what she wanted: this particular hard, hot man.

After removing pants, finding a condom (the box she'd bought in Winnemucca on a gamble), and frantic wrestling, it was the first time all over again. They both panted softly for a minute, just holding hands, not quite ready to believe. Sean began to explore, kissing her while not touching her, except to unbraid her hair and let it fall across him. When she touched his cock, he shifted them both deftly and rose above her. "Slow," he said. "We have all the time in the world." Holding her hands above her head, he first nipped softly at her breasts with his lips, then—a lifetime later—pressed into her again and began to move, slowly, taking the same eternity as that long ride across Nevada but with the sublime pleasure of touching, tickling, kissing, and sweetly mocking her desire to touch him while keeping hold of her hands, whispering that she had no choice but to lie there and feel good.

When his slow hand brought her to climax, he responded at last to her pleas and moved more urgently, wrapping her legs around him, until his shudder brought her to another climax. Moments later, when she could breathe instead of panting, he continued to tremble along with her aftershocks of orgasm.

Except he was crying. She pressed her lips against his neck to keep from crying, too.

After they murmured without words and held hands again, Sean dozed away. She slept too, letting herself drift. He woke later and was invited inside her again, neither of them having to conquer the other. When they were exhausted and traveling together toward the country of dreams, he whispered, "Put your arms around me," and grasped her so that she nestled against his back. "I can't sleep, worrying that you'll leave again."

■ ■ ■

It rained during the night but the skies cleared by dawn. When the morning sun shone bright above Zion, trees jostled by birds splashed colossal wet drops onto Eliot, who stretched on a rock at the bottom of the narrow canyon, basking in the sun's warmth. The rush of the nearby creek drowned out Pete's voice. A fly buzzed, too lazy in the sunshine to bother with Eliot.

Pete said nothing when they loaded the bikes that morning, though he'd caught her eye several times the day before, as if reading her mind. But she played erotic vamp so badly that Sean never noticed until she jumped him.

She wasn't complaining. After a pleasant early-morning hike in Zion Park with Sean's arm on her shoulder and Pete's jokes echoing in the canyon, she stretched on warm sandstone now, the weight of sunlight pressing on her body, which still vibrated wherever he'd touched her.

On that rock in Zion, Eliot smelled cedar forest and mountain water from the spray the rapids tossed into the air. And she tasted Sean whenever she licked her lips. She drowsed from lack of sleep and too much love the night before, hating to rouse herself when it was time to find Sean and Pete to ride again. Their voices no longer echoed in the canyon; she jogged up the trail to find them.

Halfway up the canyon, Pete was saying, "We meander today, right? We end up at the North Rim tonight, but we go slow and stop every hour. My ass won't take another eight hundred miles like we did yesterday."

"Yes," Sean said. "Today we relax. The previous days were just training for the real event."

He rested his arm on Eliot's shoulder as they walked the macadam pathway back to the bikes, that weight a reminder of how they walked together before, her long legs matching his stride, his boney hip pressed against hers. She and Pete noted the birds they'd seen and called up the names of each plant in the undergrowth.

"Mosquitoes!" Pete exclaimed when they passed a marsh at a bend in the stream. "I get ten points for spotting them first."

"You get one-tenth of a point," she insisted. "I get ten points for spotting the first cliff rose and five for the first fern bush."

Cloud shadows floated across the cliff faces as they prepared to ride, their bikes parked amid the bustle of tour buses unloading European travelers, station wagons carrying young couples with babies, and recreational vehicles transporting retired couples. On the way out of Zion, where the edge of the road dropped hundreds of feet to the canyon floor, Eliot clung tightly to Sean, vertiginous from lack of sleep. The sun-drenched colors, like an old-time overexposed Polaroid photo, hurt her eyes. When the bike slowed to a crawl and then wavered behind a pokey tourist in an older Lincoln town car, Eliot grasped Sean's waist, not wanting to peer down into the canyon, relieved when the road entered a long tunnel. At the eastern edge of the park, Sean stopped to wait for Pete while she clicked shots of the Checkerboard Mesa.

"Let's make love again," she said, her hands at Sean's hips. "It's like I'm starved and can't possibly eat enough."

"Where shall we go?" Sean asked, as if taking her seriously. "On this side of the road, we fall down the cliff. On the mesa side, every tourist exiting the park can see us."

"How about behind the tree on that mountain?" She pointed to a slim young cedar atop a small hillock beside the highway.

He pulled her close, nuzzling her ear, kissing her neck. "That's an anthill. We'll have to wait until later. We'll get another chance before we die."

"How can you be sure?"

"Trust fate," he said. "And don't wiggle when I'm holding you. It's bad enough that you didn't let me sleep last night. I never closed my eyes once."

"Yes, you did," she said, laughing. "I peeked several times and you had your eyes closed."

"Ecstatic reverie isn't the same as a good night's sleep," he said, stepping away as Pete rolled up alongside.

No, Eliot thought. After years of sleeping all night, ecstatic reverie was much better than mere sleep.

■ ■ ■

"Things got worse in the hospital," Destiny said, in that quiet, dead voice she'd used when she first moved to Limberlost. "Aunt Cora's scared all the time unless I'm with her."

Pete and Sean had stopped for gas and snacks at a small store near the highway junction. While they called and sent texts to their video team, Eliot had answered a call from Destiny.

"What happened?"

"The doctor thinks she had a series of small strokes." Destiny's voice was thick with stifled emotion: the girl who claimed she could bat any ball the universe sends her way. "Cora's so hypertensive, he thinks she's about to have a big one."

"Who's with you?" Even as Eliot asked, she knew the answer.

"No one. She only wants me. And I can do this." Pleading, as though Destiny was again begging to staff the market booth alone. "Only thing is, she makes me read these awful Georgette Heyer romances to her."

"Where are you sleeping?"

"This isn't about me, Eliot. I'm worried about Aunt Cora."

"I have to assume the doctors are doing everything they can. So where are you sleeping? What about school?"

"Your sister Sam gave me the key to her house. It's near here by bus. School has to wait."

Eliot kept her voice even. "Destiny, you have to be in school. We're all in trouble if you aren't in school."

"Thanks for the reminder, *Mom*."

"OK, then this is your *mother* saying you'll blow up the whole scene for yourself if you aren't in school."

"I'm not riding that ferry back and forth just to hang with those nimrods. I'd have to get up at 5:30 and—"

"We'll get you into school in Seattle. I'm calling Roslyn to ask her to help."

"Social services." Destiny shuddered at the other end.

"Roslyn is a neighbor, a friend. She won't bring social services in unless we're really up shit-creek. Tell Cora I'm pulling for her. Tell her to get well."

Eliot made one more call before Sean and Pete were ready to ride. As reliable as ever, Roz promised to get on it, requiring only a few words from Eliot to know what to do.

Friends. Blessed friends.

She texted one last message to Destiny.

Roz sent a Family Emergency note to the Attendance office. She's bringing you clothes & homework tonite. Relax. Read to Cora.

As Eliot tucked away the phone, Sean wrapped his arms around her, leather squeaking softly on leather, as he kissed her deeply, tasting of orange juice, smelling of the Zion woods-walk.

"Ah, a workplace romance," Pete sighed. "Or is this True Love? Let's ride."

· · ·

"Look at this," Pete said, his hand cupped atop the rock wall. "It's a little old fence lizard."

They'd paused at a roadside lookout just inside the Kaibab National Forest to eat a midafternoon picnic lunch of sausage, cheese, and crackers with lukewarm beer. Pete and Eliot perched on a rock wall to capture snaps and video footage of the view across the plains they'd just crossed, with the Vermilion Cliffs in the near east and the Bryce Canyon cliffs rising to the north. A string of vapor in the west proved to be jet contrails rather than real clouds to mar the blue sky. Two weeks earlier, this hillside had been hot, but now summer was over. Dangling her legs over the stone retaining wall, Eliot wore silk long-johns yet still shivered when not in full sunlight. She focused the camera but let her mind follow Sean, who prowled the trails through the trees below, out of sight.

"His belly is bright blue," Pete said about his lizard friend. "What did they call these critters before there were fences to hang on?"

"How can you tell it's a he?" she asked.

"I unzipped his jeans and peeked."

Pete stroked the lizard's belly until it lay relaxed in his hand, its eyes rolled back in its head, hypnotized. Pete's favorite trick. This was like a dozen years earlier, sitting on the canyon edge above the ranch, Pete hypnotizing some reptile he'd found in the brush. She'd been jealous, because Pete could sit so still that animals came up to him—not just the pesky ones that crawled on her jeans legs, but interesting ones: turtles, the prettiest lizards, deer mice, satyr butterflies. The grosbeaks, buntings, and juncos answered his whistles and sat in nearby junipers to watch him. She warned Pete to stay away from rodents because of disease, but once found him lulling a baby porcupine, stroking its belly the way he stroked the fence lizard now. How someone as citified as Pete moved quietly in the wilderness, she didn't understand.

"Eliot, I have to ask."

She sipped warm beer and broke off another stick of pepperoni to gnaw. "Let's see if I can answer."

"You know how your mind works when you're riding. Ten miles down the road, you forget what you worried about all day at home. With a machine like that," Pete waved toward the BMW in the viewpoint's gravel lot, "you don't even worry about every damn sound the bike makes. So what you want to forget and what you actively think trade places in your mind."

"Yeah," Eliot said. Pepperoni stuck in her teeth and burned her tongue. "My plans got thrown in the air since we started this trip. I'm thinking about what's next when I get back home."

Pete stroked the blue-bellied lizard in his hand. He said, "You're being careful, aren't you?"

"We use condoms."

"Too much information. I'm talking about reckless emotions."

"I haven't done anything reckless for years," she said, clearing her throat of pepper.

"Aren't we the supreme pair of opposites? Brother-sister, male-female, risk-safety."

He stopped petting the lizard, which woke when the stroking ceased and darted its head in search of whatever interests lizards.

"Safety is my favorite playing position," Eliot said. "There are other people in my life that I have to watch out for. Recklessness isn't an option."

"Did you add to the list of who you're taking care of?" Teasing, he pointed down the hill where Sean wandered among the piñons.

"He's no higher on the list than you are, little brother."

"Touché!" Pete set the lizard down on the rock wall, where it remained beside him for a moment. "I have lots to make up for."

"Oh no! Don't tell me you're in a Twelve-Step program for total freaking assholes?"

"I'm not that bad—"

"So you haven't yet hit the bottom of assholedom?"

Eliot sliced more cheese from the small loaf and sandwiched it between crackers to hand to Pete, who wasn't paying attention to lunch. He stared off at the red cliffs across the plain, as if he had to prepare what he wanted to say next.

"I haven't done anything truly bad," Pete said. "Some of my endeavors had unintended consequences."

"Don't make me a target of your scheme for making amends," she said. "You never screwed up anything for me—at least, not since high school. Our sister Sam, that's another story."

"Maybe I caused you harm through sins of omission." Pete stirred just enough to frighten his lizard friend, who scampered several feet along the wall.

"When?"

"Dante, for example. For all the ways he took advantage of you. I kept quiet while he exploited you at minimum wage."

"He took me in when I needed shelter. Like he did for you. And I'm not even related to Dante."

"Me either, as far as the world knows." Pete took the cracker from Eliot and bit into it with such force that crumbs showered into his lap. "His name isn't on my birth certificate."

She groped for a response. "You know Dante loves you."

"Dante and I last saw each other when he married Claudia. He didn't say ten goddamn words to me that whole day, 'cause he's so enthralled with his new beloved. Who is only five freaking years older than me. Her little sister—who's younger than me—kept saying, 'Dante is so amazing.' But all I see is a cold, dry man with steel-grey hair and a steel-grey heart."

"All I ever saw was Dante's attempts to guide you. You read more into his strictness than you should," Eliot said.

He's never given me anything of significance."

"Like his name?" Eliot stated what she knew to be the fundamental problem. "I continue to have a less prejudiced view than you of Dante's motivation for letting us live at the ranch."

"Easy for you. He's not your father," Pete said.

"No. Dante just impregnated my mother, so I've been stuck with you." Eliot prodded him with her elbow. "Anyway, our parents are in the past. The three of us—you, me, Sam—we're all beyond that now."

"Beyond what?" Pete asked.

"The repercussions of our mother's decisions. Three kids, each with a different father. Moving here, there. And then dying."

"My father owes me. I will demand my birthright." His hand beat this affirmation on the wall. This time, the lizard ran down the wall and disappeared. "You got Dante's attention because you worshipped him like all those ass-bite artists he surrounds himself with. And you let him treat you like a servant."

"That's not true," Eliot said. "Dante believes in universal love. He wanted us to learn to find security in the whole community, not to rely on a single individual." That was the lesson, though she hadn't been a successful student.

"You were all too hip," Pete said, calm again, munching his apple. "Security and fidelity are wonderful things. Or so I've heard. But with Dante, in spite of all his talk about free love, I don't see that we truly got any. You should thank the gods he's not your father."

"Yet the ranch was the first place I ever felt secure."

She gathered up the remains of their lunch and poured the last of the tepid beer over the side of the wall. A wind whipped up sun-glossed dust-devils on the north plains, each devil bright white, as if it shone with its own light.

"Dante used you," Pete said.

"Stop saying that. It's not true.

"Yes, it is. He gave you rough sketches to work from. Not detailed drawings. Dante should have asked you to sign his sculptures, since you designed and built them. And he hasn't executed one imaginative or craftsman-like piece since you left. Meanwhile, you let others take your work, your spirit, your energy."

"You have no idea what I get back from giving to others." She was tempted to tell him about Destiny, given the sad tone of this conversation, but stopped herself. Best not to talk about it until all the details were settled.

"Dante didn't give you your own voice as an artist. You still haven't claimed it."

"I'm an artisan not an—"

"And I can't tell you to shut up right now, since I'm saying you need to claim your own voice." Pete pointed to where Sean emerged from the trail in the piñons. "What are you two doing?"

"We don't know yet. He's moving to Seattle. We have all the time in the world to build a new partnership."

"Partnership? Like Jason Taylor and I have with him?"

"Ye-ess." She drew the word out, dissecting its meaning.

The sun in Pete's eyes forced him to squint against the bright light. "I want True Love for you. I don't expect it in my own life. But you deserve it. So don't screw up this time."

"Wow, little brother. Not your business."

"Except it is. I wish Sean was my brother, so I have a vested interest in your success." He focused the camera on the stooped figure of Sean walking in the piñons. "You give away exceptional, creative work at Saturday-market bargain prices. Stop underpricing yourself."

Eliot waved a hand to dismiss what Pete said. "I'm an artisan. I never wanted—"

"No!" Pete grabbed her waving hand. "You're an artist. Don't let anyone persuade you that you aren't equal to Sean in that way. Or any other."

A juniper-scented breeze burned her eyes, making her blink against the dust. She fumbled with the lunch remains. "What did you want to ask me, Pete? Have we talked about it?"

"Give me some space when we get to the ranch," he said, tucking the camera into his pack. "Don't steal Dante's attention away."

"OK. I'm thinking I should bail from the trip at Flagstaff and fly home," she said. "I have problems to—"

"No!" Pete rose from the wall, both fierce and forlorn. "I need you with me at the ranch. I can't do what I have to if I'm alone. Please don't leave me."

Sean called to them from where the bikes were parked. "Ready to ride? The Grand Canyon calls."

16.
North Rim

By the least auspicious details are our fates decided.
— Unnamed sage

ELIOT
Wednesday p.m.

"OVER HERE, PETE! I KNEW you'd find us."

Sophy's voice rasped across the dining room the moment Eliot stepped into the lodge behind Pete. The chair next to Sophy was empty; a cup of tea waited for someone to claim it. Behind Sophy, a floor-to-ceiling window opened onto the Canyon's expanses.

"I checked here first, instead of searching the whole Canyon," Pete said as he arrived at Sophy's table, Eliot tagging behind.

"You always have more common sense than most people," Sophy said. Scarcely changed after ten years, except for gray streaks in her hair, Sophy's face glowed in the Canyon light from the huge south window. She stood with open arms to greet Pete. When she let him go, she blinked three times at Eliot before grasping her hand in greeting.

"It's Eliot, isn't it? I didn't realize you were in on this adventure." Sophy covered their handshake with her other hand. "Goodness your hands are cold."

"I—yes." Eliot choked out a hello.

A tray of glasses clattered in the kitchen.

Plates clunked in the busperson's trolley.

A chair screeched on the tile floor, someone tucking in or pushing out from a table.

The kitchen's swinging doors whumped as a waitperson passed through.

She didn't remember me. She changed my life. Then forgot me.

Sophy released Eliot's hand, grasping Pete by the elbow again. "Where's Sean?"

"He'll catch up in a minute," Pete said. "He insisted he'd find you at your cabin. I made a better guess."

"So, Bad Boy, still the international man of mystery?"

"Not so much. I—"

A small, thin woman with chisel-angled cheekbones and close-cropped, stark white-blond hair came up behind Sophy. Believing her to be Sophy's traveling companion, Eliot smiled, prepared to shake hands. But the woman clenched her teeth, focusing on Pete.

"Hello, Peter Byron. Nice to see you again." The woman had a British accent. And she wasn't at all happy to see Pete.

"Louisa."

Sean came in just then, dragging his pack. He stopped at the door, astonished.

"Hello, Sean," the sharp-white woman said. "I thought I'd have a vacation, too."

Sophy rose to accept Sean's embrace. She said, "We've had a fun day, waiting for you." She slipped an arm around Louisa, as if drawing her into the embrace with Sean.

"You said your friend Iris was traveling with you." Sean sounded strained. Sophy remained stiff in his embrace.

"Iris stayed behind at the Basketmaker excavation site," Sophy said, seeming oblivious to the tension between Sean and Louisa. "Camping by a midden heap isn't Louisa's style. Don't you agree?"

"You cut your hair," Sean said, still eye-fighting with Louisa.

"The old style seemed too colonial on the streets of Los Angeles. Do you like it?"

Sean, ignoring that question, circled Eliot's wrist and dragged her into the group. They took up too much room in the aisle where the wait staff needed to pass.

"Louisa, this is my very good friend Eliot Arden. Eliot, Louisa recently joined Laconia Media."

Louisa compressed her thin lips as Sean emphasized *recently*, her violet, unnerving eyes fixed on him. "You are Pete's girlfriend?"

"No," Eliot stammered. At the same moment, Pete said, "She's my sister."

"I am pleased to meet you, Eliot. Sean's friends are my friends. Like Pete." She spit Pete's name through her plummy accent.

Sophy said, "We just finished our tea, and were about to hike. You'll join us?"

"Pete and I need to find a camp site before dark," Eliot said.

"Pete! Are you being coy?" Sophy asked. "Of course you'll stay with us. We can accommodate everyone. Especially since Iris is at the excavation site."

Pete said, "We've been riding for days. I'm happy not to sleep on the ground."

Which committed Eliot to spending the night with a new acquaintance who hated her (as Pete's sister) and another who'd forgotten her (as Sean's lover).

Sophy said, "Let's walk down the trail. Louisa wants to see the magnificent view."

Eliot saw no evidence to support that claim. However, after unloading the bikes at Sophy's cabin, Eliot found herself beside Sean's silent, grim business partner, waiting for the others to join them. Eliot in her dusty engineer's boots and leather jeans faded into the landscape alongside Louisa in her parka of batiked silk with gold fasteners and fur lining. Louisa's transparent, bone-china skin—like the ladies in Georgian portraits—came from a foreign world where windburn and sunburn never coarsened features. A reptile had given its life for the sake of Louisa's shiny hand-tooled boots. Silkworms had consumed a mulberry tree to produce her amethyst blouse. Louisa's violet eyes betrayed no clue about what went on behind the heavy, darkly shadowed lids.

"Have you been to America before?" Eliot asked, struggling to make conversation. Louisa took so long to answer that Eliot guessed she was being ignored.

"I did undergraduate work at Boston University," Louisa said at last. "But the U.S. culture has never appealed to me."

A Steller's jay scolded them from a quaking aspen. Eliot tried to think of another question, while Louisa seemed to prefer silence. Which is how they endured the wait on the cabin porch.

At the trail's head, they paused while Sophy retied her hiking shoes. The first walkway took them down a yarrow-lined blacktop path to a view of the South Rim. In the lengthening afternoon shadows, the Supai formations and higher layers of shale blazed crimson in the bright light. Eliot blinked to gain perspective, over-awed once more by that spectacular gash in the earth.

"It's too big to understand, every time I stare into it," Eliot murmured to Sophy, who adjusted her binoculars, then scanned the butte rising from the Canyon floor to the east.

"The Canyon helps us to be humble without being humiliated," Sophy said.

Eliot wandered over by Pete, who hadn't said a word since a-vowing that he'd shoot video until his fingers hurt; however in the first steps into the Canyon, he'd ceased peering through the camera, instead studying the Canyon straight on. Eliot and Pete breathed peacefully in mutual silence. Pete nudged Eliot and pointed west where two eagles soared on the updrafts.

"We deserve this," Pete whispered. "After freezing our nuts off all across Nevada."

"I still have my nuts," Eliot said.

"Look, Louisa!" Sophy called from farther up the trail. "Eagles came out to greet you."

Louisa didn't glance up. She stared at Sean. Sean watched Eliot, not the eagles.

"Come on!" Sophy called from the junction with the main trail. "If we don't keep moving, we won't get far before dark."

Louisa said, "I've walked sufficiently today. I'll sit and admire the view. Will you stay with me, Sean?"

"I need to walk," he said. "We've been tortured on our ride here. Walk with us if you want to talk."

"I'm staying here to shoot video," Pete said. "You can hang out with me, Louisa, and give advice."

"I'll walk with Sean," Louisa said.

"Eliot!" Sophy called. "You must see this!"

As Eliot joined Sophy, Louisa's voice drifted down the trail.

"Tell me the truth, Sean. Why haven't you called? Are you ready yet for reconciliation?"

After a moment, Sean said, "Are you subverting my family? Like you tried with Dante?"

...

The afternoon shadows heightened the drama of the scree and rock falls sloping gracefully down to the next staircase of terraces and cliffs. Carmine light radiated up from the Canyon, as if the cliffs breathed in vermilion and exhaled ruby vapors. Sophy chatted while they walked together.

"You live alone?" Sophy prompted.

"Yes," Eliot said. Her future change, adopting Cora and Destiny, didn't seem relevant on a stroll with Sophy.

Sophy said, "I've always been a solitary person, too. That's why my excavation adventures always appealed to my true nature."

Eliot murmured polite assents.

"My friend Iris and I hit it off so well two years ago, we've been a happy twosome, traveling together," Sophy said. "We have similar backgrounds, matching tastes and temperaments. And we went to the same schools. Neither relies on the other for money."

Eliot stopped herself from any reply. She'd listened to Sophy's warning before while repairing that abandoned garden in Amherst. When Sean headed for work in her library, Sophy sat in the shade of the garden and offered Eliot friendly guidance.

> *"One from the East and one from the West, one with an important artistic career in front of him. Love can't bridge the abyss between two cultures."*

Sophy said, "I'll be living close to Sean now that he and Robert are moving back to the States. Besides, the Northwest has a milder climate than New England."

"I wish you well," Eliot said. She sought to turn the instructional stories around on her torturer. "East Coast people often have a hard time adjusting to West Coast life."

Sophy fluttered a hand in dismissal of that idea. "Robert and I just signed a contract for the land we want. Our agent found this old farm on a charming island in Puget Sound. We expect Sean will choose to join us."

"A farm? On an island?" Eliot slumped on a crumbling limestone boulder, her heart beating fast. A pair of swifts dived over the edge of the Canyon, the white of their throats and wings twinkling in the dusky light.

"Yes. From the pictures Robert sent, the view is lovely," Sophy answered. "The agent says we're rescuing an old lady by paying full price and all back taxes. She was about to lose everything."

"How fortunate for her."

The air hummed with the heat rising from the Canyon floor and seemed to lodge in Eliot's heart, pushing in among the cracks that Sophy had knocked open. The sound of Sean and Louisa in conversation carried up from the lower trail.

"You didn't come here for a vacation, Louisa."

"Your resentment is palpable, dear heart."

"Before you harangue me, I want to remind you that the entire Laconia franchise is built on my vision. Before Laconia, you and Milo made noodle soup commercials."

That woman said, "Laconia isn't your kingdom, it's a partnership. You don't do business. You're just a cartoonist."

Sean said, "It ended between us long before now. Five more days, it's over legally. I'm not watching my manga heroes journey to the front of a Froot Smacks cereal box."

"You don't make good business decisions, Sean. You're throwing away millions over artistic differences. You can't just walk out on all of us."

Squirrels barked *chuk-chuk* and thrashed in the brush.

"Louisa, the new artistic direction isn't worth killing trees to print. Or firing up electrons to spin. Values, aesthetics, all disappeared in the last year. Laconia left me."

Eliot, her shoulders hunching up, wanted to crawl into a shell so she wouldn't hear this private conversation. On a nearby boulder, a Clark's nutcracker drawled *kra-a-a*, grating as much as Louisa's nagging, then took flight, its wings beating slowly enough that you could hear the echo as it disappeared into the Canyon.

"You're not being fair, Sean."

"I won't whore for you!" Sean exclaimed.

A proper-looking couple scurried past, shepherding two school kids and carrying a baby in a backpack. The boy wore a brand-new Monkey King baseball hat.

Rounding that turn in the trail, Sean and Louisa rejoined Eliot and Sophy.

Sophy said, "I'm not sure if our land is north of Seattle or west. Sean, what's the name of the island where Robert found land?"

"I lost track. The last place he toured was Camano," he said. Haloed by the sun where he stood among the oak and manzanita, he caught Eliot's eye and smiled.

Sophy said, "We need to start back while we can still see."

Sean gave Eliot a hand up from her boulder chair.

"Are you all right?" he asked.

"Of course. Why?"

"The disappearing light flickered in your eyes," he whispered. "Like tears waiting to be cried."

"I never cry."

■ ■ ■

At dinner, Sophy pondered the list and chose the wine, then she directed the server to pour a goblet for each of them. Pete covered his glass, refusing, but joined Sophy in chatting, triangulated with Louisa, who had little to say. Eliot willed Sean to glance her way; but he might as well be on a peak in the Canyon; he dwelt far, far from this company.

When the dessert menus arrived, Sophy chose crème brûlée for everyone, the other people at the table all too passive to make a choice. She said, "We're off to the Basketmaker site tomorrow. Louisa will get a close view of how we investigate history."

"I'm glad to see this country," Louisa said. "The movie that we work on next is a ghost story in Navajo country."

Pete snorted in distain. "Busy appropriating other people's cultures, Louisa?"

Ignoring Pete's outburst, Sophy said, "Working in the Southwest is new to me. Aren't the Navajos secretive about their ceremonies? Or am I thinking about the Hopi?"

"Our partners convinced people to let us capture certain ceremonies. Our studio is creating the special effects." Louisa then asked Sophy about wolf-spirits in Navajo lore.

"I'm not well informed," Sophy said. "People at the dig can recommend sources for you."

"Our advisors say we can't film at night, because no one goes out while sorcerers are seeking revenge." Louisa stirred her dessert, never eating a bite. "Are any people still that quaint?"

"Perhaps 'private' is a better word," Eliot said. No one even glanced her way.

Sophy asked, "What's your new story, Louisa? Is Sean's Impious Aeneas journeying to the Southwest?"

"I wish," Louisa said. She tapped Sean's hand as emphasis, but he didn't respond. "Our next story is about a dead Navajo warrior who returns as a shape-shifter to haunt his superstitious friends—"

"That's terrible." Eliot spoke louder than she intended.

"It's a good story. Our new partners love its market potential." Louisa's condescension reeked with kindness.

Eliot said, "I mean that it's just plain wrong. It's one thing when an anthropologist studies people's rites. But to make sacred ceremonies into a Hollywood movie? A cartoon?"

"It can't hurt anyone," Louisa said. She fluttered a finger, as if throwing off criticism needed no more effort than shooing flies. "People from the tribe are cooperating. They want the money this movie will bring into their community."

"Other people have sold out their own tribes before." Eliot tried to keep her voice calm.

"People need to be aware of others' beliefs," Louisa said.

"The old ways need to be left alone where they still exist," Eliot said. "At best, interference creates a cargo cult. When movies exploit and twist the old ways, they speed destruction."

"When has a movie destroyed a culture?" Louisa challenged. Her eyes drifted to Pete, awaiting his challenge. But Pete sat with his arms crossed, his jaw clenched.

No one spoke up to take Eliot's side.

"What you call superstition, other people call faith," Eliot said. "If you make movies about ninjas or samurais, it's the same as cowboys. But making sacred ceremonies into cartoons is like using St. Francis or the bodhisattvas as clowns."

"Like Sean's Monkey King?" Louisa asked. "The original Monkey King went to India to fetch sutras and—"

"That's not a religious story," Sean said, speaking at last. "It's just a novel. Like *Don Quixote* or *Tales of Genji*."

Pete finally spoke again. "And no one has practiced that form of Buddhism for centuries. So you can't pick on Sean Wentworth for cultural appropriation. Unless you want to attack Americans drawing Asian sidekicks while living in London."

Sean frowned. "I didn't realize that offended you."

"It doesn't," Pete said. "Mostly. I'm just exploring the theoretical bounds of cultural appropriation. What exactly is off limits to a white guy from the U.S.? Sean has no known Nordic blood, so no Thor, Odin, or rosemaling? Or does he restrict himself only to seventeenth century Church of England and later? Rather restrictive for exploring archetypes across cultures, isn't it?"

Sean clenched his jaw, the muscles working at the side. Louisa seemed bored, though Eliot never detected any expression change from one moment to the next.

Eliot said, "Just stop, Pete. You're being ridiculous."

"That's my role," Pete said. "You posited that Hollywood's use of Navajo wolf-spirits is inappropriate. What's the line? Or is it just that if you make money on other people's art and lore, then it's cultural appropriation?"

Eliot glanced around the table: Pete wasn't really challenging her. Sophy was busy with her dessert. Sean stared at Louisa, an expression that Eliot couldn't read. All of them with greater education and cultural experience than she had.

One from the East and one from the West, as Sophy once said.

"If your culture colonized another, or committed genocide, then commercializing its art and lore might be cultural appropriation." Eliot folded her napkin and laid it carefully on the table, like you're supposed to when you're finished. "Impious Aeneas doesn't count. It's many millennia since anyone worshipped those gods."

Pete offered a silent applause. To avoid conflict, Sophy changed the subject, asking people to describe the birds they'd seen in the

Canyon that afternoon. Soon Louisa yawned and proposed they all go to bed.

. . .

During the short trek back to the cabin, Sean walked slowly, dropping behind. Eliot lingered too, until the others had all gone inside. He cornered her on the cabin porch to kiss her, first softly, then eagerly until both of their faces were damp and hot.

"We can't sleep together tonight," he moaned. "I don't know how I'll stand it."

"You told me this morning that we'd get another chance before we die," she said, laughing, though she also wanted more.

"I'm losing faith, Eliot. This is torture, being so close but never alone. I have a thousand things to tell you. And questions to ask."

"Sean!" Sophy called. "Can you build a fire? We don't want this fireplace to go to waste."

"I'll build one in a minute," Eliot called back to her.

"You already built one," Sean whispered, tugging gently at the tops of her leather jeans.

She grasped the ragged collar of his t-shirt, whispering back. "Sean, I think your father and sister bought land on Limberlost."

"Where you live?"

"Yes." *The very same furlongs of land I coveted for myself.*

"How wonderful!" he said aloud. "The planets align to reunite the star-crossed lovers."

"Seriously?" she asked.

"Never more so." He was playful, his hands tucked in her back pockets, holding her close. Play was good. "Usually I have to push relentlessly to make the world give me what I want. This time, celestial forces have dumped bounty upon us."

In the cabin, Eliot gleaned sufficient tinder and newspaper from the near-empty wood box to coax two pine logs into flames. Louisa excused herself to make phone calls in the bedroom. Pete, relaxed and jovial, chatted with Sophy about his travels in eastern Europe. Eliot settled by the fire, leaning against Sean. While Pete told stories, Sean untied Eliot's braid and ran his fingers through her hair.

"Why do you bind this up? It's beautiful," he whispered.

This might be heaven, she thought, but said, "It gets tangled on the road."

Taking a turn at story-telling, Sean described how Eliot fixed his bike in Nevada as a comic masterpiece, with himself as a hapless clown, provoking Sophy into laughing at his incompetence in the wilderness. Louisa, hearing only the end of Sean's story, "It's extraordinary that you ride that thing."

Sean ceased stroking Eliot's hair, lapsing back into silence.

Pete said, "If we don't ride, we might as well give up living and head straight for the grave."

"It's magnificent," Eliot said. "Like flying in your dreams."

"It's dangerous," Louisa said, speaking to Sean. "People die. People get hurt and never walk again."

"Don't hex us," Pete cautioned from his perch near the fire.

"We ride aware," Eliot insisted. "It's better than staying home just to play safe."

"I'm sure," Louisa said. "But Sean can be so reckless."

Pete snorted, but stayed out of it.

Sean said, "I'm so graceful in my bog-standard caution that you can't recognize its subtle beauty."

Eliot relaxed into the pleasure of mutual understanding.

"I trust, dear friend, that you want to stay alive," Louisa said.

Sean said, "Have no fear, Louisa. There's a million things that need doing. I require all the time in the world to finish."

"All the time in the world," Sophy said, "after we get a good night's sleep. Shouldn't we turn in?"

Comfortable yet exhausted in front of the fire, Eliot agreed, yet regretted the misfortune of the bed partners Sophy had assigned. Pete and Sean had the tiny living room to themselves; Louisa, Eliot, and Sophy shared the bedroom.

Pete said, "Sean, want to walk up to the lodge for a while?"

"Sure," Sean said. "I have calls to make."

Sean pulled his boots back on, and Eliot wrestled with the urge to follow them, but it was a ridiculous impulse: she was tired, and she'd see him in the morning. He smiled impishly and mouthed the word "tomorrow" before leaving.

Nestled in scratchy white muslin sheets on the sofa in the bedroom, Eliot sensed sleep calling her name; yet for thirty minutes more, the light remained on as Louisa prepared for bed, removing makeup and repairing her claw-like nails that dripped gold, her fingers encircled with a myriad of colored stones. Eliot sought kind feelings, as Louisa took forever to douse the lights.

In the dark at last, Eliot curled into a ball, calculating the balance between blessings and curse. Every ninety minutes throughout the evening, Destiny had sent text messages from Swedish Hospital:

Much worse :(

Then:

better now! :) :))

The curse: Cora was near eighty, not likely to last forever. The blessing: Destiny managed to bluff her way through a fearsome time using her own indomitable will.

The shoreline property on Limberlost was lost. The curse: Eliot had to start over on a new plan for sheltering Cora and Destiny. The blessing: Breathing room. She didn't have to struggle to find a large down payment in a hurry.

The darkened room was shared with two sleeping women who, at best, thought her irrelevant. The curse: Sophy's not-so-subtle suggestions that the class divide between Eliot and Sean remained an unbridgeable chasm. The blessing: alone in the dark, Eliot imagined Sean's body curved around hers, how he'd kept her awake the night before, how he promised there'd be more nights far into the future.

Eliot drifted off, once more lost in road-dreams. Where she was a priestess in a cave high up a sandstone mountain, like the bluffs that hid Taoist retreats, but with red slickrock and piñon pines.

Her long white robe trailed in the dust as she climbed the path to her cave, the rustling silk dragging through undergrowth and over the rocky pathway, but glowed white. She carried a torch, illuminating the pristine snow. Her breath puffed a cloud in the cold, but her feet stayed warm and dry. In her cave, she tended a fire to cook broth and then hung herbs on a string to dry. She prepared magic potions and remedies for peasants. The moon glimmered on the snow, and the fire in the hearth cast shadows on the cave wall.

One of her disciples appeared. He tore his arm off and cast it at her feet.

"*Sifu*, my teacher," he bowed, ignoring the hole in his side that poured a brilliant red stream of blood onto her beautiful clean snow. "I am worthy, if you could but see."

She fought to mask her horror, because she was a great priestess who knew about life and death and suffering.

It was Sean, who lay prostrate, laughing.

"See," he said, "it's only stuffed. It's a cloth arm."

Treachery stretched and broke the ligaments that held her heart in place.

"This is only a movie," Sean said in the dream. "It's not real."

17.
Grand Canyon

SEAN
Wednesday Night

PETE AND I SAT AT THE bar of the Roughrider Saloon, warned by the bartender that closing hour was ten-thirty. Pete traded messages with Tadeusz and began reviewing that day's video post. I ended up walking right back to the lobby, answering a call from Jason.

"I gotta bail on your project," Jason said. Stress jammed his voice, like bad feedback. "I'm radioactive."

"No, we need you, buddy. What happened?"

"My uncle's dying. I'm in the hospital with him now."

"And—"

"The police mistook what we were doing last Friday for a crime. I spent all of Labor Day weekend in jail, because my wife never called an attorney. It's all over the web for the world to see."

"We're already rolling, Jason. It's too late to bail now. Tadeusz is linking in the tracks you sent before you disappeared."

"My name can't do you any good." Jason, who sang High Lonesome songs as if he were born to it, sounded like a character in his own compositions. "I'm so screwed."

"Look at the web comments for *Desert Crucible*. Your problems only add to the mystique." I tried to sound reassuring. "Like, how can we do this work on the back of motorcycles with you in jail? Anyway, what did you do to get arrested?"

"It'd take a book to explain."[4]

"We aren't dropping you from the project, Jason. Go check the comments online. It'll make you feel better."

---

[4] See details in *Nine Volt Heart.*

"Never read the comments," Jason said. "Didn't everyone learn that long ago?"

■ ■ ■

By the time I returned, Pete had established a long-term personal relationship with two guys at the bar. It became clear why the bar closed at ten-thirty: we were the only people there who didn't work in the park. Tourists were gone. It must be the altitude.

One of the guys, six-foot-six and strawberry blond, seemed unconscious of his size, like a golden retriever that doesn't understand he's no longer a puppy. Pete introduced him as Buddy. His pal Alonzo, five-eight like Pete but stocky, punctuated the story with muttered maledictions and hand-raps on the bar top.

Buddy said, "It all started when we got sent out to rebuild an off-trail storage shed."

"That's what we do here," Alonzo said. "Whatever we're goddamn told to do."

"Pay well?" Pete asked.

"Better'n starving," Alonzo said.

"Piss-poor joker that I am," Buddy said, "I drove a pickaxe into a skunk nest."

"A freak accident. Nest built in the shed's foundation," Alonzo said, beating a tattoo on the bar with his thumb. "Who knew?"

Pete wrinkled his nose. "We passed a dead skunk on the road up to the lodge this afternoon. The odor clung for miles."

"No shit, Dick Tracy," Alonzo mumbled.

"Three skunks ran off. One got me," Buddy said.

"Got him good, real good." Alonzo said. "Couldn't breathe around him, couldn't sit in the truck with him."

"Trouble," Pete murmured.

"Yeah. Trouble hadn't even started," Buddy said. "It pissed me off so much, I pickaxed the beast. Cleaved its skull in two."

"Didn't fix the problem," Alonzo said.

"I can understand your anger," Pete said. He circled his glass when the bartender glanced his way, then signaled drinks for all.

"That was only the beginning of trouble," Buddy said. He hunched his big body over the bar, disconsolate. "It's illegal to kill wildlife in the park. We hiked out into the woods—me stinking to high heaven—to find a place soft enough to bury the varmint."

"Shoulda' buried you too," Alonzo said. "Only way to get rid of the stink."

Buddy nodded. "Yeah. Coulda'. Shoulda'."

"Ranger still caught us," Alonzo said, tinking glasses with Pete when the bartender brought a new pour.

"Three thousand dollar fine for killing fauna inside the Park!" Buddy said, jamming his glass down so it spilled, then licking the spill off his hand.

"Shitty luck," Pete said.

"He still smells," Alonzo said, "if you got to ride with him in the pickup."

"Spent the month of August paying for a skunk's funeral." Buddy downed his drink, slapped Pete on the shoulder. "Thanks for listening, partner. We gotta hit the trail."

"*Amigo.*" Alonzo shook Pete's hand. "*Hasta luego.*"

■ ■ ■

Pete didn't even wait until the door closed behind his new friends before uploading the video and tapping notes to Tadeusz.

I tried to get his attention. "OK, what the hell, Pete? Why'd you drag Eliot into that BS with Louisa?"

He looked up from his cell. "Eliot stuck in her own oar. And rowed admirably well, if I might admire my own sister. Louisa isn't rowing in the same regatta. But doesn't know it."

"What do you think she's doing out here?" I asked.

"Executing on your endeavor to capture Americana desert life. What you're paying her for. That, and she's in love with you." Pete stared at the screen. "But she needs a voice of her own. That was good practice for her."

"I mean Louisa. Why'd she come all this way? I already made it clear that I will not return to Laconia."

"And you did a swell job of using Eliot as a defensive barrier tonight. You didn't let Louisa get near you."

Pete picked up his buzzing cell, which was hopping across the bar top, begging to be answered. He glanced at the screen and said hello, then handed it to me. "It's Tadeusz, boss. He's been trying to raise you, but your cell is switched off."

"Everyone at Laconia is screwed!" Tadeusz shouted, probably shaking his finger like he did when we debated design or story choices. "Our life's work is going to Disneyland in a clown car."

"Tadeusz, you guys still own ten percent. You can—"

"Milo is buying our Laconia shares dollar-for-dollar at our hire-date prices. One one-hundredth of the current value. That's what he'll pay us. Unless people all sign new contracts with huge non-compete clauses that forbid side work."

"You're coming with me, right, Tadeusz?"

"Dude, I'm fine. Everyone else is screwed." Tadeusz was in panic mode. "Milo is transmogrifying Laconia. Monkey is headed off to after-school hours on Cartoon Network. Where the characters just blink as the landscape scrolls by on a roll."

"Tell everyone I'll fix this," I said. Milo could not change any legal agreements while we remained partners. This should be easy to fix with a phone call to Karl. That's what I pay attorneys for, right—to keep people from getting screwed.

"By Friday at twelve o'clock," Tadeusz said. "That's how much time Milo gave people to decide. Sign a new contract or leave. When the clock strikes twelve, we all turn into pumpkins. Or mice."

On the coming Monday, escrow closed for the deal I'd struck with Milo to leave Laconia. After that, my part in the company was over. I needed to separate from Milo and begin new work now. Our relationship was dysfunctional, a creative and emotional disruption. But for the same reason that I needed a partner to invest a year ago, I didn't have enough money to buy out Milo's share. I could leave, but I wasn't rich enough to bankroll all fifteen people—only Tadeusz and perhaps two more people. That's the biggest reason why I needed HOPE to green-light full production for our new work: to start a cash flow so my team can keep working.

"I didn't intend to affect the team this way." I'd seized navigation of my own life, soaring toward a new star. But there was no way that I would toss my old team off a cliff, leaving them to fall instead of fly.

"You've always put the team first." Tadeusz's despair carried across the mountains and plains to where I huddled in a bar in outback Arizona. "It's not like Milo has one fuck to give."

I did. I do care. "I'll fix it."

∙ ∙ ∙

"And here I thought Eliot did all our fixing," Pete said as I hung up. He signaled the bartender, pointing to his empty glass.

"Milo is reconfiguring Laconia," I said. "He's buying out the team's shares." I stirred the ice, reciting back every attack my former partner had shot my way in the past week. "I can't say a word to anyone about why I'm leaving Laconia. I have no rights to Impious Aeneas or Monkey King, since Laconia owns all copyrights, from the beginning." My first act as the beneficent employer had been to show Laconia employees that we'd all share in the success, not just me. So I assigned the first copyrights to the company. "Milo nosed in to try to cut off our documentary work with Dante."

"And tried to swindle my old work from my father," Pete said, reviving the problems that arose just before we left Seattle. Pete didn't need to remind me about his bet—that Milo got a year of Pete as indentured servant if our *The Desert Crucible* adventure failed. Pete continued to grouse. "To say nothing of whatever minions Milo might have sent out to sabotage us on the road."

"I just don't believe that," I said. "Though everything else is screwed. Especially the claim that *The Desert Crucible* is a Laconia work product and doesn't belong to me."

"Milo already has a message from Karl. Maybe Louisa hasn't heard yet," Pete said. He'd finished uploading video and was viewing Tadeusz's last post, but with the sound off. "Milo sent Louisa here to pull you back into Laconia, to keep the FAIL deal from falling through."

Below Pete's shoulder, his laptop played back an animation I'd created with Tadeusz last May, with mystical beasts roaming the Sonoran desert. Overlaid with Eliot's bike being hoisted up and hauled away.

"What'd you do, Pete? What does my salvation cost?"

"Milo thought he could hold onto you through copyright law." Pete dismissed the video window with Eliot's smashed bike and opened another, clicking through a photo slide show. "You recognize these, right?"

I watched familiar images flicker on his screen, while spilling half my drink as the glass rattled on the bar top.

Pete said, "Yeah, boss, you do. The photos Eliot shot on your first Amazing Journey?"

"You just kicked me in the gut."

He closed his laptop, having made his point. "Sophy gave these to me when I visited her this summer. You both ditched a lot of stuff when you left Amherst. Sophy made me haul it all away, since she's cleaning out to move."

"Eliot shot film then," I said, remembering. "A friend of Sophy's let her use his darkroom."

"And four months later, Laconia copyrighted the original Impious Aeneas illustrations." As Pete spoke, the bartender set down the bill, pointing to the wall clock.

"I swear I didn't consciously copy." I handed the bartender my credit card, while he busily didn't listen to anything we said.

"It's just coincidence that she framed those landscapes in such evocative ways. You had to have seen these," Pete said.

"Yes, while we were still in Amherst. I'd forgotten."

"Yeah? Like a drunk blacks out and forgets?"

I swallowed a lump that didn't want to go down. "Fuck me."

"We've already covered that issue," Pete said. "Anyway, don't take this personally. A few years ago Eliot made me her agent for online sale of her photos. She doesn't put any effort into it. Says it can't be worth more than spare change. But as her agent, I asked Karl to sue Laconia for copyright infringement. Using the date-stamped negatives as prior art."

"Eliot didn't say anything to me."

"She doesn't know." Pete gathered up his electronic gear. The bartender was stacking chairs in preparation for the cleaning crew.

"But she must have recognized it, as soon as she saw the original Impious Aeneas." At that moment, I'd welcome my skull being cleaved, like that ill-fated skunk.

"Maybe Eliot has never seen your work."

"She said she admired it. She'll hate me when we tell her."

"Not possible, boss," Pete said. "She'll be mad at me, which I'm used to. She's never been even mildly irritated with you."

"That can't be true."

"Trust me."

We stood on the verandah of the lodge, not able to carry this conversation back to Sophy's cabin. The sky, now clear, displayed that litter of stars not visible in the city. Look upward: the human mind tries to form order from chaos.

"You understand why I had Karl do this for you, right?" Pete rocked on his heels, his pack over his shoulder, hands in the pockets of his jeans.

"Yes, though maybe you could've told me sooner." Like, how much earlier did I need to find out I'm a total asshole?

"Since I play the role of your bantering sidekick, I'll inform Louisa tomorrow that Milo will be leaving you alone forever."

"Nice. And I'll tell Eliot—"

"That she's in love with a guy who has a vision and the best of intentions. But who screws the pooch in reality."

"Why do I feel like the guy who pickaxed a skunk?"

The Desert Crucible Episode V
After the War

[Tadeusz: Link with the B-roll of the bike crash aftermath. Use this man's voice exactly as I recorded the story he told—no editing. Put some road hum loops behind his voice instead of music. Jason's out of jail but still hiding out somewhere. Do the best you can with what we've got. —Pete]

After I got back from Nam for the last time, I used to play with the cops. Running way the hell over the speed limit on a curvy road.

Cop pulls out and I pick up the blue flashing lights.

Whenever this happened, I'd just be singing "Yee hah!" inside my helmet. I laughed hysterically, thinking, "Here we go," while dialing my mind down to a tiny focused point and heading for that point.

I'd keep smiling and laughing as the blue lights fell farther and farther back, until they're out of sight. What a freaking blast. So goddamn funny.

It's like a little boy conjuring a band of wild Indians in his imagination. The Indians are coming, riding hard behind. They're going to kill him in the worst possible way. And the little cowboy takes off and runs his heart out, with the Indians chasing him. In his mind.

Except it's real. Which puts a crazy happy freaky mind-laugh into it.

But I had to swear off this. It's a felony in this state. So that was that. No more.

Except I did it one more time, unable to resist. Now, no more.

∞

18.
Cape Royal

ELIOT
Thursday a.m.

*I do have a sense, and I've never not had it,
of how easily things can vanish.*
—Doris Lessing

SEAN WHISPERED AT THE DOOR, waking her. "I can't sleep. Come out with me."

But before she finished dressing, the others were up, too, as if the invitation included them.

"Thanks for waking me," Sophy said. "I never like to sleep through sunrise. Let's walk to the Point and catch the sun."

Eliot waited on the porch, stealing a minute alone in the early dawn with Sean who, rather than ravishing her with kisses, cradled her in the morning chill.

"I have so much to talk to you about," Sean said, his face buried in her hair. "The mistakes I made. The—"

"Oh, no you don't," she said. "No confessions. Yours or mine."

A short, sharp laugh vibrated within his jacket.

"Eliot, I hope we can create a life, be real partners. But I have to tell you—"

"What do you mean by partners?" She stepped back as far as she could, given how close he held her. "I'm just your temp employee. I have other work to do."

"Not that kind of partner. The real kind."

"You have Pete. And your other friends, Tadeusz and Jason."

"A life partner." Sean shook her gently. "Didn't we learn that this week?"

"You mean, like married or something?"

"Yes. Isn't that where we're headed? What you want?"

"No. I never—why would you think that?"

"I've loved you—love you now. Pete says you're in love with me. Always have been."

"Yeah. Though not Pete's business to tell you. But I'm not—" She raised both hands, as if beseeching heaven. "I'm not the kind of person who gets married."

"But, I don't—" He let go. Pushed his glasses up his nose. "I don't want to lose you again."

"I'm not going anywhere. I don't want to endure another rift."

"That's why people get married. You just want to live together? Lots of people do that."

She shook her head. Hair fell out of her braid. "I don't see what good it does people to eat breakfast together every day. Do laundry. Breathe down each other's neck. Isn't it enough that you're moving to Seattle?"

Before he answered, Pete and Sophy came out onto the porch.

"Can we eat breakfast now?" Louisa said, her voice wavering from inside the cabin.

Under Sophy's direction, they all tramped up the trail to the lodge for breakfast, Sean walking between Eliot and Sophy, his arms draped over both their shoulders.

Over breakfast, Louisa remained withdrawn, Sophy exuberant. Pete, otherworldly, stared out the window. Except for Sean's hand on Eliot's knee, they might all have been on separate planets whirling through space, kept only in each other's view through the laws of gravity while the morning light gathered, revealing the Canyon's russet and rose-colored promontories.

Eliot escaped to the lodge's verandah, to trade texts with Destiny, learning that Cora had a good night and was responding to medication.

"Are we OK?" Sean slipped behind her, wrapping an arm around her waist. The ponderosas' vanilla odor drifted like incense, and the flute song of the hermit thrush played background music in the high-mountain air. "Fundamentally, I mean."

"Yes. Of course."

"I love you. It's the spiritual revelation of this trip." He kissed her. "To beat all other revelations. Of all times."

When everyone lurched back down the trail to the cabin, Sean lagged behind with Louisa, talking quietly, while Eliot fought an exasperating desire for the weight of his arm on her shoulders.

Inside the cabin, Pete and Sophy packed. Eliot, who'd taken care of her miniscule belongings when she rose, lingered on the cabin porch, watching the Clark's nutcracker scold another bird, listening as that white-haired devil spoke to Sean with the apparent intention that Eliot overhear.

"Did that woman entice you away from Laconia? Sophy says you almost wrecked your life over her once before. I thought you preferred delicacy in women."

"Eliot has nothing to do with our business, Louisa."

"FAIL Studios insist that the deal with Laconia includes you."

"Not going to happen."

Eliot disliked loud women. Scratch that. She disliked posh girls who spoke in a way that forced one to overhear. At the ranch, there was at least one apprentice each season who loudly scorned mere carpenters. At Saturday markets, one invariably appeared, bargaining down a price while dissing Eliot's work: *I've seen these knockoffs at every street market in the Northwest.*

"Milo should never have agreed to the split, Sean."

"Oh sweet Jesus. It wasn't Milo's to decide."

"He's concerned about your choices. Homemade rock videos on YouTube? Seriously?" Her voice dripped sarcasm like poison.

"I'm flattered that Milo cares."

"One business arrangement disappoints you, so you throw it all away," Louisa said. "After ten years of flaming success. And now you're hot for a country girl?"

"Great strategy. Insult what I care about most. Hilarious."

"Let's be professional. You and Milo need to find a way to compromise. He'll give you back your one-third share of the company. You'll have the majority of—"

"—of the minority portion that isn't held by Milo and FAIL Studios? No."

"We have problems—"

"—that Milo created," Sean said. "Milo's lack of honesty does not constitute a problem for me. However, his new move to screw my friends, now that's a problem."

When the two quarreling partners reached the cabin porch, Sean climbed the steps with a wide grin. He pushed his glasses up the bridge of his nose, then turned his back on Louisa to kiss Eliot. His shoulder didn't block Eliot's vision of the Clark's nutcracker.

Or of the scowling, white-hot hate that Louisa cast her way.

■ ■ ■

All packed up, the whole disparate company prepared for a tour of Cape Royal, after which Sophy would leave with Louisa for Flagstaff and that Basketmaker archeological dig. Sean slowed down the departure, on the phone in the bedroom, even after all the morning exchanges with Tadeusz were finished.

"Come on, Louisa," Pete called. "Borrow my helmet and ride with us."

"I'd never dream of it," Louisa said. She stashed a bag in Sophy's rented Dodge SUV.

"Your loss." Pete tugged on his own helmet, fired up his bike, and wheeled out to the roadway.

Eliot sat behind Sean, wrapped around him to enjoy the ride across the Kaibab Plateau through the ponderosa pines to Cape Royal. The best ride so far: morning light trickled to the understory and the curving roadway dipped and rose and dipped again along the ridge that led to the Canyon. Wild turkeys huddled at the edge of a marsh, turkey-toeing onto the mudflats in search of their breakfast. Deer leaped through the brush beneath aspens and pines, their white tails flashing goodbye in the undergrowth.

Sean's body pressed against her breasts as she wrapped around him, his ribs rising with each breath. She regretted she wasn't the rider on this perfect road, being at one with the bike. As the passenger, she tucked her thighs close to Sean's, cupped her hand over his leg for a moment, then clasped her fingers across his belly. This was an easy ride, and an easy posture, loving Sean. Later that night she'd sleep beside him when they camped.

The ride ended too soon, thrusting them into bright light at the rim's edge where piñon and Utah juniper supplanted the ponderosas. She and Sean arrived before the others, and walked in the garden, holding hands, admiring manzanita, tiny cactuses, and cliff roses while waiting for the others.

"Pete says I should be careful with you." She teased.

Sean froze.

"He meant to criticize me," she said. "He insists that I always give more than I take."

"He's right. We need to talk—"

"Not now, Sean." She didn't want to hear that morning's offer again. Too soon. "We're at the edge of a Great Wonder. Let's just be in the moment."

Sean had his hand on a tree branch, running his finger over a drip of pine pitch, two meters from the Caution sign that listed fines for disturbing flora, fauna, and rockery in a national park.

"Piñons like these grow at Navajo National Monument," he said. "It's red slickrock country there. You'll love it at Betatakin."

"Where we're camping tonight?"

"Here, smell this," he said, resting his piñon-pitch-coated finger beneath her nose. "Ambrosia, don't you think?"

"It's heavenly. If a man smelled like that, I'd be at his mercy," she said.

"Please, no. I'm at yours." He kissed her, tugging at the hank of her hair that hung free below her braid.

As the others appeared, Sophy's rasping voice carried from up the trail, asking Pete about the little cactuses. The piñon scent clung to her after they left the Sonoran garden. Pete remained behind, perched on a rock close to the parking lot, tapping his phone with typically intense concentration. Louisa commandeered Sean's attention. Sophy took Eliot's arm on the path to admire the view and, given her slow tread, they fell behind Sean.

"Eliot, what's smeared on your face?" Sophy asked.

Eliot touched her upper lip, finding it sticky. Piñon pitch blackened her face when she tried to rub it off.

"It's voodoo," Eliot said. "Sean's trying to trick me into doing what he wants."

"Sean always gets what he wants," Sophy said, chuckling at her own humor. Ahead, two slim figures walked together in stark contrast. Sean in his hoodie and leather jacket, slightly stooped, uncut dark hair sprung wild; his business partner in a silk jacket and hand-tooled boots, her white hair shellacked into a dramatic sheaf above outlandish eye-shadow. "What do you think of Louisa?"

"She seems nice," Eliot said, her voice mimicking Pete's. But Sophy didn't catch that tone.

"The last decade has been good for Sean." Sophy shaded her eyes, pretending to stare out toward the dawn light, when she was obviously watching Louisa and Sean. "He's learned the discipline of work, and it serves him well."

"Hmmm. Sean always said he learned discipline from Dante Gawain."

Sophy's nostrils flared, ever so slightly. "His Laconia partners helped him become the great success we always knew he'd be."

"I thought he was supposed to teach art at a small New England college." Eliot surprised herself with such contrariness. Then she included her own disappointment. "And paint. I thought Sean intended to become a painter."

"Sean says he has canvases coming in the container he shipped home." Sophy trumped Eliot's claim, offering a detail that Sean hadn't shared. "He'll have more time to paint in Seattle."

They reached a bench placed where the view was framed by pines and rock rose. Sophy sat gracefully and patted a place beside her for Eliot.

After a few seconds of blessed silence, Sophy said, "They live in a different kind of world than you or I. Some people have outsized fates. You can see what he's accomplished—"

"Comic books and rock videos?" Eliot said.

Sophy ignored her. "Sean was always destined for more than most people. It's like a destiny to—"

"Paint on a larger canvas?" Eliot filled in the blanks, repeating a cliché Sophy had used a decade earlier.

"Exactly." Just as ten years ago, Sophy grasped only the surface meaning of words.

"Sophy, if you're about to repeat the warning you gave me in Amherst, please don't bother. I memorized every word you said back then. I can repeat them upon command, any time you wish."

"I'm sorry but—"

"Never once have I stopped Sean from anything he wants to do. I never would."

Sophy sighed but didn't answer.

Eliot said, "I have a life of my own. I provide what I need for myself." She bit back the one bitter thought she had: *Except for the waterfront cabin on Limberlost, which you took from me.*

"I'm glad to hear that." Sophy patted Eliot's knee, which felt condescending. "Sean's obsession with you was never healthy. It's fortunate that you're a realist."

"I understand we might be neighbors," Eliot said, to keep from saying what she really thought.

"You learned of our good fortune? My father and I both have been living where land is so expensive, we can't believe what a great bargain we made."

The voices of the other couple carried with sufficient volume that Eliot heard only half of what Sophy nattered on about the gem she and her father Robert had found on an island in Puget Sound.

■ ■ ■

"She's suing us? Suing you while she's fucking you? What kind of bitch does that?" Louisa's voice screeched like metal scraping glass. "Milo called me this morning. What the ever-loving hell, Sean?"

"Her rights agent brought the suit."

"And I suppose her agent is that little bitch Pete Byron? What the hell are we going to do about this?"

"Settle, of course. There's no recourse."

"Any settlement comes out of your payout, you bastard."

"As it should. The rights infringement was my mistake."

"And your payout will be fuck-all, Sean, if FAIL Studios walks because you aren't part of the deal."

"You and Milo will find a way through it. You're always persuasive," Sean said.

"Why couldn't you leave without screwing us over?"

"I didn't set out to harm you in any way. I just want out." Sean spoke calmly, making it hard to hear his words over the turbulence Louisa created. "Your sense of—damage—is after the fact."

"*The Desert Crucible* is a colossal fuck-you to Laconia."

"My new work has nothing to do with Laconia. It's Milo who's screwing the team. If I'd known his malevolence would put the team in jeopardy, I'd—"

"Milo has the best copyright attorney in Los Angeles working right now. We're fighting this. Pete Byron can stick this blackmail attempt up his tight ass."

"I should be grateful. If Laconia wins that fight, I'll still have my full payout to launch my new work."

"You asshole." Louisa strangled on the words she spit. "You're laughing at me. You and that cowgirl bitch."

"Calm down before you choke on your own bile. There's a clear way through the mess."

"The mess that you made."

"Here it is: Laconia is being sued because I gave all copyrights to the company since the beginning. Laconia sues me for false representation. I will settle with the suit Pete brought, because it was I who claimed Eliot's work as my own. Pete, as her agent, licenses it all back to you. You can show the results to FAIL to prove that I wasn't the original visionary you all thought I was. And Laconia and FAIL Studios go forth together to make Monkey the King of children's afternoon cartoon world."

Louisa said, "That's too easy."

"I only want one thing from Milo."

"What?"

"Leave the original employment agreements with the Laconia team intact. No swindling of company shares. No draconian non-compete clauses."

"You'll just steal everyone away."

"Louisa, when Milo backs people into a corner, they'll climb out the window. Or dig a hole in the floor. Anything to get away. They aren't serfs."

"He'll refuse."

"OK. Then I remain a target in the suit against Laconia for copyright theft. I'll admit in the first deposition that I stole original art from Eliot Arden without permission or compensation."

"It was a perfect marriage," Louisa said. "That woman in her leather jacket and dirty jeans, she'll never understand you. She can't even imagine how your mind works."

"My friend has nothing to do with it."

"That rat Pete Byron did this. It's alienation of your affection. And blackmail over intellectual property."

"I didn't need Pete to persuade me to get the hell out of this, this—*relationship*. Counter-sue me, and we settle this quietly. Or my copyright theft goes viral faster than—"

"What?"

"The Desert Crucible."

"You're sleeping with that bitch. Can't you just marry her? Then give her money and make her go away?"

Sean laughed. "Like that would work. Not all people live in a world like yours, Louisa."

■ ■ ■

"Robert has engaged a surveyor and started the search for an architect and a quality builder. We'll close by the end of September and break ground soon thereafter. Mind you, it will mean a winter in a rented condo. Robert says he's already set up the perfect base camp in downtown Seattle. We'll have Sean with us and—"

Sean stood before them. "Sophy. Eliot. Ready to go? We need to hit the road to make the Monument before nightfall."

Louisa had circled toward the parking lot on an alternate path.

Eliot held a hand out to Sophy, to help her up from the bench. "Use locals so that your new neighbors know you aren't carpetbaggers. Anderson-Urquhart are the most interesting architects on the island. They'll find a builder for you."

■ ■ ■

High white clouds crossed the Canyon. Sean and Sophy traded binoculars to watch birds soar. Pete talked lenses and F-stops while snapping pictures of everyone posing against the Canyon edge. Eliot leaned against a south-facing rock, reviewing her own snaps, deleting the ones not worth passing to Pete. And replaying that conversation between Sean and Louisa, which reamed her brain like a rotary saw.

"We should be off," she said. She'd sort it out while riding.

"Yeah," Pete said. "Dante's expecting us. Probably killed the fatted calf and everything."

Sophy tucked her binoculars into her pack. "Pete, how is Dante these days? We haven't been in touch."

"Me either." Pete hid the bitterness he'd expressed the day before. "How about if everyone gets up on that ledge for pictures? Sophy, can you make it up that far?"

"Of course. If you can get me down again."

They squinted into the sun while Pete focused and arranged them as he wanted, with Sophy and Louisa in front, and Eliot beside Sean, who caressed her neck, his arm around her shoulder. Four snapshots. Then Pete helped Sophy down, and she kept hold of his arm as they walked to the parking lot. Eliot and Sean held hands and leaped down three feet to the sandy limestone; teasing, Sean pretended to trip Eliot so she stumbled, laughing, and he leap-frogged over her. Louisa remained behind on the boulder.

"Come on, Louisa!" Sean called. "Jump down. Let's go."

"Will you help me, Sean?" Louisa said.

He went back and stretched out his hand to help her down.

"Honestly, Louisa. You're the big risk-taker. Jump!"

She jumped and fell, crying out in pain, crumpling on the limestone. Sean knelt beside her.

"Louisa, I'm so sorry."

She murmured words that didn't carry.

"Can you stand?" Sean got Louisa to her feet, but she couldn't, or wouldn't, walk. Eliot came to help, asking first-aid questions to make sure nothing was broken. A badly skinned knee might be the worst of it, but Louisa refused closer examination while insisting that she was unable to walk. Sean carried her to the parking lot.

"Go on ahead, Eliot," Sean said. "Warn Sophy that she'll have to get help for Louisa."

"But don't let her worry about me," Louisa called softly.

Eliot bounded up the trail, suspicious about how badly hurt Louisa was. She explained the accident to Sophy, who was too practical to be alarmed.

While waiting, Eliot and Pete prepared to ride. They finished safety checks and stood with helmets in hand long before Sean emerged, carrying a scraped, bruised Louisa. As Sean got her into the passenger seat of the rental car, Louisa embraced him and kissed him at length.

"It wasn't your fault, Sean. Don't be sorry."

"He isn't," Pete called.

While Sophy said goodbye to Sean, Eliot offered a polite goodbye to Louisa.

"It was nice to meet you," Eliot said.

As Eliot lifted her helmet to slip it on, Louisa said, "The feeling isn't mutual, you bitch."

"I'm sorry?"

"You will be so damn sorry, dear heart. He's choosing to stay with Laconia. After he pays you off for your slag art."

Shaken, Eliot joined Pete by the bikes, tucking her braid inside her jacket and tugging on her gloves.

Pete said, "I got whiplash watching you. You started this trip needing money, mad because you had to travel with Sean. By last night, Sean committed to making you his life's partner and—"

She swallowed what tasted like heavy metal. "No, he's not. He's staying with Laconia."

"That cannot possibly be true."

Eliot, endeavoring to be cool, said, "Louisa just told me."

"She's wrong." The edges of Pete's nostrils turned white while he flushed carmine red.

"Maybe," she said. "Besides what Louisa said just now, I overheard their last conversation. What am I suing Sean for?"

"Sean didn't tell you?"

"No." She pulled on her helmet, muffling Pete's answer.

"His early Impious Aeneas artwork copied your unique photos. He got memory and creativity confused."

"So you sued him, Pete? I thought you and he were partners."

"We are. I did it to get Milo off his back."

"Is she married to him?"

"What?"

"Louisa said, 'It was a perfect marriage.' Then she said—oh screw it."

Pete blinked. Blinked again. Cocked his head. "I don't—No, I don't see that."

"She says Sean's staying with her."

In the thousand moments as Sean waved at the rented SUV and then joined them, Eliot managed to keep breathing, in spite of having been kicked in the belly.

"Let's go," she said. She climbed behind Pete just as he turned on the fuel lever and pressed the ignition switch.

"She's riding with me," Pete called in answer to whatever Sean said when they left him in the parking lot.

For twenty miles, she replayed each scene between Sean and Louisa. How Louisa used her to attack Sean, how Sophy once again worked to divide them. For the next thirty miles, she taught herself to think only of the road, which was littered with the crushed carcasses of black-and-white Kaibab squirrels.

19.
National Monument

THIS WAS LIKE IMPIOUS AENEAS'S revels after Artemis led him out of the fires of Troy.

> Oh, goddess of the wildland,
> Listen to the cries of man,
> I have only praise now.
> I am no longer your beggar.

I buckled my helmet and sped away from the canyon rim, passing the SUV. Sophy waved. Louisa stiffed me cold.

"This is so hard," Louisa said when I carried her up the trail, her voice breaking with her version of emotion. "We need you."

"You and Milo are suited to each other."

"How do we keep people happy without you? And—"

"Louisa, you have my answer. Don't screw people."

"If you won't let us protect you—"

"Protect me? I'm going to pay for my mistake. I'm protecting Laconia. Tell Milo to have his attorney call my attorney. We're done now."

"Oh, Sean. This is such a hard good-bye."

"Let Milo soothe your poor hurt feelings."

She had nothing more to say. Which suited me.

Life began at that moment.

During the ride across the Kaibab Plateau, cold tore at me with grasping fingers when I twisted the throttle to catch up with Pete and Eliot. This one time I wished we'd slow down, to watch the turkeys strut and the deer dawdle in the high meadows.

I had what I wanted most. Freedom. Love. I'd strut like the Monkey King after breaking into the Queen of Heaven's banquet. I'd eat all the peaches and drink the wine of Immortality. Then I'd stumble to the Jade Emperor's palace to eat the elixir-of-life pills. And Pete as Impious Aeneas could have more than half the peaches he helped me steal. He'd given me Eliot's secret: that she felt as I did. Our new Journey to the West united two hearts.

Ravens laughed with me now from the rookery metropolis in the tall trees lining the roadway. One dived, swooping at such a precise angle of incidence as to collide, yet I swerved and left the bird behind. Even over the roar of the bike and with the face shield closed on my helmet, I heard the ravens laughing.

The bike needed fuel at Jacob Lake. Pete and Eliot had disappeared inside the café—Pete's bike stood on its center stand near the front door. Tourists milled everywhere in a midday frenzy. A German tourist in a Winnebago backed out of the lot without checking his rearview mirrors, crushing a Honda Civic. A knot of pre-teens, combs sticking from their back pockets, wandered together giggling, texting while they talked simultaneously. Brakes screeched. The service station line moved at a snail's pace. While I waited, I fished a sweater and neck scarf from my pack. My fingers numb from the cold, I retrieved heavier gloves from the tank bag.

When my turn at the fuel pump finally arrived, I dumped gasoline on my boot when returning the nozzle to the pump. The teenage station attendant wanted to talk about my bike.

"It doesn't corner well in the twisties," I said. "And it isn't built for passengers."

"But it's fast, huh?"

"Faster than anyone needs to go." By the time I'd freed myself, Eliot and Pete were buckling their helmets and mounting the BMW to continue onward.

"I want to get something to drink," I called, pushing my bike up alongside them.

"Whatever," Pete said. He twisted the throttle and pulled out onto the highway. Eliot glanced back for the briefest moment.

Grief and dismay marred her face.

Surprised, I dropped my helmet in the gravel, accidentally kicking it when I tried to retrieve it. A little boy, perhaps four years old, ran up to fetch it, pleased to be so close to a motorcycle.

"Sean! Be careful!" a woman's voice cried out.

I whirled around, but it was the kid's mother, calling the boy back to her.

"Thanks!" I waved at the boy Sean.

My face shield was pitted from falling in the gravel.

Five miles down the road I'd formulated a good guess about her glacial stare: Eliot overheard that conversation with Louisa. And I'd failed to do as I'd promised Pete, to confess my transgression and present my case for how I'd make it right.

It should be easy to rectify this misunderstanding.

Pete adjusted his rearview mirror when I rode up behind them. I flashed a victory sign, triumphant in my freedom and happiness. Then I pulled up to ride two abreast in the lane, grinning like a demon. But a hard left turn and a litter of dead squirrels made riding a chore. I twisted on more speed to pass them, maintaining a smooth arc while choosing the clearest line among smashed rodent bodies. The rear tire slipped as I came out of the turn, but I poured on more speed, righting the bike. The engine screamed as I moved ahead of them, my laughter echoing in my helmet.

■ ■ ■

For every thousand feet the road fell in the descent off the plateau, the air heated ten degrees. A straight clear road followed the edge of the Vermilion Cliffs toward Marble Canyon, with scarcely a tourist and no highway patrol in sight. I poured on speed, winding the bike out, pushing the red line on the tachometer while the spectacle of the Grand Canyon became only a jagged crack in the torn plains. Corn grew along random irrigation ditches. The cliffs on my left seemed newly made, as if a giant had trenched his back yard over the weekend, preparing to rearrange his landscaping. Zeus and the Jade Emperor should set up a hurricane fence if they don't want mortals speeding through their back lot during construction.

The bike wanted to go a hundred miles an hour on this magnificent road. I crouched low over the tank and kept the throttle pulled down. The gods stoked their solar furnaces to burn at full heat as I traveled close to the cliffs. The wool sweater scratched, and I began to parboil under my leather jacket.

Before Marble Canyon, I cut my speed, cruising at a mellow twenty-five miles per hour, guessing where a trooper might hide in wait for unwary travelers. Not even scratching the gravel, I braked to a stop in the turnout by the bridge. I wound my sweater into a ball and jammed it back into my pack, then removed the winter-weight gloves and replaced them with summer riding gloves. After a drink of water at the fountain, I got out my pad and sat at the edge of the canyon, painting the scene where water rushed and echoed.

I drew several takes of the narrow canyon and sent them to Tadeusz in the ten minutes before the German whir of Pete's bike came up behind me. Eliot bounded off to the restroom before I made it across the lot to meet the pair of them.

"Whew!" Pete pulled off his helmet. "Hot frigging day. Finally."

"Your passenger's blood is boiling hot enough to raise the ambient temperature."

"She got stung by a piss-ant," Pete said. Still astride his bike, he folded his arms and stared at me. "You're staying with Laconia? What the hell, dude? We went through all this and you're staying with Milo? Are you and Louisa married?"

"What? No. Why the hell would you think that?"

"It's what Louisa said to Eliot after your private tête-à-tête in the bushes."

"Louisa lied. We concluded all business between us."

"However, you failed to tell Eliot about your freaking copyright infringement."

"We were interrupted at every possible chance."

"Look, *compadre*, I'm struggling to keep the bike steady because my passenger shakes like the shifting of tectonic plates."

"It's cold. Was cold."

"She's crying."

"Leave her with me," I said. "We'll work it out."

"You're welcome to her."

At the fountain, I drenched a handkerchief to line the inside of my helmet, then decided to drench my shirt, too. When Eliot returned, she stashed away her long-johns and sweater in one of the

Krauser bags on Pete's bike. Avoiding me, she walked to the fountain for a long drink. Pete nodded to me and gracefully kicked his bike into gear and took off before she could protest.

"Sean wants to talk to you," Pete shouted as he pulled away.

She glared, her arms akimbo, defensive as hell.

"A misunderstanding arose." I began.

"I think I understand." She put on her helmet and snapped the face shield closed.

"Do you? Legally it will soon be over between Laconia and me. Milo has no hold on me," I said, embarrassed to stand in that gravel lot trying to convince her at the top of my voice. "If you understand, what are you pissed about?"

"I don't want to talk. I want to ride."

"Suit yourself." I put on my water-cooled helmet. "I'd never make you do anything you don't want to."

The ride below the Echo Cliffs and up the switchback on Highway 89 toward Page didn't allow the speed I'd enjoyed in the basin below. Ten miles farther down the road, it grew too hot even with a wet t-shirt. I stopped again, causing a hostile Eliot to have to get off the bike so I could jam my jacket into a bag. I grinned because, even pissed off, she was the best person in my world.

"You ride bare skinned?" she muttered. She remained encased in her leathers, likely boiling in that shell. "Wow."

The bike only let itself get up to ninety miles an hour on this road. Pickups filled with Navajo families traveled up the slow rise, each new truck appearing just as a solid line forbade passing. I kept the bike's speed in check until passing was possible, then flew for five miles before the next family pulled onto the highway in front of me. Yet a sweet patience buoyed me. I'd tolerate anything with Eliot so close, including a slow ride on a desert highway where the bike wanted to scream.

I shifted back in the bike's seat, my hips pressing against her thighs. She retreated, sliding away for the fraction of an inch the bike allowed, her hands cupped on her own thighs as she watched the countryside. Her shift away from the center of the bike made cornering more difficult, forcing me to guide the bike with an off-center load. Whatever I'd done to offend—though I was sure it was

Louisa's BS—Eliot punished her own rear end, riding where the seat had no padding, just to ruin the pleasure of a great ride on a balanced bike.

Out in the shimmering heat, no birds appeared; nothing stirred in the landscape except the occasional trucks plying the roadway. Local craftsmen had deserted the thatched roadside stands where they sold kachina dolls and turquoise in the summer. Within fifteen miles of the city of Page, the ravens came back, but not laughing now, just soaring on updrafts. Every couple of miles another solitary hogan appeared, with no sign of life in the outlying yards.

A white plaque welcomed us to Page, which came as a rude insult after the afternoon in the burning desert: aluminum houses standing in rows of new developments, aluminum pontoon boats floating on Lake Powell behind Glen Canyon Dam. A bevy of four-wheel-drive vehicles and travel trailers crowded the streets. The towers of a coal-burning electric plant jutted into the storm-dark skies. The air clung to my skin, like it does before a thunderstorm. Ravens croaked overhead as I pulled over to the shoulder at the junction where Highway 98 leads to Navajo National Monument. Betatakin was an hour or so down the road.

■ ■ ■

Eliot took forever dismounting, rocking the bike as she climbed off. Pete wasn't in sight, and since Eliot wasn't speaking yet, I watched the horizon. The north and east held a waiting storm. Four plovers hopped in the arroyo. Killdeers cried, calling for rain in the wash below. I tried to remember which birds the Hopi called the birds of rain. The quail and the snipe—

"Which birds are rain birds?" I asked Eliot, though I might as well talk to a wall. "Yellow birds, the color of corn pollen, I remember that. And blue birds, the color of summer skies and turquoise. But I can't remember the metaphor for water birds." I pondered. "Birds flecked with white, marked by water spray—"

"Water pollen," Eliot said, begrudging that I got her to answer.

"Thank you. The very words I wanted to remember. This sky appears to be welcoming us to a spirit-quest. Are you prepared?"

"I'm not interested," she said.

"In finding spirits?" I asked, hoping she'd open up soon, and not wait until later.

"No, in stumbling around in the desert picking up dirty feathers and old bones," she said, wandering down the roadside, her voice echoing back to me. "No more finding old bottle caps like a two-year-old searching for treasure."

Lightning flashed far off on the cloud-blackened eastern horizon. She kicked at sandstone rocks, which rolled down the embankment and clunked to rest in the cheat-grass below.

Perhaps smiling too much, I said, "If you overheard my quarrel with Louisa, you might have gotten the wrong idea that we're married. It was all metaphor. She's just Milo's assistant."

"No," Eliot said. "I heard what she said to me."

"Which was?"

"Besides 'you bitch'?"

I winced. "She was in a foul mood."

"Your *friend* said—to quote—'He's choosing to stay with Laconia. After he pays you off for your slag art.'"

"God, Eliot, how could you believe her crap?"

"How could you be involved with a woman like that?" Her disgust was palpable.

"I'm not. She's Milo's—"

"And I'm your next choice, after you pay me off?"

"You can't believe anything Louisa says. I don't know how she persuaded Sophy to bring her here."

"Your sister presumed to advise me in similar ways. Just like before in Amherst."

"What? She wouldn't—"

"She gave me the same advice as a decade ago. I'm West, you're East. Never the twain shall meet."

"I'm a Seattle native. She had huge Ivy League dreams for me that I never—"

"You're summa cum laude, I'm trade school."

"That's so wrong. A warm, competent woman allowed a disorganized, schitzy poseur to trail after her, panting for love. Like I'm panting again."

She shook her head. She does that too much. "Then there was your father's goodbye handshake at Sophy's. His words: 'Dante must miss you while you're having a little adventure with Sean.'"

"Robert would never say that."

"Except he did. And then Dante took your side, Sean."

"There weren't sides. We belong together."

"Dante says Sean's the artist, Eliot's the artisan. No mere crafts-person should get in your way, begging for love. Like my mother did with Dante."

"Hell, Eliot. None of them can understand what you and I had. Have. You can't let them persuade you to—"

"They didn't persuade me."

"They divided us, kept you from coming to London."

Golden embers burned in her eyes. "Robert and Sophy merely helped me to recognize my place in the world. Louisa was kind enough to remind me that the same division remains."

Pete caught up with us, coasting to rest on the shoulder. He agreed that we should return to Page, find a campground, and wait out the stormy night that brewed on the horizon. However, in Page we failed to find a decent restaurant for dinner and so decided to get food at the supermarket. But the mall grocery store intimidated us more than the storm on the northern horizon. Scurrying down cold, too-bright aisles to buy fruit, crackers, and candy bars was like a bad acid trip. For most of that shopping fiasco, I was on the phone with Karl, making sure he squelched Milo's "let me screw you or you're fired" move on the Laconia team.

"It's slow," Karl said. "Between time zones and having to revisit the original agreements with Milo and the termination agreement. Then I have to identify where U.S. law applies, versus the portion that's the U.K. subsidiary—"

"Whoa, Karl. I'm in a parking lot, the wind's stiff enough that I can hardly hear you. Is there anything I have to do?"

"Just tell your team to be cool. We gave Milo notice not to act."

"So he stopped threatening to fire them?"

"He might blow smoke," Karl said. "But he can't start a fire."

In the gritty, littered parking lot, I made another call, to my con-tact at HOPE Productions, got put on hold. Was told to call later.

We stopped to refuel, where Pete used a sordid picnic table outside the service station to do a fast file upload. I spent time on the phone with Tadeusz, confirming that the Grand Canyon scenes would go up with no change in the story plan. Jason Taylor had finally called him, so Tadeusz was mellow about the decisions he had to make.

"Karl has it under control," I said. "I'm not supposed to talk to people directly. Can you tell people not to let Milo bully them?"

Tadeusz said, "Everyone trusts that you'll take care of business, boss. I told them you promised."

"I hope people trust enough to let the clock run out."

"The deadline is twelve o'clock. Most people say they'll hang on until the eleventh hour."

After the fiascos in Page, we went in search of the campground on Lake Powell that my map indicated lay northwest of town. Through all the hassles, Eliot let me fumble with Pete to find the right roads out of town, pretending patience with each of our three false attempts to choose a road. Electricity from the coming storm raised the hair on the back of my neck. Shimmery heat waves rose from the blacktop like an oily pall.

The Lake Powell campground hid from us among the hills and side roads. When we finally found it, it proved to be a gravel lot filled with jamboreeing Boy Scouts and the ubiquitous retirees in travel trailers. We paused by the dammed lake edge where the end-of-summer lowering of the lake left a ring like a draining bathtub. The wind whirled, blowing sand and a burning mist of water over us, stinging the sunburn I'd gotten from riding bare-skinned earlier that afternoon.

"We can't sleep here," Pete and I said simultaneously.

"And I'm hungry," Pete added, chomping a Baby Ruth bar from the grocery fiasco.

We crouched at the edge of the beach, watching the picnickers and afternoon bathers gather their ice chests and chase towels that blew across the gravel. Mothers admonished weeping children to hurry up on their barefoot scramble to the parking lot. The wind-borne gravel hurt, but overwhelming lassitude made me long to hunch inside my t-shirt rather than mount my bike to find a different camp. Ravenous, I opened a Tiger Milk candy bar, which tasted gritty and old, as though it had a long, idle life on the grocery shelf before I'd sprung it free.

"I'm not eating in Page," Pete said adamantly. "This weather is part of a negative vortex. I can't remember feeling this bad anywhere in America."

"It's just the electricity in the air," Eliot said.

We studied the map, hunting for the next campground.

"Nothing between Page and Navajo National Monument," Pete said. "It can't be much more than an hour if we go fast."

"There isn't food at the campground," I said.

"Screw it," Pete said. "We'll have breakfast in Kayenta tomorrow. I don't even want to pee in Page."

Eliot didn't argue, answering only to Pete when asked about her preferences. Each time she turned her head away, my own irritation rose, along with the pull of the electrical storm. Each small gesture was a big reminder: how she'd deserted me in Amherst.

Escaping Lake Powell and skirting Page, we stopped again at the Highway 98 junction to don rain gear, though no rain had fallen yet. A mound of black clouds threatened to envelop Navajo Mountain, smothering its bright yellow glow in the late afternoon sun.

"This is the desert, all right." I grinned at Eliot, excited by the decision to ride into the storm. "The weather hangs on the horizon like another kind of geology. It just moves faster than mountains."

Sheet lightning lit the northern horizon to the right of Navajo Mountain, casting a white glow onto Eliot's face, lighting perfect beauty and flashing in her cold, grey eyes.

"I want to ride with Pete," she said. The wind carrying her voice back to me. "Your bike is not comfortable."

"Fine," I said. "Whatever you want."

Just as I kicked the bike into fifth gear, rain misted over my face shield for the hundredth time on this demonic journey. The perfume of wet pavement and sage wafted up, but the highway's oil film meant treacherous riding until the rain thoroughly drenched the road. In my rearview mirror, the setting sun blazed in the last crack of open, unclouded sky in the west. Each time I checked the mirror,

Pete and Eliot rode in silhouette against that jagged crimson crack where the edge of the world was on fire. The hard black mass of clouds behind Navajo Mountain clutched at the ridge, but the sacred mountain of the Dineh glowed scarlet and orange.

The first finger of lightning above Navajo Mountain prodded awake images from years before, when I'd come here with Pete just before going to London. Perched on a slickrock hillside one afternoon, Black Mesa in the vista on one side, the Klethla Valley below, and Navajo Mountain to the north, we watched thunderheads dance over the mountain, never blessing the lands with rainfall. The Peabody Coal Company's electric lines and coal-slurry pipeline marred the primeval beauty over miles and miles of sacred landscape, where Navajo Mountain stood as the conductor between the heaven's electricity and thunder resting in the earth.

That beautiful mountain burned in the sunset again, and the direction it pointed was home: to go to work, not another adolescent spirit-quest.

And to fight the last battle of misunderstanding with the silent woman on the back of Pete's bike.

■ ■ ■

In spite of the hard rain, my bike hummed happily with the speed and the load it carried. The wind eased up so that I could fly. After the first lightning broke the tension, the clear, perfumed air went straight to my head. I smelled electricity among desert odors.

An hour later, the dark masses of cloud mountains folded over the burning western edge of the world, leaving us in twilight. Distant lightning still encircled the horizon, but the rain ceased.

We stopped where a road forked off the highway. Pete coasted up beside me. He said, "My map shows this fork cutting off from here to the National Monument." He pointed on the map to nine miles of graded road passing through the Klethla Valley below the Monument. Which would cut the trip to the campground in half.

Where we stopped, the desert showed no sign of rainfall. The sky cleared. Twilight transposed into night. The wind blew to wherever it lives on the Colorado Plateau when it finishes with you. I tingled from the ride down Highway 98, which would go into my sketchbook as some of the best adventure yet.

"Let's try it," I said. "Nine miles of dirt road can't be so bad. Do you agree, Eliot?"

She didn't shrug, nod, or shake her head. Her face shield remained closed.

Resolving not to engage with her until she wanted to, I squashed an impulse to beg forgiveness since I'd done nothing wrong. Well, except for that copyright thing. The next time we talked, I'd beg that she just go ahead and get mad at me. That silent hostility wasn't doing either of us a speck of good.

I followed Pete, because it was dark and I was tired, though of course Pete was, too. But between us, Pete was most likely to find the easiest way down the road. I wanted to relax, to let the desert work on my mind. In ten minutes it grew too dark to see more than what the lights of the bike illuminated. I checked the odometer—we'd already traveled thirteen miles. Pete braked to a stop.

Coming alongside, I pushed up my face shield. The smell of slickrock and juniper washed over me. The soft sand in the road, however, was too fine and deep for us to get off the bikes. A kickstand would never hold a bike in this stuff.

"This isn't right," Pete said, studying the map again with his flashlight. "Did we miss a turn?"

"Beats me. I followed your lights. That's as far as I can see," I said. The silence seemed louder than the noise of the idling bikes. No highway noise, no planes.

"There was a right turn a while back," Eliot said.

"Why didn't you say something?" Pete growled.

"You had the map. I didn't know what you wanted."

"Oh Christ," Pete complained. "Lost in the desert at night. My favorite."

"Let's just go back and find the road," I said, a deep tiredness coursing through my body. My wrists hurt and my foot cramped from all the work shifting gears on this twisty dirt road. "Will you recognize that road again, Eliot?"

"It had a sign. You'll see it when we go back."

I did not curse.

. . .

A white pickup eased toward us, so Pete and I split for opposite sides of the road. My foot sunk deep in sand on the shoulder when I stopped to wait while the truck passed. The two men and a woman in the truck watched us as if we were an interesting sideshow. None of them appeared Native American, yet out on this back road at night, they had to be locals. I willed them to stop so we could ask directions, though it seemed humiliating to be lost in the dark in someone else's homeland. Worse, to be lost in the middle of nowhere at night after going there on purpose. The pickup, as if heeding my wishes, slowed to a stop.

I wheeled my bike around to ask directions, glad that the bike was light enough to maneuver through the sand. Pete also swept his bike around behind me, but with more weight and an extra passenger, the BMW couldn't conquer the sand. By the light of my headlamp, I watched Pete's bike drop. Pete hopped off and struggled to upright it in a second while Eliot tumbled acrobatically across the sandy edge of the road. I couldn't let go of my bike to help.

One of the men, the driver, walked past me without a hello or acknowledgement, and joined Pete to wrestle the bike upright.

The other man shyly approached me.

"Hi," I began. "We're looking for the road to Navajo National Monument. But we missed the turn."

"The National Monument?" the man asked in the same way that London shopkeepers question my pronunciation, making sure they understood. The man was barely twenty and, I thought, extraordinarily handsome, super-human, his face unlined, his eyes eerily bright in the dim light cast by bike's headlight.

"The Monument is back that way." The woman leaned out the truck cab to point in the direction from which we had just ridden.

"Yes, I guessed that we passed it."

"It has a big sign," she said. "Maybe you didn't see."

I sucked air through my teeth, practicing patience.

"How far back?" I smelled gasoline from Pete's bike and heard the soft murmur as Pete talked with the other man. Eliot dusted her clothes and checked the gear tied to the bike.

"About two miles. You turn left, then go four miles and turn right. You can't miss it then." The woman smiled, her teeth flashing in the bike's headlight. Pretty, but not beautiful. Perhaps fatigue or poor health caused that ghostly pallor.

"Thanks," I said. "I appreciate your help."

Pete's BMW kicked back to life. Its headlight flooded the road.

"Why don't you follow us?" the driver asked as he left Pete and returned to the truck. "We'll show you the turnoff." He was perhaps thirty, his face round and more weathered than his friend's, his hair shading his eyes.

"Sure. We appreciate it."

We followed the truck, another white Dodge, its right rear fender mashed from a collision. Its license plate, unframed and unlit, hung from only one bolt and was so covered in dirt as to be illegible. The truck crawled along at barely ten miles an hour, so the two miles to the turnoff took an eternity.

A standard brown-and-white federal park directional sign, six feet high and six feet wide, pointed down the road.

"Four miles down and you'll find a right turn," the driver called out.

"Thanks!" I shouted back and waved. We'd thanked them an ignominious number of times.

Three miles later a road veered off to the left. We paused to stare down that road for a fraction of a second, then continued on. At Mile Four by the odometer, no sign of another road appeared. At the fifth mile, another left turn, and at the sixth mile, the road forked three ways, with no signs, no identifiers, no clues.

Pete stopped beside him.

"I think Coyote drew that goddamn map of yours."

"Were those folks Coyote's friends, do you think? Wolf-spirits? Or Navajo sorcerers, tricking us?"

"No. Maybe those tricksters work for Milo," Pete said.

"You still paranoid?"

"Just don't want to admit it's my fault," Pete said.

"You OK?" I asked, hoping enough time had passed since Pete dropped his bike that all sensitivity had been lost in the slow ride.

"Yes." Pete's voice in the dark sounded husky and strange.

"Your bike's all right?"

"Of course." His voice cracked a little. "Actually, I need you to take Eliot. I hurt my foot and my wrist. I need a lighter load."

"Fine. Anything else? You OK to ride?" I asked.

"Yes. We can't camp here in the middle of frigging Nowhere, Arizona. Let's take the right fork."

Each choice—we had to make four more decisions—we picked the right hand fork.

The sky had cleared, now so dusted with desert stars that identifying constellations was difficult. Sheet lightning and fork lightning rimmed the horizon, but so far off that no thunder echoed. Lightning and bike hum and the packed sand went on forever. Through all eternity we'd traveled, exhausted, on this difficult, twisted road, not knowing where it took us or when it ended. Twice we passed roadside encampments of pickups circled around a bonfire where Navajos came to party or to pray. Each fire that appeared offered a comfort: that humans lived out in the dark countryside. Yet these encampments seemed like the last place on earth where stupid, lost riders might wander in to ask for directions and a drink of water.

∎ ∎ ∎

Two hours after we began the nine-mile journey through the Klethla Valley, we emerged on pavement, like finding heaven's pathway. We paused by the stop sign.

"Six miles to Highway 160," Pete said through gritted teeth.

Five minutes later, we paused again where the road joined with a two-lane highway. It proved to be, however, the same road from which we'd wandered into the desert. A two-hour circle.

"Look, a paved shoulder! It's the road out of Hell." I intended to keep my spirits up. I put the kickstand down and left the bike by the stop sign. The stink of creosote bush drifted on the cold air.

Pete said, "I gotta take a break, boss."

He and I wandered a few feet out into the sage to relieve ourselves. The ground felt spongy and strange after riding endlessly through soft, shifting sands.

"Well, *compadre*, I always wondered if you'd follow me to the ends of the earth," Pete said. We rejoined Eliot, who stretched and yawned and didn't acknowledge our return.

"I said I would. But I expected you to have something interesting to show me at the edge of the Abyss."

We chomped M&Ms for energy and chugged the pint of orange juice left from the bad-acid trip in Page.

"Let's go west to Tuba City," Pete suggested. "We can find a motel there."

"Sounds good. Eliot, do you agree?"

"Whatever you decide," she said, putting on her helmet.

Joining in her rage wouldn't help a goddamn thing. I mounted my bike and switched on the ignition, revving the engine more than necessary. As I prepared to pull onto the highway, a white Dodge pickup roared past, headed east, swerving in the middle of the road. A hand reached out to wave from the driver's side.

"Thanks a lot, you worm suckers!" Pete screamed, seeming to believe as I did that the truck carried the errant-direction givers.

I peeled out of the gravel and wheeled west, twisting up the speed quickly enough that Eliot was forced into the correct position for a passenger. I put extra lean into every turn so that she had to sit right: crouch low, hang onto me, lean in the turns. We were both too tired to fight now.

Ominous yellow signs at every dip in the road warned of floods in adverse weather. The highway, dry now, showed no sign of the evening storm. I decided to trust that the storm had remained farther north and west. We'd ridden far enough from the evils of Page and the hell of Klethla Valley that nothing more could befall us.

Except I remembered that sheep grazed this land, maybe cattle too, and that a pickup might emerge from any unseen side road. Still, I twisted the throttle open and rode to the edge of what the headlight let me see of the road. The bike carried all the weight over its center now and responded as I willed it. The body behind me, wrapped around my waist, had to move as an extension of my own carcass, leaning as I leaned into turns.

The road dipped abruptly into an arroyo where a trickle of water crossed the bottom of the roadway, a warning that another dip might also hold water, perhaps more than a trickle. I eased off the throttle a fraction when we dipped into the next arroyo, but the bottom was dry, so I forgot about floods again until we passed the next yellow sign.

Then the lights of a vehicle came up from behind so fast that it scared me. Only a patrol car could move as fast as this bike. I released the throttle to cut speed drastically, not wanting to touch the brake, so my brake lights didn't report to a patrolman that I was going too fast. As I cleared one rise and started down, the headlights caught up and a ghostly white truck passed soundlessly, veering into me. I swerved, braked hard, and at the bottom of the wash, I hit both the soft shoulder and water, hating the sound of metal grating on pavement as the bike went down.

I hit the engine cut-off switch and glanced up to see the taillights and crushed right fender of a white Dodge pickup as it sped away.

"You OK?" I called to Eliot.

Gasoline reeked on the desert air. Because of the water, it was a wrestling match, getting that bike off me. Eliot, thrown into the water beyond the road, moved but didn't rise.

I called again. "You OK?"

Pain shot like fire up my knee when I stood on it. Groaning, but ignoring the pain, I went to check Eliot where she struggled to sit up in the water.

"I'm fine," she said.

The water I waded through flooded over my ankles, rising to my boot tops. I put an arm around her to help her up.

"I'm fine," she repeated. "Is the bike all right?"

When Pete joined us, Eliot and I were just done struggling to get the bike up. There was water, but hardly any sand in the clutch and brake levers. The brake lever acted right when I pulled on it. But the clutch cable was broken. I flipped on the engine switch and pressed the ignition. The engine coughed and shuddered, but then it caught.

"Help me push it to the top of the hill," I called to Pete. "If I coast to start out, I can shift without a clutch as far as Tuba City."

"I'll help you push," Eliot said. She had the bike half out of my hands and on its way up the rise before I registered what she said. It hurt like hell walking to keep up with her.

"You're sure you're OK?" I asked her again.

"I hit my shoulder pretty hard," she said, "but the sand took a lot of the impact. I bruised my thigh."

We pushed without speaking for a moment. Then Eliot said, "Are you all right?"

"I'm fine."

"Too bad about the bike. It sounded bad when it went down."

Pete rode up the hill slowly and met us at the top.

"Can you take Eliot?" I asked. "Are you OK?"

"Yes," Pete said. "Those lights over there must be the city. We can't be more than fifteen miles away."

Pete was only sort of OK. Eliot pointed to the back of his bike and took command as the rider, making him the passenger.

To save my right knee more grief, I cautiously used only the hand brake. Worried that shifting without the clutch would tear hell out of the bike, I managed minimal gear changes. Bike and man limped into Tuba City.

Looking for a place to rest.

■ ■ ■

A brief cruise through didn't reveal the motel of our dreams. We pulled into a quick-stop market and Eliot went to ask directions. She came back to repeat the convoluted instructions the store clerk had provided. A small horde of children playing in the back of a Ford pickup repeated the directions, with embellishments, so that their din made the information uncertain. I quelled my paranoia that we'd be misled once again.

The motel, overpriced and poorly lit, hardly welcomed travelers. The woman at the desk seemed hostile, though it wasn't even midnight. She had only one room left, with one double bed.

Outside, the BMW had disappeared. Eliot stood near my bike, removing our gear in slow motion.

"Where's Pete?" I asked.

"He went to find food. He said if he gets off the bike now, he'll never get back on again."

"The clerk inside thinks the Burgermeister across the street is open." I joined her to finish unpacking the bike. "Nothing else."

"That's where Pete went," she said.

Standing beside her, I felt her body quaking violently.

"Are you sure you're OK?" I asked, guessing that she'd been injured worse than she admitted.

"No. I'm cold. I'm wet and I hurt." She headed for the stairs.

At my insistence, she carried only the tank bag, and I carried the rest of the gear, limping up the stairs. The room had about twenty-five light switches, making it a chore to find the correct too-bright light needed to unpack bags.

"Wish I could wash the bike tonight," Pete said as he followed us into the room, dropping his tank bag onto the carpet.

Eliot stared at Pete, maybe too tired to answer. Then she disappeared into the bathroom. The shower thundered in the metal stall.

"The burger store across the street is closed," Pete said. "There's only candy for dinner."

"I'm too tired to chew," I said, stripping off my torn leathers and wet jeans. The flesh was cut along one side my knee. The swollen bruise was turning black.

"Oh geezus," Pete said. "I'll fetch ice from the machine."

He rigged up an ice pack with a towel and the trash bag from the room trashcan, then switched on cable news, flipped open his laptop, and ate a candy bar while he transferred files to Tadeusz. After fifteen minutes of ice on my knee and the blanket pulled over my head, I determined that life might be worth living. Flashes of that crash still played across my eyelids and echoed in my ears. It'd be days before I stopped flinching, thinking of the pavement and water coming up fast. Mercifully, Pete did not begin a mild inquiry about the accident until Eliot emerged from the shower.

"I never could read that sucker's license plate," I said. "Did you? Not that it'd do any good to report him. The local police probably could care less."

"Who?" Pete asked, surprised.

"Those guys in the Dodge who ran me off the road."

Pete frowned.

"Pete was too far behind. He didn't see us down in the arroyo," Eliot said. She braided her wet hair, tying it into a tight, severe tail. Above the edge of her t-shirt, her shoulder showed a rough red mark, glowing from the heat of the shower.

"Did they harass you, Pete? When they passed you?" I asked. "I don't know why they picked on us. It scared me when I saw how fast they came up on me. I thought it was a cop. I can't believe that truck could go as fast as my bike."

"What are you talking about?" Pete asked. "No one passed me on the road after we got to the highway."

"The same jokers who sent us all over hell out in the desert. They ran me off the road." I glanced at Eliot, who nodded. She opened the first aid kit from the tank bag, passing me a packet of painkiller tablets before swallowing two pills herself.

"It was weird how silent that truck was," she said. "I didn't hear it coming at all."

"You hit the water because you were going too fast," Pete said. "I worried every time you dipped down into a flash-flood zone."

"Sean was going too fast," Eliot said. "But they did run us off the road."

Pete choked on an M&M in disbelief. "C'mon! You call me paranoid. There wasn't anyone but us on that highway."

"Maybe it was a ghost-truck," I said.

"You're delusional." Pete snorted in disgust.

He steamed into the shower and stayed there as long as Eliot had, leaving me to watch the news with her, neither of us saying much at all. But she sat beside me on the bed, asking if the TV sound was too loud and could I see OK. And when I asked, she showed me the road-rash on her shoulder and said she appreciated my concern but didn't need to share my ice pack. When Pete came out of the shower, he rolled out his sleeping bag on the floor and burrowed into it without another word to either of us.

I hobbled in to take a shower, propped myself on the metal wall, and let the water dribble over me, then dried off with the last hand towel, all my roommates had left me. Brushing my teeth demanded as much effort as riding the bike. No weariness had ever before ground my bones against each other at the joints. Yet fatigue beat out the pain.

In the room, the lights were all off. Eliot lay on the far edge of the bed, curled in a ball against the wall. I tried to lie down and tie the ice pack to my knee without disturbing her, then tried to make my mind slow down and sleep. It'd be a relief not to be conscious for a while. But my eyes stayed open, finding shapes in the shadows cast from the streetlamp. I listened to her breathe. She thrashed and sighed, but not the same way she'd sighed that night in Cedar City.

"Maybe there aren't spirits," I whispered. "Maybe I'm supposed to learn that you can't control fate."

She didn't answer, but she rolled toward me for the first time since the previous morning. She put her hand on my arm, lightly, and left it there the whole night long. Bruised, I couldn't move closer to feel the warmth of more than just the tips of her fingers.

The Desert Crucible Episode VI
White Thunder

[Tadeusz: Sean wants to camp in the godforsaken desert tonight, so this is all you get for now. It's real desert with hogans and shit, but cut all of the Rez stuff—it belongs in someone else's story, not ours. Add the clips of Satan's Mills in Page. Sean wants to use more of his crap poetry, where you do the voice over. I have doubts, but he needs risks. Right now I blame all the world's shit on Milo. And if Jason doesn't call to help you, I'm going to kick his skinny ass all the way back to Wallingford. If we ever see Seattle again. —Pete]

Whether you call me Zeus or Thor, I am everywhere that people have named me. As a name for their fear.

For giving fire to Men.
For their wishes to receive good fortune.
For carrying their dead to eternity.

The only knowledge that people share: all are struck silent by my touch, by my hammer and thunder.

You do not want to know me up close. I'm not a bird. Birds fear me. They hide in the creosote bush, tuck themselves into the leaves and branches of the nettle-leaf hackberry tree.

I cleanse the phoenix and give it energy to rise from its ashes.

I cleanse the arroyo and prepare the seeds for spring.

∞

20.
Oak Creek Canyon

The road is never the same. Never.
— Charles M. Barker

ELIOT
Friday A.M.

THE CLATTERING VOICE WOULDN'T QUIT lecturing. Eliot just wanted to sleep, but she prepared to stand and face up to fate: it was her job to make the world right, reassemble the pieces.

The nattering voice proved to be just the damnable emphysemic air conditioner, wheezing in chorus with Pete's asthmatic snoring. Eliot ached from lying in a single cramped position. The air conditioner sucked the air from her lungs and hurt her ears, singing its repetitive song in F-sharp. Wedged against the wall in the way she was, extricating herself from the bed was a chore. As she wiggled down to the foot of the bed, her right shoulder reminded her why she'd slept in only one position.

Road pain. When she stood up, muscles throbbed in her right thigh, but not as badly as in her shoulder. At least she could move. Finding her least-dirty jeans and an undershirt, all that remained of wearable clothing after a week on the road, she dressed gingerly. Then she stretched to test whether the muscles might feel better with movement. Maybe in a day or so.

Some sixth sense told her that he was awake. Maybe not watching her, but listening. Pete's snoring had abated, which meant that he, too, would wake soon. They'd grind back into gear, and she'd have to go back to the work of making the world right. She opened the door to leave.

"See you at breakfast," Sean said.

It hurt too much to shrug, so she didn't answer.

In the café at the trading post across from the motel, an emasculated orchestral version of a Nirvana song played over the loudspeaker for the entertainment of two waitresses and six other breakfasters. Eliot bought the *Arizona Daily Sun* and claimed a table with a view of the highway, far away from any other diners. After the waitress took her order, Eliot called Roslyn.

"Is Cora better?" she asked, after replying "fine" to Roz's question about Eliot's well-being. "Have you talked to Destiny?"

"She and Cora are both in steady state," Roz said. "When will you be home?"

Eliot made new calculations, which she'd avoided during the previous day's bad-dream events. "I can fly back tomorrow. I'm stuck in the middle of nowhere right now."

"We should hear news this afternoon or Monday about your petition for temporary guardianship."

"Oh Roz! Thank you!"

"Pete's attorney did the real work. And it's not certain yet."

"Still, thank you, thank you. And I think my real estate agent found housing for us yesterday afternoon."

"Jennifer?"

"Yes. She has a three-bedroom rental lined up. Close to downtown. It'll work until I figure out the next part."

"Bless you, Eliot. I'll see Destiny at the hospital later today. I have to stop by school to pick up her homework and drop off her finished papers. She tried to call you last night."

"My cell died. I'll text Destiny. I don't know how much opportunity I'll have for phone calls until tonight."

Clicking off the call, Eliot held her breath for a minute. The Friday before, she'd started this trip to secure one goal, endured bad luck, traveled through hell, lost her original goal. And maybe a lot more. But now, at least one thing she wanted was coming her way.

By the time her Navajo taco appeared and she'd begged cream for her coffee and unfolded the newspaper to read, the other two riders limped in to join her. She persisted in studying the editorial page—a review of the successes and failures of fire prevention over the long, dry summer season—still not wanting to enter into conversation. The volume of the music had risen, making it difficult to hear what people might be saying to each other over a 100-Strings-type version of "Soul Meets Body." But some of the conversation came through.

"Yes, I have an extra cable," Pete said to Sean. "It'd be stupid to ride out in the middle of nowhere without parts."

She repressed two impulses. She did not say, "It was stupid to ride out in the middle of nowhere, with or without parts." And she did not volunteer to replace the cable. Pete could help. She studied the newspaper, learning about the feats of people she'd never met, never would meet. She ate quickly enough that she finished before Pete made it halfway through his strawberry waffles.

"I'm going across the street to do some laundry," she said. "When you're ready to take off, don't forget me."

In the motel room, clothes and bike junk were scattered all over. Normally, she'd add others' things to her load, but she took only her own clothes and left the rest. There had to be some other way to be friends, she thought, besides performing free services.

That's the problem she'd lain awake pondering, and then woke up to find still beside her: how to be close without being smothered? She dodged between cars crossing the street to the Laundromat, then cruised the double row of washers seeking an empty one. After waiting five minutes for a machine, Eliot discovered she didn't have the right change. And no one had change to trade her dollar bill for quarters.

She walked across the gravel lot to the Burgermeister, which already bustled with a brisk business in breakfast burgers. A sign by the cash register said, "No change without purchase," so she was stuck with a strawberry shake in order to get clean jeans and underwear. Back at the laundry, she plugged in quarters, then stared out the window, sucking on the stupid milkshake.

At the gas station behind the trading post, a small Day-Glo sign was taped to a 675 Triumph street bike. Modest, but red.

As soon as she moved her jeans to the dryer, Eliot cut across the haphazard highway traffic, then slowed to saunter around the bike, the dregs of her milkshake still in hand. Someone had dropped the bike at least once, maybe high-siding it when braking on a turn: the right side was scratched and dinged. The black Rustoleum painted over the damage marred the aesthetics of the bike, but there was no rust. Sitting by the highway, the bike had acquired a substantial film of road-grime.

The sign taped to the handlebars read, "$9000 OBO."

• • •

"You like motorcycles? You like this one?" the man at the service station asked. The question, voiced as a sales pitch, was an undisguised come-on, though he didn't leer outright. The tag on his shirt pocket said he was called Bob, but surely middle-aged Bob didn't own this bike. Everything about how he walked told her that riding was unfamiliar to him. He had no clue about the freedom that rested on its center stand in front of her.

"I'm used to a larger bike," she said.

"A strong, healthy girl like you can sit on the back of a big Harley, sure," he grinned. He wasn't taking her seriously, only flirting, which she ignored. "But this bike is for going fast."

Only seven hundred miles on the odometer.

"What's wrong with it?" she asked, noisily slurping up the last of her milkshake.

A Cadillac Escalade pulled up to the service island just then, ringing the bell and demanding Bob's attention. While he pumped gas and washed windows, she checked the bike's oil and battery, and pulled on the levers to check that everything worked right. When Bob returned, she was standing astride the bike to feel the suspension and to check whether the rider's position suited her.

"There's nothing wrong. It's just scratched a little," Bob said. "My son-in-law got it, but then he joined the army. Now he writes how he's got another woman and won't be coming back here." He shrugged. "I'm selling it so my girl can get some money."

As the guy went on to give other reasons for the price, she examined the bike, not wanting to signal what that For-Sale sign did to her pulse rate.

"People always want new bikes," he said. "You can't get parts here, so people only buy Kawasakis from the local dealer."

She lost track of what he said about how he didn't want it sitting around on his lot any more, but people here don't have that kind of money. How much of what he said was real, she couldn't tell; he prolonged the conversation just to flirt with her, which only wasted her time.

"I want to ride it," she said. "How long did it sit here? Did you leave gas in it so the carburetor's screwed up?"

He frowned. "I don't have time to take you for a ride, sweetheart. I'm the only one here, and I got to work."

"I want to take myself for a ride," she insisted. "Here, you can hold onto my driver's license. I have a motorcycle endorsement. I'm staying at that motel, so you know where to find me."

"What if you wreck it?" His voice sounded strained. It took a bit of an effort for him to pass from flirtation to seeing this as business.

"I guess if I break it, I buy it. I'll be back."

She finally coaxed the key from him. The engine started as soon as she touched the ignition switch, and she took off down the highway out of town, forgoing a helmet. The handlebars pulled her forward, stretching her sore shoulder pleasantly. Her foot pressed the brake pedal without hurting her stone-bruised thigh.

Turning left on Highway 264, she rode out past Moenkopi, the Hopi village at the edge of what used to be the Navajo-Hopi joint use area. Twisting the throttle open to see what the bike could do, she found a live, healthy machine. It didn't scream as she wound out the engine, and it didn't roar like Sean's bike, but it took corners as though it hungered after them. In fact, she'd have to exercise discipline to keep its speed down, because it wanted to go fast. When she wheeled it around after a few miles to bring it back to town, two pickups in front of her on the highway needed passing. When she dropped speed and shifted down, then opened it up to pass, the pull of acceleration thrilled her as the bike passed five thousand RPM.

Her rearview mirror showed only empty road; both trucks had already disappeared.

Back at the station, Bob busily tended to a several customers and hardly nodded to acknowledge her return. Her heart beat hard. She clenched the handgrips to keep from shaking. To calm herself, she skipped across the highway again to remove her clothes from the dryer, colliding with a young Navajo woman in blue jeans waiting to use Eliot's machine. Back at the station, jeans and underwear jammed in her shoulder pack, she feigned a casual, disinterested posture, not even glancing toward the bike while she waited for Bob. When she got his full attention again, she feared that the guy might smell her eagerness.

"I'll give you seven thousand fifty for it," she said, "if you'll take my bank card," hoping she sounded like a hard bargainer.

He shook his head. "It's a good bike. I can wait for my price. Besides, I lose three percent on the bank fee if I take your card."

"If it's your son-in-law's, how can you sell it?" She veered away from the bargain, suddenly suspicious. "Do you really have the papers?"

"Yeah, sure," he said quickly. "He didn't have no credit, so I signed for him. The papers got my name on them. I need at least eight thousand."

"OK," she said. "But give me a tank of gas and let me change the oil. You let it sit out here too long. It's not good for a bike."

More cars pulled into the station, ringing the bell cord at the service island. Before he ran to offer service, Bob took her offered credit card automatically.

"Where can I wash it?" she called to him.

"There's a hose behind the station. Use the soapy water I wash windshields with."

He called in to verify her card; the deal was closed. She owned her own freedom. She finished the oil change quickly, thanking Bob while ignoring that he watched her backside the whole time she worked in the service bay.

When she returned to the motel, the other two bikes sat in the parking lot, the Ninja's cable repaired and most of the luggage already fastened to the bikes. Upstairs, her companions discussed the route for the day: skirt Flagstaff, then down Oak Creek Canyon to the ranch outside Sedona.

"The question is whether Eliot has agency in this." Pete spoke the first words she heard as she came in the room.

"I'm always a free agent," she said.

"We're talking political theory," Pete said. "It's about a person's capacity for individualized choice and action."

He had that expression—one's brother knows ahead of time that he'll get smacked for what he's about to say. She wouldn't rise to his bait.

"You're paying me," she said. "My agency begins with my choice to be employed, and then how I comport myself during employment. At each point, I make choices to form my world the way I want. Isn't that agency?"

"You sure you want to give up on Navajo National Monument?" Pete asked Sean, changing the subject.

"I chased enough spirits yesterday to last me awhile," Sean said. She hadn't noticed at breakfast, but the right side of his face looked as if he'd been in a fight. Though not bruised so badly that anyone need feel sorry for him.

She helped carry the rest of the luggage downstairs before saying, "I have to take my tank bag back, Sean."

"Huh? Why?"

Pete figured it out first, smiling. "Goddamn, Eliot."

Sean grinned as he handed her the tank bag. "It's perfect. Exactly what you'd do."

He congratulated her, while Pete asked what she paid and commented on its suitability for the road ahead, but she was surprised by how much she appreciated Sean's good wishes. Caught off guard, she let him hug her, and found it too easy to return his quick, friendly kiss. The bruises and road-rash made it hard for either of them to unbend or press for more. But standing beside her own bike again, the resolution to all dilemmas didn't seem so impossible, since she was free now to ride however she pleased. Like receiving a benediction.

■ ■ ■

After two hours on the road, the new bike had become a familiar extension of her body. The shift from passivity to action meant a shift in how she experienced the landscape. The earth came alive, birds flew everywhere overhead, and small desert critters scampered along the roadside. Until that morning's ride, the entire two thousand miles of the trip had seemed like a waste, but she could see the horizon now, see where the highway led.

Blacktop rolled by, but it wasn't until after Flagstaff, where the road started winding down into Oak Creek Canyon, that Eliot remembered in her bones how good living on earth is. The bike, with its lower center of gravity, asked her to ride it in ways her old bike never had. While her BMW rusted in a wrecking yard in central Nevada, she gave her heart away to another love. Here in Arizona, she crouched low over the Triumph and leaned into the turns, getting more pleasure than she usually believed she had a right to.

And Pete, as always, liked the ride down Oak Creek Canyon enough that he wheeled around just before Sedona to take the whole ride over again. Eliot swung around to follow him. The other bike, its rider still bruised and hurting too much from their misadventures, rested near the bridge outside of Sedona while Pete and Eliot indulged their old belief that any ride worth taking was worth taking twice. Rejoining Sean, they loafed in the cool along the edge of the river and ate a late lunch, talking about nothing much at all.

The late afternoon became too hot as they entered Sedona. The Saturday tour buses disgorged tourists and shoppers who swarmed into the roadway without regard to crosswalks or common sense. The masses were in search of craft vendors, curios, and photo opportunities. The riders dodged the multitudes and headed for the road out of town that led to the ranch.

Heat shimmered above the pavement while Eliot thought about remodeling her shop, making it ready to inhabit a new course of life. Creosote bushes and ephedra replaced sage in the undergrowth. Scrubby oaks and jojoba lined arroyos, growing wherever enough water seeped down to nourish their roots.

At first, she welcomed the sun's heat, but as they got closer to home, the air became thicker. She didn't want to complain after the long days in the bitter cold, but the farther they dropped in elevation, the more life seemed to be baked out of the air, except when the road dipped into a cool pocket along a north-facing embankment that never cooked in the sun.

For most stretches of the road, the weight of the atmosphere bore down oppressively. The air inside her helmet turned to jelly. Her bra and t-shirt clung, sticking to her sweat. She'd forgotten how she hated the heat. She'd ridden across the rain-infested western

U.S. just to broil her brains and sweat in heat and dust. Still, the bike felt good, pushing down the highway.

. . .

At the turnoff to the dusty road that led under the power lines to the ranch, Eliot parked near where Pete had stopped. She wanted to keep riding, although her hands were numb and her wrists sore from the day's ride. But she sat quietly while Pete psyched himself up, waiting for Sean to join them before heading together down that road to the ranch. Sean had been a far slower rider all day. Pete fiddled with his remote wireless to upload Eliot's memory cards with the still shots from that day's ride. She took carefully framed shots of the ranch, using her best camera. When her phone rang, it was Karl, Pete's attorney.

"I have good news," he said, without bothering to say hello.

Eliot listened with what she thought was amazing calm, given that her chest was ready to break open with sunbaked joy.

"You've got ninety days," Karl said. He listed the rules and requirements that she had to meet before the next review. Destiny was under her guardianship, as soon as she appeared in Seattle to sign the papers.

"Thank you," she said. "It's perfect. You've done well."

"Anything else I can do?" Karl asked.

"Yes, pull that copyright suit that Pete asked for."

The line was silent. Finally: "I don't advise that. You have such a strong case, Eliot."

"Pete wasn't aware of prior oral commitments."

"OK, if that's what you want."

"Please, Karl. End it today if you can."

Pete listened, though the last part was likely all he understood. He stared at her, as stern as someone's little brother can be.

"What are you going to say to Dante?" Eliot asked, ignoring his stare. "Have you decided?"

"I've rehearsed it many times over the last few days. I shall be as eloquent as the goddamn wind." Pete sighed. "No, I don't know what the hell I'm going to say."

Eliot cleared her throat, but didn't respond. The sound of Sean's bike echoed from up the highway.

"Fight for what you want," Pete said. "Don't just settle for less than the whole enchilada."

"That's what you're telling yourself about Dante?"

"No. It's my advice to the lovelorn. Demand what you want."

"There's no use fighting battles that everyone wants you to lose," she said. "I have a life. I'm going home to live it."

"You're settling for less than you want or deserve," Pete said.

"BS. I do not lead a diminished life. I have everything I need, and most of what I want. That beats about ninety-eight percent of the world's population, from what I can tell."

Sean roared up the road, gliding to rest beside where Pete and Eliot waited.

"What the hell," Pete said. "Let's go home."

He switched on his bike's engine and rode slowly down the twisty driveway to the bottom of the canyon. Sean followed immediately, but Eliot sat at the top for a moment, shooting pictures and listening to the sounds fade in the arroyo, what you hear as a bike goes away from you, leaving you alone.

She followed when the other two bikes thundered over the wooden bridge. She'd ridden down that road on other bikes so many times that she could do it blind. Every bump and rise on the road was the same as years before. The bridge over the arroyo, though, was far worse for the wear. They parked at the end of the driveway, which was deserted save for one oversized 4WD truck.

She glanced around what had once been home. No sign that anyone was now in residence.

"Dante, your prodigals are here!" Pete called from the porch. "We rode through hell to get here!"

A crash echoed inside the house, followed by the distinctive sound of a pump-action shotgun.

"I warned you bastards to keep away!" Dante's voice screeched from the shaded interior.

"You damn asshole!" Pete shouted. "It's me, Pete! Your all-time favorite bastard."

He banged open the front door and stomped inside. Eliot pulled off her helmet and shook out her sweat-damp hair, viewing what had once been home.

Ten years is a fraction of a second in the life of the mountains. The hillsides hadn't changed at all, but every building was transformed. The greenhouse had crumbled. An adobe tool shed slumped, as sad and downfallen as ancient pueblo ruins. Several outbuildings had been abandoned, as if no one tended any chores since she'd loaded her truck and driven away. Her old cabin lacked a window and most of its roof. The garden had been abandoned, too, except for a few discouraged blue-corn stalks. The gravity-fed irrigation system had collapsed, but before it did, someone had let the water run too long, provoking a landslide at one end of the garden. The whole landscape was dried to the bone. No trace of water ran in the creek at the bottom of the canyon. The dust-rimed oak trees bent their heads, dispirited in the heat.

Sean abandoned his bike and banged open the screen door behind Pete. There was no reason to dally in the tumbled-down ruins in order to allow Pete a private greeting.

21.
Dante's Circle

SEAN
Friday Night

THE HOUSE WAS IN MAGNIFICENT disarray: suitcases and trunks stacked near the door as if ready for transport; artifacts scattered beside packing boxes or cast in a pile by black plastic trash bags or abandoned midway between piles; all awaiting decisive action. No artwork or desert-gleaned treasures remained on walls and window ledges, just sun-faded shapes marking their past lives.

My vision, through the year's planning and this ride across hell, was that once again Dante Gawain ambled out onto his porch, meticulous, tanned in the desert sun, delicately thin-boned with a dancer's grace, paint brush in hand, greeting us as crickets sang in canyon. We'd experience one more time the indomitable creative force of the man who brought us together, taught us how to see the world and how make it new.

We found Dante and Pete in the kitchen. Pete hugged Dante in greeting, a European style embrace, the shotgun now in Pete's hand. Dante stepped back. Tears brimmed over the red-rimmed edges of his eyes. Pete took the shotgun out to the back porch and expelled all the shells.

When Dante glanced over to greet us, the white-hot sun through the window cast his shadow over us. A diminished shadow, scarecrow-thin rather than willowy. His long hair, premature-grey for a quarter century, was now white, lank, lusterless. He pushed locks behind his ears as he squinted to see who had entered; the carved bones and ridges of his skull stood out, framing watery blue eyes. A long red mark streaked Dante's cheek; not the rough road-rash like I had from rubbing across pavement, but a stinging red mark as if he'd been smacked with a bare hand.

"Come in, kids. Welcome to the mad house."

"Where is everyone?" Pete said. "Why are you here alone?"

"Are you thirsty?" Dante asked. "I've got beer and some sodas. Bottled water."

"I'll get it," Pete said.

He fetched beers for all four of us and poured Dante's into a glass. Then he made Dante sit at the kitchen table, which was piled with china and tableware waiting for a packing crate. Eliot sipped at her drink. I gulped mine, greedy in this heat and dust for any liquid, dehydrated from that day's ride, my lips already chapped from desert air. Then I fetched power cables from the bikes, since Pete and I had been without charged phones for a few hours.

When I came back, Dante was fiddling with the jumble on the table, wrapping a cup and trying to fit it into a small box. And still not answering Pete's questions.

"Damn it, Dante, why are you—"

"Oh no, Peter! I broke it."

Shards of blue china nestled in folds of cotton wool inside the little box. I made out the wing and eyes of a bird figure; the rest were unidentifiable pieces.

"That Dresden cup was your mother's favorite thing," Dante said. "It was her grandmother's. She had a pair of them, but I can't find the other one."

"I have it," Eliot said. "I can give it to you to replace this."

"No, that wouldn't be right," Dante said. "I have no excuse except clumsiness for ruining this one. Perhaps someday you'll let me paint the whole one."

Pete took the cup's box from Dante's hands, which seemed to lift a spiritual weight off my old master.

"Sean, what happened to your face?" Dante asked. "You look like Peter that time we had to scrub his face with a brush when he crashed in the gravel."

"Why are you here alone?" Pete asked again, not leaving space for me to answer. The two guys were only interested in each other.

"The well's dry. The cistern's empty. When those fool friends of yours showed up with cameras—"

"They aren't my friends. The opposite," Pete said.

Dante chewed on this thought, his boney jaw grinding. He nodded. "Just as well then. I sent everyone away last month. We haven't had rain since May."

"Do you have to truck in water?" Eliot stared out the window at empty water jugs stacked haphazardly on the back porch.

"Yeah. But I don't want the bother." Dante sipped his drink in a miserly way, only touching its contents to wet his lips. "The beggars have been driving me mad all summer. There's so much I want to paint, but some fool wants this or needs that from me. Claudia cranky all the time. The gods sent this drought so I could get time alone." He set his glass down. "Except for you kids—I'm glad to see you. You can take care of yourselves, thank God.

"Where's Claudia?" Pete asked. "She's not going to Europe with you? What was that message about water and horses?"

"She changed her plans." Dante absent-mindedly rubbed the red mark on his cheek.

"What's this?" Pete took Dante's hand. A deep cut ran from the tip of Dante's ring finger to his wrist. Most of the blood had been wiped away, but clotted beads of dried blood knitted the edges of the gash together.

"I cut myself. I haven't had time to fix it."

"Dante!" Pete said, exasperated. "It'll get infected. You'll end up crippled, painting with a brush held in your teeth."

Pete grabbed a clean cloth from the mound of unpacked kitchen goods and flipped on the faucet to wet it, but the pipes only moaned and shuddered in protest.

"There's no running water," Dante said.

Pete went out to fetch the first-aid kit from his bike. Eliot searched for a jug of water for washing and tried to make small talk while Pete was gone, but Dante didn't have much to say.

I chose a soda from the refrigerator after I finished the beer, offering one to Eliot. As I set it on the table, the bottle nudged a card, the paper too brilliant-white amid all this detritus. Lifting it, I read Milo's name, with a blue-inked phone number and the message: "*If you change your mind.*"

"Thanks," Eliot said, accepting the bottle. "I'm so thirsty."

My hand lingered as she took the soda from me. Pete came in. I nodded to the door, silently asking her to leave with me.

"Not yet," she whispered.

Pete took fastidious care in cleaning the wound, pausing each time Dante winced from the antiseptic.

"Don't be such a baby," Pete said, at the tenth wincing. "You should ice this before I dress it. Your hand is swollen."

"There's no ice. Go ahead and put a bandage on."

"Holy crap, Dante! Do you know how to take care of yourself?"

"I've been lost in thought since I finally got the chance to spend time alone."

"Not to hassle you," Pete said, "but what happened with you and Claudia?"

"She decided she wanted children." Dante laughed mirthlessly. "I wasn't very nice about it. I said I already had the best possible child, so she'd have to find another inseminator."

Pete pulled to tighten the bandage.

Dante yelped, then took a breath. "I'd forgotten that I could be such a bastard. That's why she's coming after me about water for her horses."

"She's too young for you," Pete muttered. "What else is she taking, besides your land?"

"Nothing of your mother's," Dante said. "I'm standing here making sure of that."

While Pete finished dressing Dante's hand, the musty heat of the house drove me outside. The day's hot dust hung in the air, with no trace of breeze to disperse it. I went in search of whatever now passed for an outhouse, then settled for peeing on a tree.

As I was buttoning up, Eliot emerged from the house with an armful of food from the refrigerator. She set it on the verandah's dining table, and proceeded to compose sandwiches out of dry bread, cheese, and wilted lettuce.

"You're limping," she said. I couldn't tell if it was an observation or a criticism.

"Yeah, knee hurts like hell. And there's no ice here."

"Can you believe this place?" She slammed mayonnaise on bread with a vengeance.

"Dante was never a good manager," I said. "Without you."

"He hasn't even eaten today," she said. "Whoever Claudia is, she should go screw herself for leaving him alone like this. Along with everyone else who was staying here. He's obviously not well. And it isn't just Dante's usual bitchiness."

"If he and she disagreed—"

She scowled. "You don't leave a weak partner in hard times. You suck it up and do the right thing. He clearly needs a doctor."

"But you—" I started to say.

Her cell buzzed on the table. She glanced down, then picked it up and walked over to talk under a palo verde tree.

Dante's voice drifted out through the screen door.

"Peter, I should have returned your mother's things to you. She's on my mind constantly these days. We were so different, that was the real tragedy. Don't make that mistake, getting involved with a woman from a different universe." Dante's voice faded for a minute, then rose again. "Where there's no bridge that unites the two worlds."

• • •

I stretched out the last of the road kinks. The loose, aging boards creaked on the verandah with each movement. In spite of bruises from that bedeviled tumble off the bike, and in spite of a hard day's ride, I felt good. Though hungry. Waiting patiently, assuming one of the sandwiches would be mine, I sat on the porch swing to watch the last daylight fade. The swing's rusted chains and loose boards squeaked in the dusty evening, joining the rasp of cricket calls in the canyon.

A dust-filtered beam cast a Pre-Raphaelite halo around Eliot. I stared until my eyes watered, either from the dust or from seeing her harsh beauty illuminated in ways that I've never accurately caught in any drawing. Just as she glanced my way, clouds scudded across the horizon, eclipsing the last of the sunlight. In the moments we regarded each other, electricity filled the heavy, dissatisfied air, seeking the strength to coalesce into a storm.

"This isn't how I thought it'd be," I said. She glanced up, but didn't answer. "Dante taught me how to live as an artist. How to greet the creative spirit each day. To stay disciplined. Now, to see him so—"

"Diminished?" she said. "He's ten years older than when we saw him last. And he's ill."

"We have to talk," I said, my voice creaking like the ill-tended porch planks. "It's never good when you and I stop talking."

"What to say?"

Electricity stirred itself around us, trying to get from the ground back up to heaven. The rousing electricity had the hair on my arms standing on end. I shivered in spite of the heat.

"I understand why you were mad at me yesterday. I'm sorry I used your material. Stealing someone's art is the worst bloodless crime."

"But I'm not ticked off. Those photos were yours."

A lizard rested on the window ledge near where I sat, craning its neck in search of moths and other dinner, the pounding of its heart pulsating at its throat and stirring the shadows when nothing else moved.

She said, "While we traveled, I snapped pictures. Lots were my own ideas. But the ones Pete has, you constructed the composition. You wanted them to paint from later. They were always yours. Created for you."

The ghost bodies of oak trees shivered in the late twilight, but hot, dead air still oppressed breathing and movement on the verandah.

"How can you not be pissed off? I'm no better than Dante, using you without even—"

"I'm only unhappy that you don't remember how we read each other's thoughts. Completed each other's stories and drawings."

"But I do remember. I want that again, Eliot."

"Yet you didn't remember we created those images together."

Doves cooed under the tamarisks, calling to each other to come in out of the electric-charged night. The canyon rocks seemed to call out in longing for thunder; the oak trees begged to be relieved of the torturous waiting for lightning to strike.

She said, "None of us got enough sleep last night, and we rode too far today. Let's eat some food. Call Dante and Pete."

While we munched sandwiches, Pete kept watching Dante. Finally, he set down the last dried crust and reached over to feel Dante's forehead.

"You have a fever."

"It's hot." Dante swiped away Pete's hand.

"You're hotter than that. You need a doctor. I'm taking you to urgent care."

"Foolish business, son. We'll sit on plastic chairs, cooling our heels all night."

Pete paused at that—"son"—then pushed ahead. "Get a book to read. Where's the key to your truck?"

Dante scrunched his nose in disgust. "I'm not riding in a closed vehicle, smelling you. When did you last bathe?"

"Last night. I probably beat you."

"It's your clothes then, Peter. You're filthy."

"So are you, old man. I'll change—if you haven't tossed out the clothes I left here."

Dante waved in the general direction of the bedrooms. "Didn't ever touch anything of yours."

"You go change, too. Do it now, Dante. We're leaving."

In two minutes, Pete returned in clean, if aged, jeans and t-shirt. "This isn't turning out as we planned," he said, understating the case. "Tell Tadeusz that the final episode of *Desert Crucible* doesn't include a triumphant tour of Dante's circle of art."

"Of course," I said. He didn't have to ask. "Give me the video you took above the canyon. I'll upload files for Tadeusz. He has older sketches I made. We're prepared to substitute art for reality."

"Don't share anything that shows how it is now," Pete said.

Eliot said, "Pete, either go with Dante to France or get him up north with us. He can't live here."

Pete sniffed as he nodded in agreement. "I'll stay and get him better situated. It's my turn this time, isn't it?"

"You did say you had reparations to make for family," she said. "Looks like you don't have to demand your birthright."

Pete said, "Looks like I'll spend the night reminiscing about our mother, whom I can't remember."

"I remember her as beautiful, but probably from pictures," Eliot said. "I remember her whispering stories in my ear at bed time."

"Inside just now," Pete mused, "Dante said our mother wasn't really insane, that it's not like people say."

"The misfortune," Eliot said, "is that most likely no one ever knew her."

. . .

Pete was searching a map on his phone to find Sedona urgent care when Dante reappeared, dressed now in the holiday clothes I remembered: a white linen shirt, now well-worn at the cuff edges, and linen trousers, a woven belt keeping them from sliding down his skinny hips.

They crossed to the parked 4WD truck. It struck me that there could be no doubt that Dante and Pete were father and son: the same slight build, the same wild blue yonder eyes. Pete slipped an arm around Dante's shoulder, as casual and guy-like as possible, but still: supporting Dante over the pot-holed driveway.

After they drove away I fetched my recharged phone and two more beers from the kitchen. There wasn't enough left in the cupboards and refrigerator to feed a single human through another day. Twisting off the top and handing a bottle to Eliot, I collapsed on the battered old sofa that had crowded the verandah for at least fifteen years, hearing it groan with my weight, though I don't weigh that much. I set my bottle on the plank floor and began texting instructions to Tadeusz. He sent a quick answer, unfazed by the change in plans for our Web post finale:

If things were different, they wouldn't be like they are.

While I was texting him back, promising that I was about to call Karl to confirm that Milo wasn't screwing over the Laconia team, my cell rang. It was Tadeusz.

"Dude, the deadline Milo gave the team was this Friday."

"It's still Friday." I looked at the date on my phone to be sure. "The deadline's twelve o'clock tonight."

"The deadline was for noon, not midnight. And London time, not where you are."

"It's—" I flipped back to reality from desert dreams. "It's, like, five o'clock Saturday morning there, right?"

"Yeah," Tadeusz said, "that's why so many people resigned. Remember when I told you yesterday that they'd wait until eleven o'clock? Milo kept blowing serious steam on people all morning."

When it was noon in London, I was lying sleepless beside Eliot in Tuba City, a melted icepack over my knee.

"I'll fix it," I said once more, less confident this time.

All I could do this late on Friday was to leave a message for Karl. I thumbed through my email and voicemail for the first time since lunch.

"Best I could do," Karl said in a voice mail stamped five o'clock Pacific time, "was to pull the plug. Your deal with Milo won't close on Monday. You and Milo are still married, and Laconia is still your child as much as his."

I started typing emails, one by one, to each team member: *"I'm still the boss. You still have a job on Monday."*

• • •

Eliot remained at the verandah table, sipping at her drink and gazing at the shadowy ghost-town wreckage of the ranch, which was lit only by the yellow light cast from the house.

I tugged at her hand to get her to join me on the sofa. "Come on. I'm too stiff to make love to you or even figure out how to seduce you. Let's be friends."

She didn't argue. She sat and rested against me. Far away, the thunder rumbled. The crickets, frightened, quit singing for their mates. For a moment, the only sound was the whoosh of doves in flight, echoing against the slickrock walls. Then the crickets clacked together again, sounding first nearby and then far away, calling from the bottom of the canyon.

I traced her hand where it rested on the filthy arm of that ragged sofa. "Soon I'll be in Seattle. Next door to you. Pete says you've never seen my work. I'd like to show it to you, to explain what—"

"Pete's wrong," she said, smiling with that goddess-like expression of mercy. Mercy for an idiot. "I've seen every creative act of yours that's public. In your Impious Aeneas work, I can see how you made each line, and which parts were done by other artists."

"But I haven't seen your work," I said. "I'm more than a fool. I was curious, but never asked."

The thunder rumbled again, perhaps twenty miles away. Sheet lightning flickered in the eastern sky.

"Let's just listen to the desert and worry another time," she said. "I'm too tired to talk."

My arm rested more heavily across her shoulder.

"It's good, having your arm around me again." She whispered in my ear. "I've known truly fine woodworkers, artists, metal smiths. Yet nothing compares with you. And whenever I consider seeking human warmth, I imagine your hands. Your arms." She leaned back against me. "Every possible lover comes up short."

With no damned thing to say, we sat in silence while lightning danced on the horizon. Her head became heavier on my shoulder, her breath rising and falling quietly.

She was asleep. Slowly, careful not to wake her, I wriggled away. In the house, I found a worn India-muslin cloth and covered her, then left her sleeping on the verandah. I rolled out my sleeping bag on the porch and tried to doze, but the night's heat and the lingering undischarged electrical storm kept me awake past midnight.

The thunder and wind should have aroused each other to break the tension, but the clouds occluding the stars were sterile: nothing broke the dry, electric heat in Dante's canyon.

■ ■ ■

In the night I got too hot in the sleeping bag and crawled out of my jeans and shirt, which were damp from the heat.

When the Inca doves and Bendire's thrashers set up their bird-din at dawn, I awoke, dehydrated and stiff. I stumbled painfully out of the sleeping bag and into the kitchen for water. The plumbing groaned and choked like death before I remembered there was no water in the well. I got a jar of water from the refrigerator and chugged it greedily, spilling it over myself. Out in the driveway, Eliot was packing her bike to leave.

I grabbed my jeans and ran out to stop her.

"Where are you going?"

"I have to leave today," she said.

"No way. Wait. We'll leave together." I stood in front of her bike, my jeans still unbuttoned, prepared to grovel.

"Sean, I'm needed at home. I'll catch a flight out of Flagstaff. Tell Pete to fetch my bike and ship it later."

She went to the verandah for her helmet. I was still standing in the potholed driveway barefoot, buttoning my pants. "Eliot, please."

Only the white-winged doves shut up to listen.

"Eliot, don't do like last time. Back then, just one of us could have said, 'Stay with me.' I'm begging now."

She was ready to ride. Her eyes were slate-grey and fiercely determined. I took a step back, but her bike was there. So I straddled her bike: she had to listen to me.

"I promise to make it all good," I said. "Stay with me."

Pete drove into the lot just then, alone, parking Dante's truck near where we stood in the dust. He emerged from the truck and stretched. He said, "They're keeping Dante for at least one more night. For observation."

Neither Eliot nor I answered, since we were locked in metaphysical battle. She was Kali on the verge of spontaneous combustion, and I wanted to surrender.

"Get off my bike." She spit each word.

"We're supposed to be together. Are you afraid?" I didn't say it right. I wanted mercy. She thought I wanted a fight.

"Are you calling me a coward?"

"Never. I—"

As if riding a bolt of celestial fire, she bounded onto my bike, jerked it to life, and screeched in a blur of gravel and dust across the lot, then launched the bike like a rocket where the road arched away to climb up out of the canyon. She leapt from the bike just before it flew off that rackety wooden bridge and tumbled down the rocks to the canyon's bottom.

A covey of doves, startled by the crash in the canyon, fluttered from among the boulders, curving up in a trajectory of fright, then arching down to settle in the creosote bushes in the lower canyon, white wing-patches flickering in the sunlight.

Eliot rolled free, then stood and walked away while that bike continued to career down among the boulders. Hearing the clanging of metal cracking against slickrock hurt my heart.

Pete scratched his nose, watching where the doves settled while the sound of the riderless broken bike echoed in the canyon.

"Whew!" I said, faking calm assurance. "Glad it was the bike, instead of me."

"Should we rebuild it?" Pete said. "Or sell it as parts and buy a better bike?"

"What?"

"Just a joke you wouldn't get," Pete said. "I told you not to leave the key in it."

"That bike was such a pain in the ass."

"Then this reduces the number of hassles in the world."

"We better make sure she's OK," I said.

"She got up and walked. Leave her be until she cools down."

We climbed down the arroyo to make sure that the broken bike wasn't leaking fluid into the creek bed. Then we sat on the verandah for a long time. Pete fetched a couple of beers from the refrigerator, since there was nothing else for breakfast. We listened for sounds through the trees.

Pete said, "Dante's things are packed already. I'm going to close the place up. I spent the night trying to convince him to come to Seattle. But I might end up leaving the country with him."

"How much of what we plotted for the last two thousand miles turned out as planned?" I asked.

"You won the Internet. You have a green-light meeting with HOPE on Monday. But that's not what you're asking, is it, *compadre*?"

"Suppose you got a second chance with the person you loved most in your life," I said. "What happens?"

Pete said, "I'm going for a second chance with the man I resented most of my life. I haven't got a clue what will happen."

"Is there a shortcut to avoid making the same mistakes?"

"Careful! Remember our last shortcut, following a map drawn by Coyote?"

As I tried to laugh, Pete's cell buzzed with a text message. All this way, through thousands of miles of deserted U.S. landscape, we were never more than a buzz away from our hellhounds. Over Pete's shoulder, I saw the screen splash "Unknown" as the sender's ID. The message had a Web link, which Pete clicked.

And we watched a night-vision video, showing us making fools of ourselves on a dirt road we never should have followed, somewhere in the general vicinity of Jackass Canyon. The long bare arm of a white-boned demiurge waved farewell at the end of the clip.

Pete clicked to play it again. A 404—File Not Found message appeared. "Milo-fucking-Speiser," he said. "Can't even hire people who are loyal to him." Then he started to laugh, like I hadn't heard for a couple of days.

"Forgive me for calling you paranoid."

"Worse for you, boss. Looks like you have to give up believing in desert-spirits and fate. At least we won the bet."

"Yeah, but he's not paying off." I summarized Karl's news.

"I always knew he'd weasel out," Pete said. "Though that's an insult to weasels. At least he can't make me work for him for the next year."

I wondered whether I'd be so lucky.

Heat already rose in waves from the ground as we scrutinized the arroyo, waiting for Eliot. We'd both ridden our memories and thoughts into the sand, and hadn't much to say. Just waiting for the next part of life to begin.

Pete said, "Remember that old thumper of yours, that Triumph? It's still sitting out in Eliot's old workshop."

"Does it work?"

"Likely it's seized up inside. You didn't drain any fluids, did you, when you parked it there?"

"I had other things on my mind. I was in a big hurry then."

"If you don't want it, I think I'll tinker with it while I'm here." Pete was quiet again for a while. "I'll take a truck of stuff to Seattle, wherever Dante decides to settle."

"Good. Eliot wants you to fetch her bike from the Flagstaff airport and ship it to her."

"What are you up to?"

"First, getting to the green-light meeting in L.A.," I said. "Guess I'll rent a car in Sedona. I beat my body enough for all the enlightenment I need this year. Time to get back to work."

"You and Eliot work anything out?" Pete asked.

"Not yet." I pointed to the arroyo where the bike had died. "But I'll do whatever she wants. As soon as I know what that is."

"Shoot, I was hoping she'd finally find her own true voice with you," Pete said. "And you and I'd finally be real brothers."

. . .

Pete, exhausted, went in search of a bedroom with air conditioning, promising me a ride into Sedona when he woke. I filtered rusty water from a jug and made coffee, then tried to wash up before stuffing my sleeping bag and preparing to leave.

I was tossing my gear into the back of Dante's truck when Eliot hiked up from the lower canyon, helmet dangling from her hand, jacket open in the morning heat, her t-shirt soaked with sweat. She went inside and came back with a bottle of water, and then leaned against the palo verde tree, watching me pack.

I wanted to say everything, all at once. "I made mistakes, Eliot. I thought you abandoned me. Back then, I assumed that you'd come with me, but I never actually asked you. And our friends persuaded you otherwise."

"Persuaded me?"

"Yes, but even with their interference, that ten years' of separation was my fault. I didn't ask for what I wanted."

"Sean, what would I have done in London?" She sipped at the water, letting it dribble down her sweat-soaked chin and neck.

"You could have joined my team and—"

"Be real. I need power tools. Room to roam. Room to be alone." More trickles, wetting the collar of her t-shirt. "Moving between here and Puget Sound is all the transplanting my roots can tolerate. How could I exist in London, just to be with you?"

I'd never considered her desertion as self-preservation. "But doesn't love conquer all?"

"No. It's obvious that I couldn't follow you," she said. "And it would have been wrong to beg you to stay with me."

"Stay here? In the U.S.?" Which I'd never considered once after that night Robert begged me to join him in London. There had been no desertion. The entire loss—ten years—it was all on me.

"My decision then was simple logic," she said. "I gave up my greatest desire so you could be a genius painter. And instead—" she jabbed a finger at me, "you're a cartoonist."

I muttered, "Mixed media animation artist."

"What?"

"What greatest desire? Yesterday you refused to marry me."

She squinted in the sun, the light too bright. The birds finished their morning quarrel in the arroyo, and for a moment, only the fading squawk of the piñon jays answered me.

"To laugh," she said. "To go to bed together. To make things every day. To be loyal in ways neither of us ever knew before." She shifted where she stood by the tree. The sun was encroaching on the morning shade. "None of which would be possible if I had followed you to London back then."

Seeing her head bent so abjectly, I stooped to begging. "I'm headed to Los Angeles for my Monday meeting. Please. I wish like hell that you'd come with me."

"I have to fly home now," she said. "I can't go with you."

"Then I'll see you in Seattle? As soon as I finish my business in L.A.? We have all the time in the world to rebuild our friendship."

She closed her eyes. "I can't make you part of my everyday life right now. I have to take care of Destiny."

"This is our destiny. I believe in it, heart and soul. We—"

"Destiny is a fifteen-year-old girl on Limberlost. With enormous talent and no one in the world to take care of her. I just became her guardian."

"Oh." I replayed all the phone calls I'd interrupted, wondering what cue I missed. "You never said anything."

"I avoid talking about what I most want. It keeps the universe from thwarting me," she said. "While we played in the desert, Destiny sat alone by her aged ill aunt. There's nothing ahead for her—just like me at that age—if I don't pay the universe back for the chances I've had. I need to leave today, right now, for her sake."

"I had no idea." My mind raced over what I knew of the fabric of her life, her work, her friendships. All I envisioned was the multiple canvases where I'd tried to sketch the goddess Artemis.

"If I don't leave now, I'll miss my flight." Her helmet in hand again, she left the shade to set her water bottle on the porch and walked to her bike. "Please understand that I can't live with myself if I let others down. When you're in Seattle, you can—"

"Sit on your doorstep and beg you to be my Artemis again."

"Artemis?" she scowled. "I'm not your goddess of the freaking wildland. I'm a goddamn person who spent a significant portion of my life being in love with you."

When her bike's electric ignition clicked, I imagined the ground trembling as her engine thundered to life.

"I didn't mean to wreck your bike," she called over the noise of the Triumph. "I didn't see that gaping pothole between the bridge and the road until it was too late. Tell Pete to get it fixed."

My phone buzzed as her bike rumbled over the bridge.

"Yes?"

"Mr. Wentworth?" A pleasant-sounding woman introduced herself as the assistant to the HOPE representative who had arranged the Monday meeting. "I'm asked to pass on praise from HOPE for your fine work on *The Desert Crucible*. You've certainly found an excited audience."

"Thank you."

"Also, we want you to know that Monday's meeting is being postponed."

"All right." I'm not happy. "What's the new date?"

"It's indefinite. HOPE would like to wait until your legal issues are resolved with Laconia and FAIL. We're sure you understand."

When we finished with the pleasantries, I clicked off and called Karl. His number's on speed dial.

"It's Saturday, Sean."

"Yes, Karl. And you're in your office. So escrow doesn't close on Monday? That's the price of keeping my team employed?"

"Worse. You have—"

"Not another estoppel? What the hell more can I estop?"

"Milo doubled-down on our breach of contract threat. He filed suit himself. For breaking an implied covenant of good faith and fair dealing through acts of bad faith."

"Fuck me."

"I believe," Karl drew it out, as if he enjoyed the moment, "that Milo Speiser intends just that. He's unhappy that the Laconia production team resigned. He's accused you of stealing them and so wants to be made whole."

I guess after you complete your spirit quest and find True Love, you just go back to everyday life. Otherwise, you'd just run forever. And now I didn't even have a bike.

The Desert Crucible Episode VII
Coyote

[Tadeusz: Overlay the drawings with the video from above the ranch. This is a wrap—no closeups at the ranch. The voice-over is Pete—age it to 70 years. If Jason doesn't call, just run a 60-cycle hum behind it. Or, hell, a Ducati. I'll see you as soon as I can get a flight to Seattle. —Sean]

You knew me from your earliest dreams.

When you stood where the air smells of mesquite fires in winter and dust in summer. Where the Sonoran desert gives way to junipers and oaks on the hillsides and yields to sycamores and tamarisks at the canyon bottoms. Where wind whistles in the fall, and heat crackles under the cliffs as spring turns to summer.

You stood on the wood-planked bridge over the dry gully, breathing the blue air of twilight beside the first lover you declared to be the mirror of your soul. The essence of life. A mortal sent from the gods. When life held bright, wild possibilities.

Your lover's flashing eyes return to you in dreams, to say what you always knew: only memory endures.

You think every day about what I taught you:
This is the way of Seeing that started the Renaissance. Here's the medium that binds paint to canvas. Use real lapis for blues. Choose Lead White to capture the reflection of light in your lover's eyes or foam on water.

Listen at twilight to what the world whispers to you through all that noise—your heartbeat, that jet overhead.

It's not relevant whether there were bodhisattvas. Or gods manifesting as men.

Or whether you can speak with the demiurges that live among the sacred rocks and springs.

You are always standing on that bridge at twilight. Just listen. Keep working.

∞

22.
Flying A

We have it in our power to begin the world over again.
—Thomas Paine

ELIOT
Twelfth Night

"DESTINY, FOR PETE'S SAKE, PUT on your safety glasses."

"Pete's in France, Eliot."

"Very funny. Use safety gear if you're going to be here. Otherwise, go to the library."

"They're so ugly."

"Not as ugly as construction debris sticking out of your eye."

"That might be a new look. No one at my school…"

Destiny explicated a lunatic fancy about taking over the Cyclops clique. But she put the glasses on.

"And gloves, Destiny. Get over here and help me with this."

We were installing the last framing for a new wall in my shop remodel, which had to be done before the drywallers came on Monday. Since it was a market-free Saturday—the first one following the Christmas season—Destiny begged to help me. Her help always includes much more conversation than I'm used to while working.

In late October, we all acknowledged that Cora needed more professional care than the amateur assistance Destiny and I tried to provide. We had good luck finding a place for her, near downtown. Destiny and I had been sharing a rented apartment that didn't suit either of us. Nix on the moss-green walls and loam-colored carpets. We required more than one tiny bath and a one-cupboard kitchen, plus a good deal more than a miniscule living room that accommodated no activity other than TV viewing, which neither of us was interested in. She and I both spend all our free time working in the shop. We needed to be living here, which spawned this remodel.

The project is driven by the best news of the year: Child Protective Services extended Destiny's situation with me for another ninety days, and is almost certain to approve permanent guardianship. Roz and Karl worked together to prove that I'm providing a stable routine and appropriate housing. That housing story will be even better by the end of this month when we have another bedroom, a second and better bath, and a real kitchen. I'd pushed the plans through the Village's building department. The subcontractors finished work on electrical and rough plumbing last Friday.

All of which I managed in the same way I proved to CPS that I have a reliable income, based on that *Desert Crucible* job.

That income was padded by the settlement Laconia tendered, which they'd sent before Karl could kill Pete's suit. One fat payout, plus residuals. Forever. I'd cashed the first check with too much glee, thinking of the pain Milo endured when he signed the blasted thing. It was paying for hardwood floors in the bedrooms and nicer bathrooms than any house I've ever lived in. It also paid for digging up the blacktop pavement that surrounds the shop, since the Village's architectural review board believes that commercial spaces used as private residences make the town seem tacky. *"Not in keeping with the Village design aesthetics."*

Though it hadn't bothered the Village council for the last eight years while I'd camped out alone in my father's Flying A station.

The rest of the money would cover Destiny's education. First, everyone agreed that she needed to transfer to the arts academy in Seattle. As much as I argued with the local high school for the right instruction and opportunity for Destiny, it's more than they can do.

Admission to the academy was a snap, since Destiny already has a portfolio deeper than the stack of drywall waiting to be tacked onto the studs in my shop. The barrier to overcome had been Destiny's resistance to catching an early-morning ferry into the city. Fortunately the only two kids on Limberlost with whom she has any affinity attend the academy. The ferry terminal is three blocks from my shop—closer even than the local high school. And the academy picks kids up and drops them off at the Seattle landing.

Destiny and I then agreed on the coat and boots that would make an inconvenient commute tolerable. She's thrifty: a guy's peacoat and plain leather boots, which she then tooled and painted to her personal taste. Classes start at the new school on Monday, and Destiny has been in high anxiety over the change, which affects the duration of attention she can allot to any task. For example, following a heaving sigh:

"So now I spend every day with those prancing prats."

"Only one person we met was gay," I said. "That woman in the junior sculpture class, the one you liked a lot. And gay slurs are not acceptable."

"I'm fine with gays. Maybe I'm gay. What's your point?"

"Words have meaning. If you don't know what 'prancing prat' means, then you shouldn't be using that phrase.

"Is this what my life has come to?" Destiny cried. "A morality lesson every five minutes?"

"Guess so. Sucks to be you."

We stopped talking about school. Instead, we talked:

— How closely to space the nails for the frame of the chase that would hide the air-exchange duct for the bathrooms.

— How not to shoot yourself with a nail gun. Also, remember no one can hear you talk over the air compressor.

— Whether the kitchen needed the recycled concrete counter that Destiny wanted, or the butcher block I preferred.

— How to preserve the Flying A mural on the shop's exterior, which the Village architectural review board wanted gone.

Destiny believes all things are possible. "I know we can move it. I saw a video once about how they moved the murals in medieval Spanish churches and preserved them in a museum."

"Catalunya," I said. She'd shown me the video weeks before. "It wasn't Spain then, wishes it weren't now."

"Whatever."

"Seriously." Living with a teenager will destroy my diction.

"Okay-ay." Destiny was concentrating, using the finger method I taught her to estimate nail spacing. "But I think that Catalooney method might work."

"Yeah? Even if you had a million-dollar grant and a bunch of art historians to move it, the sign is painted on brick. Not plaster."

She huffed. "I'm going to take a look. Maybe we remove the bricks by hand and reassemble them inside."

"Fine. You'll need to number every single freaking brick and make a scaled sketch."

Destiny was out the door, yelling back, "You betcha!"

I continued nailing the overhead frame, the task which was likely the root cause for Destiny's sudden need to examine the exterior mural. Destiny may be a bit taller than me, and beats me at manual dexterity, but she doesn't have the same major motor-muscle mass. And she hates doing anything overhead that requires physical strength.

A chilling, wet January wind blew through, rattling all the Visqueen plastic stapled over the kitchen wall-to-be, raising a cloud of construction dust. A whirlwind sent sawdust over my boots.

"Shut the damn door, girl!"

The front door clicked.

"Excuse me. Ms. Arden? Ms. Eliot Arden?"

Swinging the cord of the impact hammer behind me, I jumped from the ladder, sending up another cloud of dust—it was only the fourth rung, but that move always shuts up guys who harass me when I work on a crew. Very machisma.

"Yes?"

Pushing up my safety glasses, pulling off my dust mask, I faced a ghost from the future. In a Burberry raincoat, which no man in Seattle wears.

Robert Wentworth.

"I bought a sculpture of yours over Labor Day, Ms. Arden. I believe you've been storing it for me."

Robert's bassoon voice sounded like Sean's, but split-reedy, quavering like an often-played 78 RPM record. Looking at Robert was like gazing into Sean's own hazel eyes.

Coughing from the dust, I cleared my throat. "Certainly. We're storing it over here."

Under two layers of plastic tarps, buried behind the Saturday market barrows and shelves and the other large sculptures that never, ever sell at the Limberlost Saturday market.

Except for one, when Robert Wentworth bought the welded Motorhorse from Destiny.

• • •

Destiny slammed back through the front door. Robert was turning two hundred seventy degrees to study the metalwork hanging from nails on the upper shop walls, protected from the construction by sheer plastic painter drops.

"What laser cutter do you use?" he asked.

"We use hand tools," Destiny said, having answered this question at every Saturday market since the dawn of market time. "We're not Luddites. Some of our—Eliot's tools are electric, especially for woodwork. She's not that patient. But most metalwork is manual."

Robert held out his hand to Destiny. "Hello. We met before. I'm Robert Wentworth."

"I remember," she said, shaking his hand graciously. "You bought the Motorhorse. Ready for delivery?"

"It's been a whole season and more. I feel guilty about leaving my horse with you so long," he said.

"His upkeep has been easy." Destiny pointed to the plastic-wrapped pile in the center of the room. "He hardly eats anything. So we aren't adding any boarding fees."

"Generous," Robert said.

"Do you have a crew to haul it for you?" I asked. "If we'd known you were coming today, we'd have gotten it ready."

He glanced my way and smiled. "Obviously it will be an inconvenience to move it today. I'd best make an appointment. But I came to inquire about other work. I'm building a house, and my architect said you're the best resource for specialty metalwork and woodwork. Do you have time to discuss possibilities for the doors and wall screens?"

Even though cash isn't short this year, the idea of working for this man presented an unusual challenge. Yet what do we live for but to push ourselves in new ways?

"Of course." I pulled off my work gloves, unbuckled my tool belt, and dusted my clothes before approaching him to shake hands. "It's cleaner in the kitchen, which is my office until we finish here. Do you want to come in?"

Destiny was on her tiptoes with anticipation.

We had two chairs in the kitchen.

"Destiny, do you mind fetching coffee from Casa D, so we can offer our guest more than bottled water?"

Yes, the plumber had roughed in all the new pipes, but the only running water in the place was the original tiny restroom.

"Sure, Eliot. Be right back."

Robert took the seat inside the clear plastic walls and set a small drawing on the table. "This is as far as the designer has gotten with the ideas I brought him."

Studying it, I tried to discern the figure. I knew Robert's architect. Her clients typically want salmon carved out of burl wood, either leaping waves or lurking in shallows. Or a heron tiptoeing amidst wild irises. Modern Pacific Northwest iconography. Styles derived from the original inhabitants, or art nouveau-*cum*-hippie, or heavy-metal spirit fauna.

"Mythic?" I asked "I don't recognize the figure."

"From two lost cultures," Robert said. It's Artemis holding the peach that Monkey King stole from the Queen of Heaven. To sustain us until we reach enlightenment."

I pushed the paper back across our tiny table and fought to keep from folding my arms into a Pacific Northwest defensive posture. "I'm not the right person for this sort of job. And my time is fully engaged until summer."

"Pete Byron says you'd be perfect," he insisted. "And I have all the time in the world."

Pete went to France with Dante. No one had seen him since September, so the likelihood of Pete referring customers my way: slim.

"There are other local artists. I'd be happy to introduce you."

The front door banged open as Destiny kicked it with her boot, her hands full of coffee and croissants in a cardboard tray. The January wind rustled the plastic tarps and walls, and whipped up sawdust and debris, plastering the transparent wall.

"Oh my God!" Destiny exclaimed. "Guess who's at Casa D. I about peed my pants. Tadeusz fucking Nowak."

"Language, Destiny." I said it automatically, a habit I'd already gained from living with her.

"I mean, wow. This beats when Jason Taylor came to see you." Destiny busily sorted coffee and napkins on the table, not noticing what passed between Robert and me. "Yeah, Jason Taylor has a Grammy nomination. But he's kind of a dweeb. Cute, but a dweeb. Tadeusz is, like, gorgeous."

Robert thanked her for the coffee. "Tadeusz came along to help move my sculpture. But I don't want to disturb your work today."

"You could bring him over here, Destiny," I said, now suspicious that Robert had other company.

"He's hanging with some old dweeb," Destiny said. "It's not like he's lonely."

Robert smiled. "Yes, I believe some people also consider Sean Wentworth rather a bit of a dweeb."

"No." Destiny was adamant, though I wasn't sure on what basis. She didn't possess any details of my September employment. "Sean Wentworth is like the best. His Impious Aeneas is an inspiration for a generation of artists and—" Destiny, midway through gushing, noticed the drawing on the table and stopped. She glanced at Robert then.

"I can guarantee he's a dweeb," Robert said. "I'm his father. Do you mind going back out in the rain to tell Tadeusz and Sean that I'll be a moment yet? I would appreciate the favor."

"Order some lunch for yourself, Destiny." I gave her some bills from my pocket. "Don't let Yuri comp you for food. He already paid me for that door repair I did. He doesn't owe us more favors."

"I know," Destiny said, eager to split. "You told me a hundred times."

"Sucks to be you," I said.

"Not today it doesn't!" She ripped the door open so hard that it bounced on the doorstopper. "I'm going to talk to Tadeusz Nowak and Sean Wentworth, while you're here eating dust."

· · ·

"I spoke once in unfortunate ways," Robert said as the door banged closed. "I am sorry."

My hands were wrapped so tightly around the takeout cup that the lid popped, spilling hot coffee on my lap. My Carhartt workpants, however, were so crusted with builder doo-doo that the coffee ran down onto my boot, where it seeped in past the laces and tongue. Though not so hot by then.

"You have nothing to apologize for, Mr. Wentworth."

"That is nice of you to say. Please call me Robert." He sipped at his coffee, decided it was too hot, and set it aside. "I have been castigated and humbled to be reminded of my discourteous behavior."

"Please!" I held up a hand, finally able to let go of the strangled coffee cup.

"And I'm being ill-mannered now," he said, "by forcing my apology upon you. However, you'll also be uncomfortable when Sophy apologizes for meddling. She wasn't raised that way."

"It's not necessary, Robert. Truly."

"If we're going to see each other on the streets of this town for the coming years, I believe it is essential."

Someone had to get us out of this stuck conversation. Me staring at my dirty hands wasn't going to do it.

"How are your construction plans going, Mr. Went—Robert? We noticed that you broke ground." *On the land where I'd planned to live,* I did not say.

"Please come visit the site and tell me that it goes well. I don't have another expert to give me reassurance." Robert glanced at his watch. "Shall we join the others at Casa D? I understand the heart of Limberlost drinks coffee there each morning. Perhaps you can introduce me."

· · ·

Resembling a bad community-theatre production of *Singles*, a crew of hip dweebs in hoodies and jeans huddled around the back table.

Sean sat drawing on his pad, staring out the window where pedestrians battled a twenty-mile-an-hour wind to cross from Curl-Up-and-Dye on this block over to the Raven's Nest, the preferred morning destination for people who need a lot of milk foam in their coffee. And gluten-free cinnamon rolls.

Beside him, Destiny chatted with Tadeusz. He's more strikingly handsome than I'd remembered, especially with that shaggy Wolverine haircut. Tadeusz listened intently, leaning forward to look at what Destiny shared on her cellphone. My new hyper-guardian self noted that Destiny sat between two older men in a stiff student-before-the-master posture.

Roz and her husband Harley Owens sat in the nearby booth, chatting with Yuri, who stood with a pot of coffee in his hand. As Robert requested earlier, I introduced him to his new neighbors.

"You're the man?" Yuri said. "The one who saved Cora Waddington? I'm happy to shake your hand. Welcome to Limberlost."

Destiny glanced up, hearing Cora's name. She waved for me to come to her, just as Roz and Harley were inviting Robert to join them for coffee.

I boldly slid into the booth beside Sean.

"Hi, Eliot. May I introduce Tadeusz Nowak and Sean Wentworth?" Destiny had taken over ownership of her new friends.

I reached across the table to shake Tadeusz's hand. "We met briefly once. I admire your work."

Sean set down his pad and stylus and dropped a hand into his lap. Then, lightly, it crossed into mine.

Just like we used to do.

"Eliot and I know each other," Sean said. "We exchange email every day."

Destiny amped dismay. "Oh no! You're the guy she writes that old-people's mail to?"

"It's not old-people's mail," I protested.

"Most definitely is." Destiny quoted from our daily email exchange. "'It's windy here today. Seattle grey till May.' 'Made a nice black-bean chili with cornbread.' Like you plagiarize the world's most boring Facebook posts."

"You shouldn't read other people's mail," I said. Good lord, I'm turning into a next-generation version of my censorious father.

Destiny sniffed. "You leave it open all through making dinner. I have to walk by it, like, a hundred times before the dishes are done. How can I not see it? Why do you leave stupid one-line emails open for, like, an hour?"

Sean's right cheek twitched, ready to laugh, but I was still compelled to say, "You also aren't supposed to tell the rest of the world what you read in other people's private mail."

"What's to tell?" Destiny said. "Except to warn people that I'm likely to die from an overdose of banality."

"Was that a word on your last vocabulary test?"

Yuri arrived then, with a professional armload of toasted cheese sandwiches and fries, deftly passing plates around the table. Me, I couldn't swallow a bite under these circumstances.

"We're practicing, Destiny." Sean finally spoke. Like me, he wasn't that interested in his cheese sandwich.

"Like fate?" Destiny said.

Tadeusz said, "Hey, boss. You keep claiming you don't believe in fate."

"Let me restate," Sean said. "Destiny, we are practicing. Full stop. Neither Eliot nor I believe in fate."

"What are you practicing?" Destiny said.

"Everyday life," Sean and I said, simultaneously. Which was an unnerving first effort at performing everyday life together in public.

"Better hope practice makes perfect soon, Sean," Tadeusz said. "Right now, everyday living is awkward. We're all camped out at Pete's house."

"We're earning our own way," Sean said. He explained details he hadn't yet shared with me. When I asked him to stop recruiting me into his plans for working and living with him, we agreed not to discuss details of our various predicaments. All that chaos distracted from what we needed most: to understand each other in deeper ways. "Pete paid six months' lease in advance. We live there and use it as a studio."

Tadeusz shrugged. "It's more space than we had in London."

Sean said. "Soon, we'll have—"

"—real contracts, real payments," Tadeusz said, as if they frequently finished sentences for each other.

Since Sean had begun to eat and needed both hands, I slipped mine over to his thigh and asked the business question we'd been avoiding in email. "Are you free yet?"

"Freedom is a state of mind," Tadeusz said.

"How true is that!" Destiny exclaimed, snapping her fingers.

"Yet in one story, the White-Bone Demon sucks men's souls and minds," I said. "Leaving a walking husk."

Sean said, "Tadeusz and I just submitted our final work to help reboot the Monkey franchise. FAIL agreed that the story and art directions planned for the first film were—"

"A freaking fail," Destiny said, dipping a French fry into the pond of ketchup on her plate. "The whole world noticed when the preview trailer appeared on the web."

Tadeusz said, "We created a new story arc and suite of images for the next three stories." He offered Destiny his phone, and she immersed herself in flicking through the images. "You can look, but do not tell anyone what you've seen."

"Your last goal was to leave Laconia and Monkey King behind as quickly as possible," I said, but softly, not as a challenge.

Sean twitched. "I was in too much of a hurry. To get everyone out of court and back to work, I agreed to a slower transition."

Tadeusz said, "FAIL bought out both Sean and Milo, and took over Laconia management. They kept the whole team on staff, with better compensation."

Though Sean and I had agreed not to discuss each other's business while we felt our way into a new friendship, I couldn't stifle my curiosity about his nemesis. "Does Milo run Laconia for the new owner? With Louisa?"

Sean and Tadeusz exchanged looks.

Tadeusz said, "After the problems with Laconia staffing and the battles over intellectual rights—"

"Yours, mine, and ours," Sean murmured.

Tadeusz continued, "And after FAIL execs compared audience response to *The Desert Crucible* with their Monkey King debut—"

"Debacle," Sean said.

Tadeusz said, "They chose a new creative director and producer for the Monkey reboot, starting with *Havoc in the Heavenly Kingdom.*"

"Milo is out?" I asked. I'd never met the guy, but I'd like to know that I never will.

Sean said, "He's in Canada, seeking funding for a Haida First Nation ghost story."

"And Louisa?" I asked, not surprised that Milo hadn't learned a single lesson.

Tadeusz said, "Our new FAIL masters promoted her. She's assistant to the manager of the New World subsidiary redistribution for FAIL media." Tadeusz put a hand over his handsome mouth, covering a smile. "Minus North America, Argentina, and Brazil."

"So FAIL defeated the White-Bone Demon?"

"The meanest thing I ever heard you say, Eliot." Sean dropped his hand to cup mine, resting on my thigh, like when we rode together. Except over my filthy Carhartts, stiff with construction slime and sawdust.

"Milo's fire burns as hot as ever," Tadeusz said. "Pete keeps stoking his fury by mentioning the video clip that proves Milo contributed to your bad luck on the road."

"We made our own luck," Sean and I said, as if we'd rehearsed it, causing Destiny to glance up from Tadeusz's phone and Tadeusz to sit even straighter in the ruby-red Naugahyde booth.

"We always do," Sean said. "Like right now. FAIL has freed us to start new work with HOPE Productions. But our new storyline is all Northwest."

"No Monkey, no deserts, no borrowed stories," Tadeusz said.

"Yet retaining Sean's marvelous blue palette," Robert said from the neighboring booth.

Yuri appeared just then, bearing a plate loaded with Ukrainian holiday treats: little crescent cookies with walnuts and cinnamon, buttery *kolachy* filled with quince, and honey and spice cookies that I think are called *medianyky*. However, I know for a fact Yuri's life in the Ukraine under the Soviets involved no such medieval or Christian traditions.

"Yuri! Thank you," I said. "You're so kind."

"It's Twelfth Night," Yuri said. "May you have sweetness and many good things in life and in the new year."

I stood to embrace him in gratitude, and because I needed to hug someone at that moment, but our table was too crowded for me to hug the one I wanted.

Destiny watched Sean doodle. She bent down close, as if examining actual pixels. Then she took the pad away from him to study a couple of inches from her nose. She passed it to Tadeusz, who stared down at it.

Sean reached for the pad, but Destiny scooped it up first.

"He's proposing, Eliot. Say yes. It's so romantic."

"Sean isn't proposing. He knows better."

"Yeah? This sure as shit isn't one of your daily boredom bombs in email." Destiny's hair flew loose as she thumped the table to confirm her truths.

"Language, Destiny."

She thrust the tablet in my face. I closed my eyes.

"You have to look," she said, adopting the tone I use whenever she hits the limit of my endurance.

Rather than Artemis or Impious Aeneas, or even a raven on the desert wind, Sean's drawing transformed the scene from outside Casa D into that story-poem I'd read in Nevada. An aged woman clutched her cloak against the wind and rain, a crooked walking stick in her other hand as she crossed the main street in Limberlost Village.

Below the drawing, Sean's stilted calligraphic script read:

> *"Will you please do me the honor of allowing me a place in your everyday life?"*

"C'mon, Eliot, say yes," Destiny begged.

Sean said, "Any space will satisfy me, that doesn't create an inconvenience."

"She always says yes if I wait and ask at the right time."

"I have all the time in the world," Sean said, his hand moving up my Carhartt-armored thigh.

"She'll say yes," Destiny said, vehemently confident.

"I can speak for myself," I said, just as confident.

Notes and Acknowledgments

The highways and most towns in *Artemis in the Desert* are real. Once upon a time, real people on real motorcycles followed this route and endured extraordinary, unseasonal weather and bad coffee. However, those real people were practical and suffered no similar degree of human angst in their travels. The characters and activities in this story are wholly fictional and do not represent real events or real people, living or dead.

Chapter 1, "Lost Point Road": The real deer was on Highway 101 along Hood Canal. This is a fictional deer.

Perhaps, like my partner, you searched the web for Limberlost and found it in Indiana or Missouri. Like the deer, this Limberlost is fictional.

Chapter 3, "Limberlost," and later chapters: No actual bikes were harmed in the creation of this story. All the dumped bike scenes in this story are either the product of my imagination or were told to me by strangers in bars where I went to watch Sonics basketball games. I can't account for how I became confessor to dumped bike stories, but I never knew those guys' names or met them again, so these scenes are not revealing your personal secrets. Also, unhappily, the Sonics left Seattle, and since then, I haven't been told new dumped-bike stories. Maybe no one dumps their bike any more.

It should be noted, however, in situations like the one in which Eliot first dumped her bike in Leschi, you might wish to kick a barking dog that charges at you when you pass on a bike. Fortunately, as humans, we have higher conceptual physics capabilities, so we can accelerate just when the dog thinks it has the right trajectory for ankle nipping.

Chapter 4, "Seattle" and other voice-overs: I am grateful to Bruce Barker for text contributions to help explain the thrill of riding.

Also in Chapter 4, bike models were chosen by Chip Barker; however, I'm grateful to him for a good deal more than that.

Chapter 10, "Winnemucca": The Winnemucca Hotel on South Bridge Street is now, rightfully, on the National Register of Historic Places. Sadly, you missed your chance for the decades-long dining experience.

Chapter 16, "North Rim": It is not possible to show up at the North Rim during seasons when it's open and obtain an empty room at the lodge or in the cabins. You will find yourself driving far back up the road, out of the park, begging for a campsite.

Chapter 17, "Grand Canyon": I overheard the skunk story in the bar on the North Rim. If anything remotely similar happened to you, I don't know who you are, how tall you are, the color of your hair, or any other details about the story other than the involuntary skunk-slaughter. So this tale is fictional; it isn't about you.

Chapter 19, "National Monument": Quote from E.A. Stewart provided specially for this publication. See the *Accidental Heretics* series from Jugum Press.

Chapter 20, "Oak Creek Canyon": It is generally recommended that you ride down this road at least twice on each visit. Once is never enough.

About the Author

ANNIE PEARSON lives and writes in Seattle. In addition to the *Rain City Incidents* series, she also writes the *Accidental Heretics* adventure series (as E.A. Stewart).

The *Rain City Incidents* series focuses on life in contemporary Seattle and its environs, among people whose work drives their hearts' desires, often in conflict with other love affairs.

Annie Pearson posts about writing and eclectic project planning at www.anniepearson.com.

From Jūgum Press

RAIN CITY INCIDENTS SERIES by Annie Pearson
When bad things happen to quirky people under grey skies

The Grrrl of Limberlost
A murder in a Seattle coffee house. A murder on a decaying boat dock on Puget Sound. Samsara Byron, the security expert, insists this has nothing to do with her. She's busy fending off an attack on the world's cyber infrastructure—if she could only get a cell signal.

Nine Volt Heart
He said, "I love you." She said, "You don't even know the real me." He said, "Great title for a song. Key of G? Can we try close harmony?" Jason, the singer-songwriter, and Susi, a music teacher, meet by accident in Seattle. Secrets, songs, and stalkers quickly entwine their lives in unpredictable ways.

ACCIDENTAL HERETICS SERIES by E.A. Stewart
Lost in the Languedoc Crusade

Bone-mend and Salt (Book 1)
Fight or beg for mercy when enemies turn an unjust war against you? Three ruined crusaders battle conspiracy and disaster while trapped in the new war against the Cathar heresy. Swords and grit must defend against deceit.

Trebuchets in the Garden (Book 2)
How do you prepare for the dawn of the Inquisition? In the Languedoc, three embattled crusaders seek justice and respite amidst terror, siege, and conspiracy—as zealots prepare to ignite the next heretics' pyre.

ECLECTIC FICTION

Bad Reputation by Ajax Bell
A close-up portrait of pre-AIDS Seattle that illuminates dark corners, where homeless kids cluster for safety near the revitalized Pike Place Market. *Bad Reputation* contrasts the deeply personal need for friendship with the universal dilemma: people aren't always what they seem.

www.jugumpress.net